DANIEL M DURICK

The Dark Matter

THE TETRAD CYCLE BOOK 1

First published by Druid Lake Inc. 2024

First edition

ISBN (paperback): 978-1-966053-01-9
ISBN (hardcover): 978-1-966053-00-2

This book was professionally typeset on Reedsy.
Find out more at reedsy.com

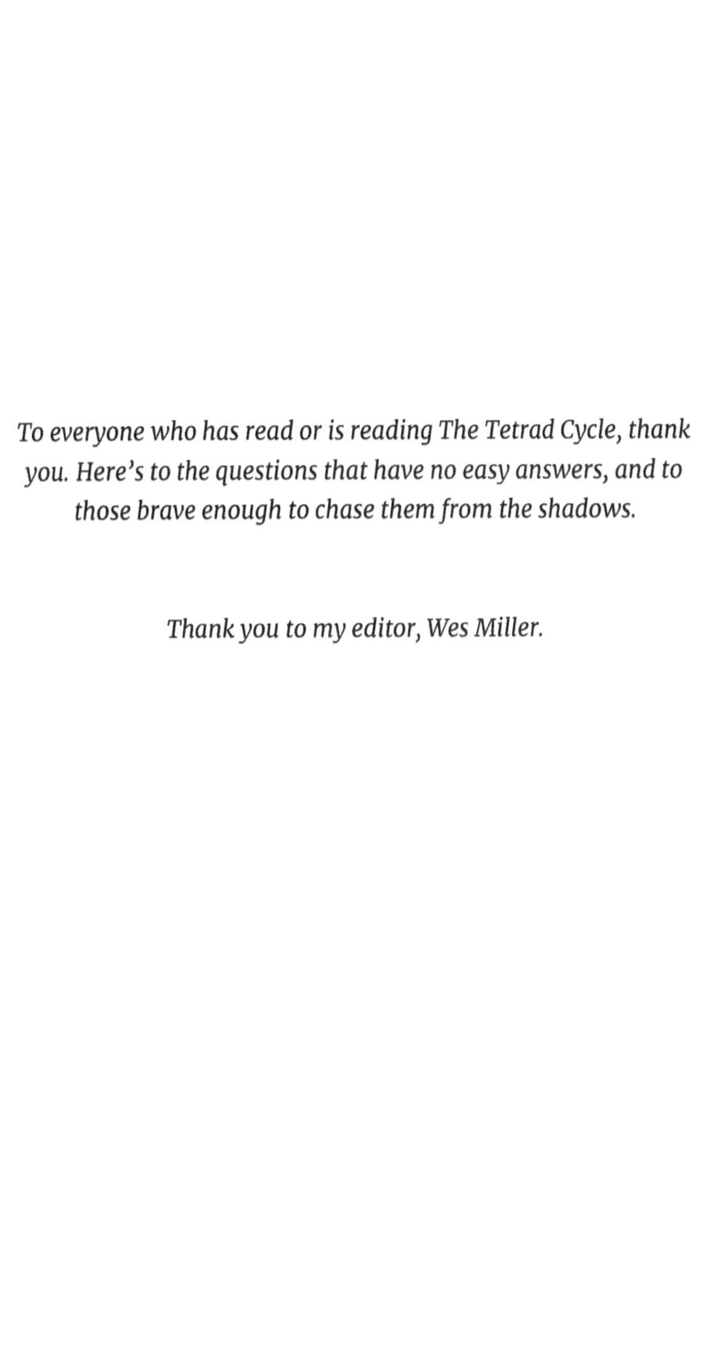

To everyone who has read or is reading The Tetrad Cycle, thank you. Here's to the questions that have no easy answers, and to those brave enough to chase them from the shadows.

Thank you to my editor, Wes Miller.

Contents

Prologue

Katherine O'Reilly had never contemplated suicide. But now the professor of Cosmology and preeminent expert on dark matter prepared to kill herself.

Closing her laptop's lid and pushing back from her desk, she walked to the wall where the image hung. Her crowning achievement of 57 years. The first true photograph of dark matter. Stretching over the brown leather couch beneath, she pulled it down and slid it behind a bookcase.

Pictures are hung to be remembered, people hang to be forgotten, Katherine thought.

She turned for the window, passing her desk with her planner open to tomorrow, April 14th, a day she would never see. Two lectures, an interview with The Astrophysical Journal, and lunch with her boyfriend.

Outside, the blue sky of the warmest April day on record shone, and eight stories below, busy students followed pathways to classes or lunch. Young men and women, beaming with optimism on the pleasant day, wore shorts and t-shirts to soak in the sunshine. Some of them she recognized.

She placed her hands against the top of the window's frame, pushing it up a crack, then positioned her fingers under to lift it open completely. It creaked with age and tossed dust.

The air rushed in and woke the skin of her face.

Katherine placed each palm on the windowsill and lowered her body. Pushing forward, she stuck her head out and rested her stomach between her hands. The wood pressed against her diaphragm, making every breath more laborious. She stretched her back, arching herself further out of the building.

Like a fulcrum. The load from the epiphany a burden too heavy.

With a gentle nudge from her feet, her weight shifted enough to send her body out. Katherine closed her eyes and relaxed her muscles. Her body rolled as gravity pulled her.

Or maybe it's less of a pull and more a push.

Among other bloody and messy consequences, the intense impact of the still frozen ground sent the air out of her lungs. But before she could feel pain or hear the students' screams, she was gone.

I

Part One

"For my thoughts are not your thoughts, neither are your ways my ways, saith the Lord. For as the heavens are higher than the earth, so are my ways higher than your ways, and my thoughts than your thoughts."

- Isaiah 55:8-9

Chapter 1

Beads of ice, pushed by the harsh winter wind, battered the windshield of Reed Jacobs Jr.'s cruiser. From the side of rural Route 4, lined with tall pines, he watched the frozen sandstorm. A low whistle accompanied the vibrations from the cold air rushing over the car. He waited for his next call or ticket recipient, alternating between the bitter view and the thick study guide for the National Detective /Investigator Test propped against the wheel.

Reed grabbed his coffee from the center console and took a sip. The "Sally's Gas" cardboard sleeve felt cool. *Almost time for another cup to help get through the night.*

The dashboard's clock ticked to 10 p.m. Reed returned his coffee and retrieved his cell from the passenger seat. He tapped the buttons to call Wendy Joyner.

It rang twice before she answered. "Hey, hon."

"Hey, babe," Reed said while looking into the frozen night.

"I'm just getting into bed. How are you?"

"Good. Studying up for NDIT since it has been quiet. You do some Tweeting today?" Reed asked. Wendy worked in marketing for Bridgewater Health, the area's largest health-care provider. She held a position on the marketing team and focused on social media. The two met at the gym over a year ago.

"It's 'X' now. You need a new joke."

"How was it?" He moved his book to the passenger seat.

"Meh. Elizabeth's still being a taskmaster."

"That sucks. You have more to offer." Reed turned on his vehicle's headlights and takedowns. Meant to flood an area with light, the intense beams reflected off the onslaught of flakes to white out his view. The ghostly scene might have sent shivers down others' spines, but Reed had yet to meet a problem that couldn't be solved with his muscles.

Wendy's tone shifted to defeat. "Yeah, I know."

"Hey, did you run Badge?"

"It's so cold!"

Reed shrugged. "Yeah, fine. It's awful out there. But in the morning, okay? He needs to get out."

"Fine, okay."

"Miss you," Reed whispered.

"Hey, did you get to ask Detective Prosser for advice on the test?"

"Naw, he gave me the cold shoulder as he ran off to something." Reed flicked off the lights. Without them, he could see further into the blizzard.

"I want you to make detective."

Reed huffed. "The test comes first. Then I have to convince Chief Oberman for the job."

"Babe, she thinks you're just like your dad."

Reed raised his free hand to the steering wheel and wrung it like a dishrag, slow and deliberate.

Wendy continued. "Will I see you in the morning before I leave for work?"

"I think I'll be hitting the pillow when your alarm goes off."

"You don't have to work so many doubles."

"It's not forever. Just till I get a house." He released the wheel.

"Still. We could go to Florida to visit your mom. It's almost April, and it's still freezing! I don't remember a winter this long."

"I just told you." Reed moved his cell away from his ear. "I need to focus on the house."

"K. Whatever."

Reed tapped the dash. "Alright, I have to get back at it. But wanted to call to say 'hi'."

"Thank you."

"Love you. Sleep well. And don't let Badge sleep in the bedroom."

"Be safe."

Reed disconnected and tossed the phone on the dashboard.

He didn't need to be reminded that others saw him like his father. Brash. Impulsive. Overly aggressive for the job. Every damn day when he'd walk up the stairs to his desk, he'd pass the photos of various ex-cops, department chiefs, and other notable officials nailed to the cement block wall. Each sat in full uniform and next to the American flag. Inscriptions on the plaques included various accomplishments or dedications. Reed would always place a hand on the one for Reed Jacobs Sr. and say, "Hi, Pops." He'd then wipe a finger across the brass plaque, under the name, where an inscription should have been. *Should have been.*

Reed roughed up his short hair, and at six-foot-four, his hand brushed the roof of the car as he did. He grimaced. The hours in the gym helped him in his job, but made sitting in the cramped cruiser uncomfortable.

The wind continued howling, driving snow and hail against the glass. Reed flipped the switch to turn on only the red of his overheads. The snow appeared like an unending splatter of blood. He swapped it for the blues, and the flakes transformed. He switched it back and forth, red to blue and back again, until he set both to a steady burn. Ahead, the scene bled from one color to the other.

Setting it to full activation with rotating beacons made the outside look like a disco.

The snow thinned, and the pitch of the wind's whistle faded until the pattering of ice stopped. The cabin was silent. But Reed noticed something in the distance. He leaned forward. "What the hell?"

He grabbed the wheel and pulled closer.

The snow continued falling, but at a hundred feet ahead. Between him and there...nothing. Down the road, Reed could see the blanket of white descending in straight lines, undisturbed by the once gusting wind. But nothing reflected his overheads.

"What's going on?"

Reed opened the door and stepped out onto the empty road. The cold hit him instantly. Without his jacket, it filled his shirt. He spun around to check the surroundings. Each way, walls of flakes crossed the road and ended somewhere in the thick trees. He seemed at the center of an area protected from the storm. Or in the eye of one.

"Strange." He reached out to feel for any precipitation. Nothing.

"Hmm." Reed looked up. The sky was black. No stars or visible clouds. "Going to have to call the weatherman about this one."

Suddenly and all at once, the sky opened up, sending sheets of ice pellets into Reed's face while a blaring horn blasted behind him. Reed twisted around to the headlights powering towards him. He leaped to the side of the road behind his cruiser, rolling on the ground in frozen dirt and snowpack.

The car horn screamed, followed by the screeching of wheels. Reed's body came to a stop, and he pushed himself up. The silver sedan careened off the road, where it slammed into a pine tree.

Then all the noise stopped, to be followed a moment later by the return of the gusting wind. Reed went to one knee as the ice collected on his eyelashes. He pounced up and into action, rushing across the road to the car and slipping along the way.

"Shit. Shit. Shit!" he cursed as he realized he had been standing in the middle of the road, and may have caused the accident.

Reed approached the shallow embankment and slid to the vehicle. The frozen trunk stung his bare hands as he braced himself against it and hustled to the front. He pushed aside branches to force his way closer. With the headlights broken, only the dashboard's LEDs provided illumination.

"Hello? You okay?" Reed called out.

As Reed reached the driver's door, he heard a groan. Branches had broken through the windshield and surrounded a young woman. Blood dripped from a wide gash on her forehead and ran down her puffy white winter jacket. A quick check of the cabin confirmed she was the only one inside.

Then the smell hit him. Gasoline.

The branches scratched Reed as he reached into the car to place a hand on the woman's shoulder. "Hey, you with me?

Can you talk?"

She looked his way, her pupils half rolled up under her eyelids.

"Okay, I'm going to get you out of here. Hang tight." Reed tried the door handle but it didn't budge. Pushing the sticks aside with one hand, he poked his head inside the cabin. Reed found the unlock button and hit it repeatedly before trying the door again. No luck.

He tried the back door. No response. Reed circled the car to try the other side. Again, no door would open. He looked around and inside the car but found nothing useful. He hit the radio on his shoulder. "Car 4-4-0. Need ambulance, STAT. 11-80 on Route 4, three miles east of Sally's."

"Fuck," Reed said as he stepped over the gasoline puddle forming under the car. Snow crunched under his boots as he moved to the back and lifted himself onto the trunk. "Don't worry," he called out. Reed steadied himself, placing his left foot flat on the lid and bending his knees. The muscles in Reed's legs tensed as he raised his right boot and drove it down on the back glass. A single two-inch crack appeared.

A gust of wind swept gasoline fumes and ice crystals into his nose.

Again, he raised his foot and stomped. A series of fractures spider-webbed out. Reed turned to face the cracks and launched his body. The frigid air brushed his face as he descended and clubbed the back windshield with all of his weight.

It crumbled beneath him, sending him into the back seat and almost wrapping him in a glass blanket. He hurriedly kicked it away and grabbed the roof to pull himself out of the car. Sliding off the trunk, Reed rushed to the driver's door, flexing his frozen fingers as he moved.

The woman inside sat staring at her bloody hands. Her eyes were now focused. "Oh, God."

Somewhere deep in the forest, a pack of wolves howled.

"Can you undo your seat belt, miss?" The woman didn't move or answer. "K, almost got you. What's your name?" Reed asked as he reached inside and searched for the seat recliner.

The woman responded with another groan.

Concussion? Reed thought as he blindly hunted for the lever. He looked back at the puddle and, not seeing any open flames, returned to the driver. "I'll have you out of here soon. Help is on the way."

As Reed pushed his shoulder further into the cabin, a sudden spark and small fire emerged from the crumbled engine. It licked the tree trunk.

The woman gasped.

"Don't worry about it," Reed reassured her. "We got this."

Moving his hand forward, Reed found the latch and pulled it. The swift movement of the woman's body dropping back and abruptly stopping alerted her. She raised her arms toward the ceiling. The cabin amplified her scream, "Ahh!"

Without hesitating, Reed ran to the back and dove on top of the trunk. He reached for the woman and clutched her wrists. As she scratched at the air, Reed tightened his grip. The fumes now filled the cabin.

"Come on!" Reed pulled her closer to him. His biceps flexed, stretching his uniform shirt. Then he pressed his knees on the bumper to lift her further out.

With her body on the trunk, he heaved her onto his shoulder and ran to his cruiser. The thin ice under his department-issued boots caused him to slip with each stride. "Got you! Got you!"

The woman mumbled.

At his vehicle, he opened the back door and gently lowered her. He pushed her feet inside and closed the door before retrieving flares from his trunk.

The snow reached two inches deep on the road. He lit the warning signals and laid them across the scene, both in front and behind it. Reed looked back at them before returning to his car. They glowed red, like depictions of the fires of early humans.

He grabbed his first aid kit from the trunk before closing it and returned to the cabin. Inside, he turned to the woman, who was rubbing her eyes as she lay on her back. Reed could now smell the alcohol on her. *Thank God.*

"An ambulance is on its way. Can you tell me your name?" he asked as he retrieved the pressure bandage.

The woman rolled onto one shoulder, pushed herself into a seated position, and then slid down into a slump. "Amber."

"Hi, Amber. I'm Officer Jacobs." Reed reached back and pressed the bandage to her head. "EMTs will be here soon. We just want to hold this to your wound until they arrive."

Amber placed her hand over the fabric and held it in place. She opened her mouth, but before she could utter a word, her vehicle exploded with a visceral roar. The back end lifted off the ground. The trunk lid flew into the woods. A ball of black smoke and fire rose and disintegrated in the wintry air. The cruiser shook from the blast wave.

Reed took a deep breath and called for a fire response team.

The girl's eyes reflected the flames outside as she stared.

Flashing lights strobed a half-mile out, an ambulance and a

cruiser crawling over ice. "The EMTs will check you out. Then you're going to do a sobriety test."

"Great," she responded with a hiccup.

The blaze flashed and now engulfed the tree. Needles sparkled orange, then curled black and crumbled to ash. A gust caught the inferno and spun it into a towering fire devil. Snow danced around it. Reed watched Amber rest her head against the window, her eyes fixed on the destruction.

"It's so beautifully awful," she whispered.

"You okay, Amber?" Reed asked, looking back at her.

Amber's attention lingered on her car, her eyes half closed. The window fogged from her breath. "What's left after you watch your life burn away?"

Reed exited the vehicle and motioned for the ambulance to pull up beside his cruiser. The night air bit at his face. The tree burned. He tipped his head to the sky, his mind drifting between the odd weather occurrence earlier and Amber's words.

Chapter 2

Detective John Prosser received the call shortly after sitting with his coffee outside of Bluebakers, his favorite spot for his morning brew on a sunny day. He sat alone. Like he always did.

Around him, groups of patrons, energized by the warm mid-April day, entered and exited the small shop. Prosser could hear the buzz in their elevated voices. In his mind, he turned over what he might do between cases. Somewhere beneath that, he heard Sarah's voice chiding him to make a friend or two at the office.

Then the call came.

Dispatch called it a "likely jumper" at the University of Bridgewater, though Prosser corrected them. All they had was a body and some exterior witnesses. It's possible the victim was pushed. Regardless, the situation already gnawed at the detective as unusual since campus deaths were typically substance abuse-related or suicide. Perhaps this was the latter, but that would be curious in its own right, as it more frequently claimed students as the victims.

As he got behind the wheel of his black Ford Explorer, his cell alerted him to a text message from Chief Oberman.

Getting calls on UofB body. see me at hq immediately after. be delicate.

Prosser scoffed at the last sentence. Working with Oberman for decades and supporting her through her rise up the ranks, she saw him in action and knew him as a thoughtful, thorough, and *delicate* detective.

So the unusual request got him thinking. It meant those calls she received were probably from people with pull. Perhaps political power or wealth. The intrigue arrived early.

He parked in the lot at the front of the University of Bridgewater Sciences building and grabbed his notepad to tuck it into his light jacket. In less than a minute, he turned the corner of the gray stone building to see the crowd of students and staff gathered at the scene. Four uniformed officers stood between them and the black tarp covering Doctor Katherine O'Reilly's body. He left the path for the grass; the ground was hard, only beginning to thaw after the unusually long winter.

Detective Prosser's duties typically took him into the densely populated part of the city. Only once in his two decades as a detective did he have to venture onto the University's campus, which occupied Bridgewater's southern border and abutted the Elm River. Nonetheless, as a lifelong resident, he knew the campus well from attending sporting events and parties while he studied Criminal Justice at the much less prestigious Community College down the street.

"Detective." Officer Cooley, who had stationed himself at the body, nodded to him.

Prosser lowered himself, careful not to touch his khakis to the damp ground, and lifted the corner of the thick sheet for a view of the body.

"What do we have here?" he asked Cooley.

"Professor Katherine O'Reilly. Her office is up there." He motioned to the open window on the next-to-top floor. "It's eight stories."

Prosser already knew who she was from Dispatch. A respected professor and scientist, almost sixty years old. No kids. Not married.

Katherine's eyes bulged from the force of the impact. The back of her head had shattered, brain matter splattered across the dead grass. Her mouth gaped from the relaxing of her jaw muscles, but pointed to the heavens in an agonizing and soundless scream.

Prosser replaced the cover and looked up at the window. "Secured?"

"Oh yeah, Petey's on it."

Prosser looked at Cooley. He recognized the tone. Many on the force hazed Peter LaFontaine for his exuberance, but Prosser appreciated the young officer's diligence and enthusiasm for the job.

"Good. Do we have any witnesses?"

"We've been collecting."

Prosser stood. "I'm going up. When the coroner arrives, tell him not to leave before I talk to him."

"You bet."

Prosser returned the way he arrived. As he walked, he made note of the crowd. No one seemed out of place. Students stood in clusters, whispering, thumbs moving across phone screens. Older faces, probably staff or professors, had gone red, leaning into one another.

He took the stone steps up to the doors of the Sciences building and went inside, where he rode the elevator to the eighth floor. As the door opened, Officer LaFontaine perked up from his station halfway down the hall.

Prosser approached Katherine's office, and the young, blond-haired man talked excitedly. "No one has come in or out, Detective Prosser. I also have the head of security getting the footage from that camera down there." He pointed to the small white enclosure in the far corner. "I asked for the last eighteen hours. I figured that's good enough."

"That's great, Officer. Thank you." Prosser would have preferred to speak to security first, but at least the footage was requested.

Prosser reached for the chipped and dull brass doorknob and smiled at LaFontaine before entering the office, shutting the door, and lowering the shade over the window to the hall. He took a deep breath and looked around the room. A bookcase to his left, a couch along the adjacent wall, and another bookcase across from the first. Katherine's vintage desk on the right wall and a few feet in front of the open window.

The only thing that surprised him was the complete lack of anything to surprise him. Nothing looked out of place or disheveled.

He retrieved his notepad and pen. Though he'd have photos of the scene, he had the habit of jotting down various elements of interest or items to investigate further. Starting at his left, he made his way around the room.

The natural wood bookcase almost reached the ceiling, and publications neatly lined the shelves. Prosser recognized one of the hundreds: *A Brief History of Time* by Stephen Hawking. The remainder often had titles he didn't understand, like *Quantum Field Theory*, and a volume that ended with *Physical Kinetics*.

He moved to the couch. Above it, a bright empty space

surrounded by sun-beaten paint, with a nail at the top. *Missing art*, he wrote on his pad. Maybe the only thing odd about the room.

The second bookcase offered only denser materials, so Prosser moved to the desk. *Uneaten cupcake, day planner.* He opened the laptop. The screen lit up, its background a photo from the Hubble Space Telescope that he had seen a hundred times. And at the center, the password prompt.

He shut it and looked around the room. The blank canvas of the wall caught his attention again. *If something had been there, where could it be?* He walked to the couch, knelt on the middle cushion with his right knee, and reached down between it and the wall.

Nothing.

Then he noticed the protuberance from behind the bookcase just feet from him. A large frame.

Prosser moved to it and pulled it out, holding it at arm's length. The strange abstract photo reminded him of the thermal camera footage in ghost-hunting television shows. It hinted at structure, like the Hubble picture from the laptop. Blocks of red, orange, and yellow surrounded others of deep black and blue.

The sound of the door opening broke his focus. He turned as Dr. Manjusha Sharma, the University's president, entered the room. She wore a purple blazer over a white blouse and black slacks. The skin around her eyes was still red. Prosser only knew her from news articles. She joined the University three years prior and came highly respected.

"Detective?" she asked.

He leaned the photo against the couch and turned to her. "Yes." He stepped to shake her hand. "It's nice to meet you, Dr. Sharma. Apologies for the circumstances and my condolences."

"Thank you."

Prosser waited for a question, but she offered none.

"Do you know what that is?" He pointed to the photo he had retrieved.

"Yes, that is Dr. O'Reilly's first image of dark matter. Quite an achievement. She developed a new imaging method because traditional photography could not capture it. She called it a Quantum Gravity and Dark Matter Interferometer. It visually captured dark matter through an array that harnessed the interference patterns caused by the matter's gravity."

He nodded and smiled politely. "Interesting. It was tucked behind the bookcase there. Do you know why?"

He noticed tears welling in Manjusha's eyes. "After this morning, I can imagine Dr. O'Reilly feeling devastated and perhaps not wanting to look at it."

"This morning?"

"Yes, after the Elisha."

Prosser shook his head. "I'm sorry?"

"Oh, of course. The Elisha is, well *was*, a satellite made possible by Dr. O'Reilly's work on dark matter and energy. She proved her hypothesis with that image and received funding for Elisha to further her study. A remarkable advancement in technology. The launch was this morning, but I'm afraid the rocket exploded."

"That must have been difficult to see."

"Definitely so. She couldn't even bring herself to be present for the launch; her nerves wouldn't allow it. So to then see all of her work destroyed, it must have been too much."

Prosser nodded. He didn't like the fact that Dr. Sharma

seemed so confident in what drove Katherine to take her own life, if, in fact, that was what happened. But he also observed that the instincts of those closest to victims were often correct.

Prosser clarified. "So, and apologies for being so frank, you believe she jumped after the rocket exploded?"

"Yes. It launched at 11:15 this morning, and I received the call about Dr. O'Reilly a few minutes later."

"I understand it must have been hard for her. But couldn't there be more to it?"

Manjusha looked at him sharply. "This was her life. You must understand that, for Katherine, Elisha was her reason. It's why she lived. Many preeminent scientists are this way."

"Of course. I'm sorry if I offended."

"No," she responded matter-of-factly. "You're doing your job. Regardless," she reached into a pocket to hand the detective her card, "if you need anything or have further questions, please reach out. I'm sure you understand the campus needs me now, but I wanted to introduce myself."

"Thank you for doing that. And for enlightening me. It sounds like Katherine was a brilliant woman."

"Indeed."

Prosser watched Manjusha leave and noticed the woman standing in the doorway of the office across the hall.

Chapter 3

The red and blues of Reed's cruiser lit the night and raced across the frontage of the rural hardware store. Its glass front doors gave back only the lights' reflection. The parking lot sat empty, save for the two patrol cars—their course marked by tracks in the dusting of snow.

"He's in there somewhere." Officer Keyes held his flashlight pointed up at the small and open side window, his other hand tucked under his arm for warmth. "I heard about that accident the other night. Crazy shit, you diving into the car like that."

Reed shrugged.

The two were responding to the silent alarm triggered by a break-in. Keyes arrived first to see the man's bare feet sticking out from the side window, heels scrabbling against the siding.

"I'll go." Reed retrieved his flashlight and headed to the same window.

"You sure, Jacobs?"

"Yeah."

"You don't have to go jumping into every window you come across. We can wait for the owner with the keys."

Reed huffed. "That can take hours."

Reed approached the building and looked up at the window.

He stretched for the bottom of the frame, planted his boots against the wall, and muscled himself up. Propping himself on it, he shone the light across the empty bathroom he found inside.

Through the open door into the store, he called out, "Bridgewater PD. I'm coming in. Come out with your hands visible."

With no immediate response, Reed dropped and caught himself so he didn't slam against the floor. He stood and aimed his light into the store, revealing the end of a display of screws and nails.

"Bridgewater PD." Reed pulled his pistol and lifted it to his flashlight.

Peeking out from the bathroom, he found no one. He saw the patrol cars' lights gliding along the floor and ceiling as he moved with his back against the wall toward the front of the building.

The register sat quiet and undisturbed, its cash drawer closed. In past cases like this, Reed would notice the obvious cash grab. That meant the drawer was thrown onto the floor to collect any money stored underneath. Seeing it in place was curious.

"Come on out," he demanded.

Over the roar of the wind, Reed heard soft wheezing and shone the light to his right. Three rows down, pale flesh shifted between the shelves like something hung out to dry.

The man stuck a foot out from the aisle, dark from frostbite, with long nails and dirty skin. The cricket-call wheezing continued in bursts.

"Sir, you need to come out now. Slowly. Show your hands."

Reed trained his light and weapon as he circled for a better look. The man's leg stretched out, dirty and hairy. Another step, and Reed saw his crouching torso, devoid of clothes, with red marks spotting his chest and arms. The man clutched a shelf as if he might fall into the depths of space. His white skin reflected the flashlight's beam.

Reed took another step. The man knelt, staring at nothing in particular, or something very specific only he could see. His eyes opened wide with terror, his mouth ajar and gasping. His hair was disheveled, and his graying beard was matted with spit, ice, and dirt.

The slow movements continued.

"Sir?"

His eyes remained lost, unresponsive to Reed's voice or the light sweeping across his face.

Reed called over the radio strapped to his shoulder. "Four-Four-Zero. We've got a potential medical emergency here." Confirmation of the EMT's dispatch followed the crackle of the radio.

"Sir, can you stand up?"

The man's hands still gripped desperately, and being naked, he didn't seem to pose any risk. Reed holstered his weapon and tucked his flashlight away, leaving the headlights and overheads from the cruisers outside as the only illumination.

"Sir, I'm Officer Jacobs. Can you tell me what's going on? It's quite cold not to be dressed."

His odd movements stopped, though his gaze remained fixed. Reed stepped closer and removed his jacket. He placed it over the stranger's shoulders. "I have medical help on the way."

The perp's chest heaved before his mouth opened for a scream, but no sounds arrived. His eyes strained against the muscles and tendons of his face that pulled at them.

"Sir, tell me what's going on."

The man's jaw clasped tight, and he looked at Reed. Neither spoke. Reed held the stare.

Reed pushed the *Talk* button on his radio. "Four-Four-Zero, where's that ambulance?"

"En route, Officer."

"ETA?"

"Unknown."

The man relaxed his fingers and let go of the shelf. His body dropped to the floor, his arms and legs falling to his side. He leaned his head back against the display of bird feeders.

The ambulance's oscillating siren alerted Reed to its approach. "Help is on the way." He stepped closer and leaned over, gently taking the man's icy wrist. "I'm just checking your pulse. Your heart rate is high. Did you take any narcotics?"

With no response, Reed continued. "I'm going to unlock the doors for the medical professionals. Please remain here."

Reed moved to the front double doors, where he unlocked two deadbolts and pushed them open.

Keyes jogged in. "You find him?"

"Yeah, catatonic or something."

Reed led his peer to the man, who remained slumped over.

"Sir, help is coming." Reed took his hand. "Is there anything you can tell me that will help the EMTs? What's your name?"

The man's eyes looked at Reed, but still seemed somewhere else. He held the officer's hand like a child might hold his father's, a security blanket in a large and frightening world. Keyes stood watching.

Reed lingered as the EMTs checked vitals and attempted

to get the man to communicate. They wrapped him in warm blankets and placed him in the ambulance to be taken for evaluation.

"Weird man," Keyes said as he got into his patrol car. "I'll catch you later. Have a safe night."

"Later, Keyes."

Reed leaned against his cruiser and let a long breath go, watching it dissolve into the cold. After a video call to Wendy to say 'goodnight', which included a brief visit with Badge, he returned to the cruiser.

Night shifts often worked like this. Long stretches of inactivity followed by intense moments of domestic disturbances, accidents, or criminal activity. Reed prepared for it with a turkey sandwich, two Red Bulls, a protein bar, and water—all in his cooler riding shotgun.

At 11 p.m., he parked his patrol car off the side of Route 4, where it intersected with a road that led to neighborhoods. With the lights off, he could sit unnoticed and wait for someone to run through the stop sign or exceed the 40-mile-an-hour limit.

As the quiet set in, he exited the car to stretch, placing his hands on his lower spine and extending back. The bitter air rushing up his jacket helped revive him. The police radio broke the calm with loud static followed by the friendly voice of a female dispatcher. "Hey, Jacobs, can you head to the Collins farm?"

Reed recognized the voice as Officer Cindy Fitzpatrick, whom he had known since elementary school. "Hey, Cin, I can. What's up?" He got in and started his car.

"Unidentified disturbance. Someone messin' with his cows."

"On my way."

He was only a couple of miles away. Reed turned on his beacons, not bothering with the siren, and continued down Route 4.

Chapter 4

Prosser smiled at the woman, who appeared to be in her thirties, with swollen eyes and cheeks still blotched from crying. He stepped out into the hall and introduced himself. "Detective Prosser."

"Hi, Professor Stanier." She wiped her slacks before shaking Prosser's hand.

"You knew Professor O'Reilly?"

The woman clenched her jaw, lips pressing together. She gave a single, tight nod.

"I understand this is hard, and my sincere condolences. But maybe you could help me. Can you tell me when you last saw her?"

"This morning. We came in at the same time and walked up together."

"Anyone else walk with you two?"

She squinted. "No."

"How did she seem? How were her spirits?"

Stanier relaxed. "She was excited. It was a big day, and I think the warm weather made everyone a bit happier, anyway."

"So she seemed happy?"

"Oh, yes. Definitely."

"Did she seem like anything was on her mind? Preoccupied?"

"I got the sense she was anxious about the launch. But not upset or anything." She leaned against the door frame.

"Right, the...Elisha?"

"Mm-hmm. That's right."

"What about before this morning? The previous week or month. Anything unusual, out of place, inconsistent with her?"

"No, nothing." Stanier shook her head.

Prosser glanced past her into the office. Black-and-white portraits lined the walls. Einstein, Hawking, a guy writing on a giant chalkboard.

"You teach science?"

"Physics."

Prosser nodded. "Did you know her long?"

Her smile emphasized her round cheekbones. "Many years. She was my favorite professor when I was in graduate school."

"Oh, so she taught you, huh?"

"Yes. She is...was inspiring. She loved her work." Stanier clasped her hands in front of her. "A favorite teacher of many students, which made her tough competition." She chuckled. "Students often selected her as a speaker at graduation."

"Why was she so popular, do you think?"

Stanier's eyes circled the hall. "She pushed our boundaries of what we should consider possible. She questioned everything. If you made any statement of truth, she challenged you to break it down. To deconstruct it. To rip it up and pull it apart until you had just a shadow of what it was before. And that was the kernel of truth. The only truth. And for young and curious minds, it..." she looked around again, "it got you eager to discover new things. To expand that truth to something larger."

Prosser nodded slowly. "What about outside of work?"

"We were friendly, but not friends, I'm afraid."

"Do you know what she liked?"

"She never really talked about anything but physics, cosmology. It was her life."

Prosser thanked the professor and crossed the hall to Katherine's office.

Chapter 5

Reed had grown up across the street from the Collins farm, close enough to smell the manure on hot summer mornings, close enough that old Joseph's granddaughter Sadie was a fixture of his childhood. Since her father was never in her life, and her mother was often in trouble, Sadie lived with Joseph and his now-deceased wife.

It had been about twenty years since Reed last set foot on the property, and as it came into view, he thought of all the days with Sadie. They played Marco Polo in the corn rows, their voices swallowed by the stalks, pretended to race the rusty John Deere along the fence line, and fed the cows handfuls of grain. Last Reed had heard, Sadie had moved her life south.

He pulled into the semicircular driveway and turned off his lights. Collins, still in his dirty overalls, waited on the small porch at the side door of his home. Reed glanced across the street at the house he grew up in, the one his mother sold after his father passed. It looked vacant and neglected. The shutters hung askew, windows had punch holes, and the siding tore away from the insulation. *What happened to the family that moved in after us?*

The Collins' house, though, was large and well-kept thanks

to the fortunes they made selling the land that composed much of what Bridgewater is today. They held on to several acres for themselves and never lived like the millionaires they must have been.

He turned off his car, exited, and rounded it to approach Collins. The farmer still stood at the door, motionless. Fifty yards behind the home, the red barn sat dark and quiet.

"Mr. Collins," Reed called out as he approached and reached for his flashlight.

"Well, well, if it isn't Mr. Reed Jacobs himself," the man's grumbling voice struck the still night air.

"How have you been?" Reed reached out a hand, and Collins took it with his large mitt.

The years of farming built Collins like an ox. Unshaven, deep wrinkles carved into his face, and fingernails rimmed black. He appeared aged by dirt. Collins examined Reed's eyes. He looked from one to the other like an optometrist.

"You okay, Joseph?"

"Good to see you, son."

"So what's going on?"

He smirked and motioned to the barn. "Somethin' was disturbin' the cows, causing all sorts of trouble. Seems peaceful now, though, you think?"

"Certainly is," Reed agreed. "Why don't I take a look, anyway? Make sure you don't have any stupid frat boys looking for cows to tip."

Collins smiled. "You do that."

Reed nodded and crossed the field to the barn, his flashlight raised and pointed ahead. The squeaking of Collins' rubber boots followed to the barn's large open doorway. Reed entered.

Across the door he had entered, a matching one led to the dark night beyond. To his left, a once-white wall chipped and scuffed from years of abuse. He turned to the right to look down the long building. Dirt, wood, and hay packed the floor of the walkway down the middle. On either side, pen after pen of Holstein cows all slept undisturbed.

Turning back to the wall, he found the light switch, but with multiple flicks, the space remained dark. He positioned himself at the head of the path and crisscrossed the barn with the flashlight. The cows all seemed disinterested in his presence.

He continued walking and checking the pens. The stench had him taking short breaths. The silence of the setting rang loud in Reed's ears.

He opened his mouth to call out for anyone hiding, but before he could make a sound, a cow pushed itself up. It slammed against the wooden pen as it did. Another followed. Then another. A symphony of *bangs* and *thumps* rumbled through Reed as they clumsily lumbered to their knees and hooves. Standing, they turned their heads to Reed.

"The fuck?"

Reed swept the beam back across the barn, his wrist tightening, the light jerking. His thumb found the grip of his pistol. With their eyes reflecting the light, Reed glimpsed sudden movement. Something short ran from the furthest pen on the right to the left, ducking under his light. It appeared like a moving shadow, without discernible details, and didn't reach a cow's neck.

"Okay, hide and seek is over. Come on out, I saw you." He kept his light trained on the last stall and flicked the strap holding his gun to his hip.

"This is Officer Jacobs with Bridgewater PD. I need you to come out now."

He waited.

"If I have to go and get you, I'll be pissed." Reed felt the early pangs of the anger that had gotten him in trouble. *Easy Jacobs*, he repeated to himself. *Breathe.*

With no response and with the animals still staring at him, Reed inched toward the far end of the barn. He kept himself between each row, out of the reach of their mouths, and they turned their heads to continue watching him as he passed. Reed moved the flashlight back and forth, checking every other pen on each side. As he approached the last few stalls, he kept it trained on the left.

"Alright now, let's go," he said, hoping for something in return.

Reaching the last corral, he aimed his light, painting it across the floor. Besides the cow, just hay, wood chips, and crap.

"Fucker."

Then, as one, they went down. A single resounding thump of flesh and bone against wood and dry grass that Reed felt in his sternum. They flopped their heads down to return to sleep.

Reed made a fist and shook his head. He guided his light up and down the rows toward the front of the barn.

Again, he caught movement. This time, the thing was already at the door Reed had entered just moments earlier, and it ducked outside. The gray formless entity blurred from motion, but Reed made out hints of spindly limbs.

He jogged back to the front of the barn. "Fucker's going to get it."

He reached the door and yelled, "Hey!" but Collins waited alone for him outside and under the dim moonlight. "Did you see who just ran out?"

"Who?" the old man asked.

Reed motioned in the direction it went. "Yeah. Someone ran out of the barn here."

"Nope."

"Shorty, little guy."

"Nothing came out. Been standing right here."

Reed glared at Collins in disbelief. Something ran out; he knew it. Maybe he couldn't reasonably make out what it was in the darkness, but it wasn't nothing.

"Maybe it was a raccoon or something."

Collins examined Reed again. His rough voice punctuated his point. "Nothin' came out."

Reed dropped it; there was no sense in arguing with the man. "Okay, I'd say there's nothing to worry about then, huh?"

"All clear," Collins said matter-of-factly. "Now, come on in a moment. Get you some coffee."

The old man started walking toward his home.

"I appreciate it, but I'm on duty. Need to get back out."

Collins continued. "I don't hear your radio goin' off."

Reed followed but aimed his feet at his cruiser. "Yeah, but I have to be on the road."

"Consider it community relations."

Reed's shoulders went slack, and he turned toward the house. "Sure, that's fine."

They walked to the home over patches of dead grass and beaten-down snow. Collins took the two steps up the side porch and kicked off his boots. "Keep yours on, 'case you need to run. Don't worry about the mess."

He entered through the screeching metal storm door into the kitchen, and Reed followed. "Sit." Without looking back, Collins pulled one of the wooden chairs out from the table.

The cop sat and watched the man take a mug from a cabinet and pour coffee from the maker by the sink. The kitchen looked much like it did when Reed saw it almost twenty years ago. It had been maintained and treated well, as it was clean and had new appliances.

Collins moved close to Reed and looked down at him, placing the coffee on the table. "Pie?"

"No, thank you. Seriously." Reed didn't want another argument.

The old man turned and went to the seat across from his visitor.

Reed looked around the room and smiled, mainly for the benefit of his old neighbor. "You've really kept the place nice," Reed said with a motion of his mug before taking a sip.

Collins didn't respond to the compliment and instead asked in a gruff voice, "Why didn't you come back, Reed?"

Reed swallowed the coffee hard. He set the mug down. "What do you mean?"

"Why didn't you come back?" The table creaked as Collins leaned his weight on it. He clasped his hands together.

Reed looked at the man with a blank stare.

The farmer shifted back again and crossed his arms in disappointment. "You tellin' me you don't remember?"

"I'm sorry. I don't know what you're talking about." Reed moved his feet as he thought about just getting up and walking out. He didn't have to put up with the bullshit, and as strong a man as Collins was, Reed was a good 40-plus years younger.

But he didn't move out of respect for the families' histories.

"You were eleven," Collins said it like a punch. "You and Sadie were playing out the back there," he motioned behind him. "Under the tree. Playing..." Collins' eyes trailed off as he searched back in time. "Well, I don't know what you were playin'. I was in here; Mary was upstairs."

Reed remembered the tall and thick tree they would often play around. It had a small dirt patch under it that they would dig in. He also remembered Mary, Joseph's wife, well. She died of cancer a decade ago.

Collins sat quietly a moment, then continued, "Then you come running in here through that door behind me." He pointed to the one across from the door they had both entered that provided access to the other side yard. "Screamin' like a toddler. And you go runnin' to the front." He moved his arm to point to the front room and its exit outside. "Don't even make sense. You runnin' in here just to run out there."

Collins worked his tongue against his dentures. "Then you go on home across the street. Barely saw you after that."

Reed thought back and moved his eyes to the floor. Memories came of playing at the Collins' farm and spending time with Sadie. The animals, scarecrows, and equipment. Then they just didn't hang out anymore after about age 11, and he couldn't place a finger on why.

"I'm sorry, Mr. Collins." Reed looked back up at the man. "I really don't remember that...event in particular."

Collins nodded, his gaze locked on the cop. "Well then." He took a deep breath and stood. "I guess that's it. You had better get back to protectin' and servin'."

The chair legs scraped against the floor as Reed rose, leaving his coffee on the table. He felt the farmer's heavy hand land on his shoulder as he reached the door.

"But one thing now, Reed," the old man's voice came with a squeeze.

"Yes, sir?"

Collins took another deep breath. "You see, Sadie struggled not having you around to talk to about it."

"About what?"

Collins ignored the question. "So I think it best that you take some time. You take some time when things are still, quiet-like, and consider. You think back on that day 'bout twenty years ago, and when you remember, you come on back here."

The man shook Reed, then released his grip. "Any time, I'll be here. I'm always here unless I'm not. But you come back, and tell me why you never returned."

"Sure, Mr. Collins." The odd lecture made Reed feel like a kid again. "I'll do that."

Collins smiled. "Yes, I rightly think you will."

Chapter 6

Back in O'Reilly's office after the conversation with Stanier, Prosser admitted to himself that the unraveling story made sense. Katherine dedicated her life to research that culminated in her satellite, only to watch it be destroyed. He understood someone feeling lost, knowing there was no second chance at their life's pursuit. But he continued his due diligence.

At the window, he saw the coroner examining Katherine's body inside a perimeter of tall, blue plastic sheets. The officers now stood between the fence and the thinning crowd.

Then Prosser noticed the four new onlookers. They huddled together at the outer edge of the students. All male, with buzzed or cleanly cropped hair, black sunglasses, strong postures, and muscle definition. They wore plain, non-branded t-shirts, shorts, and running sneakers. From the eighth floor, Prosser saw one with bright blond hair.

"Spooks?" Prosser asked himself. *Why are spooks here?*

He removed his glasses and stepped back to lean on the desk.

Prosser had dealt with Feds once before, at a rail accident along the border with Springfield. The official story was that a train hit a stalled car on the tracks, and the two people inside didn't get out in time. Their bodies and vehicle were torn apart.

That narrative didn't make sense from what the detective saw in the few minutes he had at the scene before the Feds arrived. A forearm rested ten yards from the tracks, severed above the elbow. The wrist was stripped to tendon and vein, the hand hanging by threads of meat. And a blood-soaked white zip-tie dangled from the torn flesh. Whomever that arm belonged to was tied to something in the car.

An older gentleman had approached Prosser as he walked around the scene taking notes. The man smiled, put his arm on Prosser's shoulder, and took the notepad, flipping its cover closed. "Detective, we appreciate your help here this morning." The man stopped walking and turned Prosser's body to face him. "But we'll take it from here. Why don't you go home to Sarah and Charlie? I heard they just got back from getting groceries."

The detective did as asked, understanding the unspoken threat. He checked on his wife and infant son. Sarah could tell he was on edge, but he brushed it off as being due to witnessing the bloody aftermath of the train accident. She accepted the lie. But he locked all the doors, shut all the windows, and hovered around them for days.

Prosser kept his own private investigation alive after dark, after Sarah fell asleep. He found the victims' social profiles, which had all been created in the month prior. Outside of the accident, the department's Incident Management System held no reports on them. Nor could he track down employment or birth records. It was as if they had never actually existed.

He replaced his glasses and crossed his arms as he stared at the men below. His mind went back to the rabbit hole he had spiraled down into after the train accident, and to the article he had found about the whistleblowers. Two government contractors had secured legal representation to blow the lid off the U.S. Government's collusion with drug cartels. The day of the accident, they both went missing. From the photos he found of them online, Prosser was confident they were the individuals killed by the train.

That's where he stopped his unofficial work on the case. He could never let anything go if it meant not knowing something, but he had reached a point where further investigation would have drawn attention to his efforts.

Not this time, he thought. *Not this time.*

Turning away from the window, Prosser clenched his fists as if clutching at the truth. He wouldn't let go this time. This time, he'd go as far as he needed.

Fucking spooks. Why?

Finding the answer would mean thinking steps ahead of the spooks. That would be the only way to ensure he discovered why Katherine O'Reilly had apparently committed suicide. Not knowing would eat him alive.

He reached into the jacket pocket on the desk chair and found a set of keys and a key fob for a GM vehicle. They rattled against his own as he placed them in his pocket. Prosser took out his phone and switched the camera to video mode. He scanned the entire room with it and went across each shelf to capture the book titles. After tucking his cell away, he grabbed the laptop and slipped it under his jacket, holding it with his left hand.

The detective looked back out the window. The men were gone.

They're probably on their way up.

He opened the office door and took LaFontaine's hand. "Come."

"What's going on?" the cop asked.

They headed away from the elevators, to the stairwell Prosser knew was at the other end of the building. Behind them, the hallway remained vacant. Prosser opened the door to the stairs and pulled the officer in behind him.

"Hey, what's this about, Detective?"

With the echoes of the stairwell, Prosser whispered and slowed his pace. He smiled at the man who might have been in his mid-twenties but looked 18. "I need your help."

"Of course. What?"

"I need you to go straight to campus security, tell them you need the footage now. Don't let them stall. Then bring it right to me. Tell no one you even have it. Hand it to me, don't leave it at my desk or anything. Okay?"

The man nodded. "Yeah, I got it. Give it to you and tell no one."

"That's right. If I'm not at the station, you know where I live?"

"Yup, over on Pleasant Street."

"That's right."

The men reached the double doors out to the side of the building, and Prosser opened it a crack before allowing them to exit.

"After you get the footage, tell the coroner I had to leave and will call him. Thanks again, Officer." Prosser headed for the parking lot at the front, with LaFontaine going in the other direction, deeper into the campus.

Prosser pulled out the GM key fob, held it up, and clicked unlock. A large white SUV facing the road blinked its lights.

Running to it, he checked for any onlookers, but found none. He opened the driver's side door and noticed the garage door opener clipped to the visor. "Perfect," he said as he pulled it off and slid it into his jacket.

After a quick look into the center console and the back seats, finding nothing of interest, he went to the glove box. "Gotcha." He snatched the vehicle registration with Katherine's home address, then shut and locked the car.

With still no Feds in sight, he walked to his vehicle a few rows over. He slid the laptop under the driver's seat before getting in. The Explorer weaved through the parking lot and rolled out onto the main road.

Chapter 7

Reed pulled his vehicle into Sally's Gas, a gas station and convenience store off of Route 4 in rural northern Bridgewater. The glow from the business's lights was the only illumination for over half a mile. They colored the pine trees between it and the acres of dark open land behind.

He let out a slow breath after the odd business with Collins and let his mind drift back to Sadie. For the life of him, he couldn't recall what had sent him running from that yard so long ago.

A cow or chicken got loose and ran at him and Sadie. No, that doesn't sound right.

They were digging or rummaging around the tree and saw an enormous spider. Nope.

A wolf or coyote out in the corn? No.

Sadie tried to kiss me? He chuckled.

He let the question go and stepped inside. The usual night clerk, Patch, attended the register, standing between it and the display of lighters and gum. Reed had never actually seen him sitting.

"Free coffee for first responders," Patch said in the uninterested tone Reed expected.

The store was otherwise empty, also as usual. It was small, with a row of refrigerators with glass doors illuminating the back wall. The lighted panels at the top advertised Coca-Cola, Gatorade, and Fiji water, and the large Owl Creek Brewery bird glowed brightly among the wares.

"Thanks, man!" Reed waved at the clerk.

Reed turned left to the coffee stand and filled a paper cup halfway, then slid on a cardboard sleeve. After a single packet of sugar, he snapped on a cover and took a few steps to the doors.

"How's tonight been? Any trouble?" Reed asked.

"Is this where we start the witty banter?"

The kid looked 20 years old and was articulate. *Gas station attendant* didn't seem appropriate for him. He should be in college somewhere.

"What witty banter?" Reed asked.

"This witty banter."

"This is witty?"

"From what I hear, for Bridgewater's finest, our neon display of gas prices is witty."

Reed sipped the coffee. "Are you disparaging a uniformed police officer?"

"Is that illegal?"

"Well, it's not witty." Reed shrugged.

Patch crossed his arms. "So now you're the wit police?"

"It's a dangerous job."

Patch changed the subject. "Boring night. Listening to the snowflakes hit the ground."

"Why aren't you in school?" Reed asked as he stepped toward the counter.

"I chose a life of debt-free destitution over the alternative."

"Let me guess, debt-ridden destitution?"

Patch placed a finger on his nose.

"Well, do me a favor. Do something."

"Is this nothing?" Patch opened his arms wide to exaggerate the expanse of his responsibilities.

Stepping closer to the register, Reed could see a thick book open and resting on the black stool behind the kid. "What are you reading?"

Patch half glanced back, as if needing to see what Reed meant. "It's a book on Python."

"The snake?"

"No, not the snake. It's a coding language."

"Ah, computers!"

"Yes, computers."

"So you are going to do something with your life!" Reed lifted his cup in a cheers motion and took another sip.

"I'm developing an online game."

Reed nodded. "That's great. When I see you at night, I want you to tell me how you've progressed since the last time we talked. Okay?"

Patch shifted his weight to one leg. "Who are you, my dad?"

"Just someone that appreciates shitty gas station coffee and some witty banter."

"Deal." Patched relaxed his arms.

Reed moved to the doors. "Cool, have a nice night."

"Go get the bad guys, Officer."

Reed pointed to his cup. "Thanks for the coffee." The cold air hit him as he pushed out the door, his boots printing shallow tracks in the dusting of snow. Behind the wheel, he made room in the cup holder for his coffee and looked up as he started the car. As he did, a vibrant green praying mantis rose from under the hood and stood on the windshield. It stared at him.

"The fuck?"

Motionless and unnatural in the cold weather, it sent shivers up Reed's spine. The triangular head with long antennae held large black eyes, darker than the night.

Reed looked around, then realized the sensation of being watched was coming from the bug. Its eyes seemed to infiltrate his own and deposit something squirming inside his thoughts. Reed brought his hand to the top of the steering wheel.

He couldn't remember the last time he had seen one, but the thought suddenly came to him that it should have green eyes. And these weren't just black. Reed felt if he looked at them for too long, he'd lose himself. They would suck him into another plane, never to return.

Just as he was about to shoo it away, the mantis hopped up, its wings expanded, and it flew off into the night.

* * *

"Reed, got your regulars," the familiar voice came over the cruiser's radio.

"I was enjoying my turkey sandwich and Sally's burnt coffee, Cin."

"Highland Park, unit 30."

"Got it."

Putting down his food, Reed flipped on his cruiser's flashing lights. The call would be a good distraction from the odd evening at the farm and the insect that seemed to want access to his psyche.

A couple of miles later, he came to the Highland Park condos, a block of 200 identical units. The dirty beige siding matched the mud along their foundations, and the carports' roofs sagged at their centers.

Reed parked his vehicle at the small roundabout at the center of the complex, where he saw Judy and Dilly Bombard arguing outside for the neighborhood to witness. Reed kept the lights on and approached the couple.

"What is it tonight, newlyweds?"

Dilly, a rotund man whose gut hung over his sweatpants and out from under his t-shirt, had one arm stretched on Judy's shoulder, keeping her at bay. Judy had positioned herself to face Reed and swung an arm to knock Dilly's off her own.

"Fuckin' Dillweed is what it is!" she hollered.

Dilly kept his mouth shut. Judy had on her once-fluffy slippers, which were now soaked. She also donned a heavy flower-print robe. The two couldn't have been over 50, but looked closer to 70.

"I'm seeing you two too often now," Reed said as he stood close. "What's it about that you need to disturb your neighbors?"

Judy huffed and crossed her arms. The door to the couple's second-floor unit was wide open.

"Well?" he asked.

"Dilly crushed my smokes."

"Ain't good for ya'," the big man wheezed.

"You're giving out health advice now, Dill?" She looked him up and down.

The man squinted at Reed.

"I said I was quitting," Judy explained.

Reed moved his arms like directing airplanes on a tarmac. "K, inside we go so I can get back to real emergencies?"

Each sneered in agreement, and Reed followed them up the wooden stairs. Judy went first, and Dilly followed with one hand on the rail and the other on the outside wall. He took each step with care, heaving his weight painfully.

Inside, Reed guided them forward as he shut the door. Judy took her spot in the recliner, and Dilly remained standing in front of the sofa. Their living area needed fresh paint, but they kept the floor free from clutter.

Dilly adjusted his shirt. "She been quitting for a long time."

"It takes time, Dilly. And those ain't cheap no more," she scowled.

Dilly waved his arms and matched her volume. "We could use the money!"

"Then get a job!"

"I got disability! You got nothin'. You get out and get a job!"

Reed raised a hand. "Jesus Christ, Dilly, you don't fucking sit, I'm going to show you that Weebles do fall down."

The couple stopped bickering. Dilly leaned to his right to place an arm on the couch and lowered himself to the center cushion.

"Do you think you two can talk this out and keep your business up here?" Given Dilly's size, it surprised Reed that he ventured down the stairs for his spats.

"Yeah, we're okay," Judy said with her eyes locked on Reed.

"Look, I keep coming out here because people call when you're fighting outside. They just don't want to hear it. So I have to drive out to get you to come in. And my patience is running thin. How about just working it out in here? Stop wasting resources for your little arguments."

"She gets so pissed, I gotta get air."

"So, you tell me the plan. How are we going to prevent calls to the police?" Reed tightened his grip on his belt.

Dilly shuffled in the seat, and Judy stared at him for an answer.

When none came, Reed sighed. "Fine. You do you. But someday you won't let up, and I'm going to really lose my shit."

They looked away.

"Judy, you feel safe with him?" Reed had to ask in order to leave. Recording their answers in his report would give him the cover if something were to happen later.

"Yeah."

"Dilly, you feel safe?"

"Sure."

"Great, have a good night and stay inside."

Reed opened the door and turned to close it.

As he moved to the stairs, he saw the praying mantis on the railing. It stood upright, on its four back legs, with its front extended wide as if waiting to attack. Just like earlier, the black eyes stared at Reed.

"What the fuck?" he laughed.

Reed half turned to knock on the Bombard's door, but then realized they'd offer nothing resembling wisdom.

"Isn't it too cold for you, dude?"

The mantis didn't move.

Reed shook his head and descended the stairs without looking back.

The mantis's gaze followed him.

Chapter 8

Prosser approached Professor O'Reilly's single-story ranch home from his SUV, looking up and down the street for occupied cars monitoring the house. The suburban neighborhood was filled with similar homes, made unique with paint colors and landscaping. Katherine's was white with blue shutters and a slight incline to the yard.

Not seeing anything suspicious, Prosser turned into the driveway and up to the garage. The LED on the garage opener glowed red. He tapped the button, waited for the bay to rumble open, pulled in, and killed the engine. The door groaned shut behind him.

The empty space, save for a rake and broom that hung from hooks on the wall, had plenty of room for Katherine's larger vehicle. The door at the side of the garage led Prosser to a small mudroom with an old, dingy tiled floor, barely big enough for two people to stand. To his left, he found a glass door to the backyard. He opened the door to his right, revealing steep steps to a dark basement. Ahead, the opening to the kitchen.

He stepped through to find an old-fashioned white refrigerator with rounded corners and a small top freezer. The rest of the kitchen kept the vintage style with pale blue walls, white cabinets, and a deep porcelain farmhouse sink.

Through a spacious opening in the wall to the right, above a buffet table, he could see the living room. He passed through the adjacent threshold to find the area sparse. A couch, two side tables with old lamps and books, and two recliners. No television. It didn't appear a room much lived in. A large bay window, covered by thin, silky curtains, looked out onto the street.

He picked up the small photo frame that rested on one of the side tables. It showed Katherine and a man in a selfie pose. They each wore heavy jackets, and behind them loomed a mountain of bright orange, red, and yellow trees. Prosser studied the man's face. He'd seen it somewhere, the scene, maybe. He pocketed the thought along with the photo, sliding it free and into his jacket. He set the empty frame back as he'd found it.

Prosser moved to the hall, which held four rooms. The first on the right was a spare bedroom with a twin bed, a roll-top desk, and a tall dresser. To the left was a small, windowless bathroom. Further down, what appeared to be Katherine's bedroom. The queen-size bed was made, make-up products were scattered across the top of a dresser, and a mirror stood in the corner.

The last room caught his attention. Unlike the others, its contents spread across desks, the floor, and bookcases. One area seemed to be the primary workplace: a tall, rough wooden workbench with various small tools, microchips, and wires.

Prosser moved to the closest bookcase. The publications included guides to electronics and micro-processing, in no particular order. Many appeared hastily placed on shelves, with some even upside-down. He took a series of photos of the library.

The floor held a collection of broken circuit boards in one corner and vacuum tubes in another.

On the workbench, Prosser found screwdrivers, clipped wires, and other electronic parts. At the center of the workspace sat a black metal box, a single thin silver wire curling from the top like a stray strand of hair. He picked it up. It was dense and heavier than it had any right to be for something about the size of a few stacked cell phones. He turned to the window, its shade burning in the afternoon light.

If the Feds were at the campus, they surely would come here. If Prosser was to understand what they were after, he had to be gone before. Otherwise, he'd be railroaded again. Another circuit around the room turned up nothing. Holding onto the strange box, he walked back down the hall to the living area and looked out the front window for any sign of visitors. All clear.

Prosser went to the garage and got into his SUV. He slipped the box into the back seat with Katherine's laptop and opened the garage door. The tires of his Explorer squealed as he sped away.

Chapter 9

After a workout at the department's gym and a quick shower, Reed drove home with the rising morning sun. The long stretch of road held few buildings, with acres between each. His house sat 50 yards back, a lone tree at the center of the expansive yard. The paint was peeling and everything sagged, but he had it rent-free.

Behind the home, a football field-sized yard abutted a preserved forest.

As he entered the tattered foyer, Badge jumped from his soft bed by the fireplace in the adjoining living room and ran over the chipped wooden floor to his owner. The long-haired, gray and black German Shepherd reared onto its hind legs and licked Reed.

"Hey, buddy!" Reed bent down to hug and pet him before slipping off his jacket for the rack and boots for the muddy rubber mat.

He crossed the sparse living room, its white walls washed gray by years of fireplace use. On the left, his second-hand couch and rickety coffee table. Above the hearth, the faded and framed print of Bosch's *The Last Judgment* triptych. Next to it, an antique clock on the mantel. A stiff wooden chair sat in the corner. Beside it, a lamp whose yellow shade only made the room more unpleasant. Reed lived so minimally that the quarter-cord of wood was stacked directly on the floor to the left of the fireplace, while the lone tools, a singed poker and ash shovel, leaned on the brick surround.

The nicest thing in the room was Badge's orthopedic bed.

Reed moved to the kitchen and drank straight from the tap. Not seeing Wendy, he headed back to the foyer and up the stairs with the dog following. Reed found her in the bathroom, readying for work.

"Hey, babe," she said as she put on a subtle pink lipstick. Wendy was 5'5" in heels and fit. Her defined calves sprang from her skirt, advertising her dedication to the gym. Her reddish-brown hair fell past her shoulders.

Before he could answer, Wendy's earrings, deep black triangles that Reed didn't recognize, caught his eye in the mirror. They seized him. His skin crawled. The shapes swarmed at him like wasps, and he was stepping backward before he understood why. Between Wendy and the mirror, the triangles multiplied and closed in.

"What are those?" he asked, motioning to the jewelry.

"I got those yesterday, you like?" Wendy smiled.

"No."

The room tilted. His legs buckled and he caught the doorframe. He fumbled down the short hall to the bedroom and locked the door behind him. Reed knelt to one knee just in front of the bed and placed a hand on his forehead.

"Breathe," he whispered.

The cold floor almost woke his mind. He needed another minute. He took a slow breath and looked up at the walls, their paint cracked in long, wandering lines. The lone dresser had uneven drawers, and the windows were milky with age.

"You okay?" Wendy asked after the gentle knock.

"Yeah, one minute," Reed said as he felt the sweat bead on his head.

The thick wood door muffled her voice. "If you don't like the earrings, I can return them."

"Sure."

Reed hurried to the window to free his mind from the tension, not believing his own words. *Come on, you're not a controlling dick. What's going on?* He took a deep breath.

"What are you doing in there?"

"Uh," Reed looked around before rounding the bed to open the small closet to grab sweatpants. "Just changing."

The doorknob rattled. "Can I come in?"

"One sec." He threw his jeans into the basket on the floor and jumped into the sweats.

Reaching for the doorknob, the vision of the jewelry stopped him. "Do you have those on?"

"The earrings?"

Reed could see her questioning face in his mind. "Yeah. Take them off."

"What?"

"Please?"

Wendy scoffed. "Fine."

The door scraped against the frame as he opened it to his girlfriend standing with her arms on her hips.

"What was that?" she asked.

"I don't know."

"Reed, what's going on? Why are you freaking out?"

Reed dropped to the bed. Wendy moved to stand over him, and he recognized the look, the same measured, almost clinical appraisal she gave the skinny guys who struggled at the gym.

"I have no fucking clue. I saw those and just lost it. It's nothing."

She placed a hand on his shoulder. "You're stressed or something. Maybe you need to eat."

"No. No, that's not it."

"You're not getting enough sleep."

Reed stood and walked away from the bed. Shortly after meeting Wendy, a fight broke out at the gym while they exercised together. Two behemoths of men started brawling, and Reed rushed into the fray to break it up. He got hit numerous times before successfully pinning one man down while fending off the other. Through bloodied vision, he glimpsed Wendy's wide eyes. He knew then what she desired most was strength.

"What is it, then?" she asked.

"No idea. But, it was a weird night."

Wendy nodded like she was pretending to understand. "Okay. But don't pull that shit." She chuckled, but Reed didn't find it funny.

"Can you return them?"

Wendy straightened up in surprise. "The earrings? Seriously?"

"Yes. You did offer."

"Yeah, I guess. That's really fucking odd though."

"I'll buy you a pair of something else."

"Fine."

She headed back for the bathroom. "I have to finish getting ready."

Reed made himself breakfast and played fetch with Badge

as Wendy got ready. After saying goodbye, he sat in the living room in silence with his dog curled up at his side. He thought about those triangles and the unfamiliar feelings that welled in him. Badge groaned and rolled onto his side.

Where did that come from? He had no answer to his own question.

And what about Joseph? What was that about? And that mantis? Was it the same one? Reed got dizzy from the thoughts and the long night.

He retired to the bedroom, pulled the shades down, shut the door, and turned out the lights. In the darkness, Reed stripped to his underwear and got under the covers.

Within minutes, he was asleep.

* * *

My hand is on the trunk of the maple. Its bark carved deeply with lines. I run my fingers down them. Rough.

Sadie's here and playing. Running around it. Dodging me.

The sun sparkles off the pollen in the air from the fields of wildflowers and corn. Like stars during the day or visits from fairies.

Sadie's blond hair whips at the fairy dust.

It feels warm.

Sadie has stopped.

She's looking at me.
For something.
She wants something.
Terror.
Her eyes.
Her eyes aren't happy anymore.
Horror.
She wants something. From me.
To protect her.
She wants me to protect her.
Silence. Silence all around.
Stillness.
Nothing's moving now.
Sadie just...bent over in a wail.
I can't look up.
Something won't let me.
I need to protect Sadie.
Tears in her eyes.
I can't look up.
Her mouth is open.
She's screaming. A black cavernous mouth.
But no sound.
I can't look up.
It won't let me.

* * *

Reed woke screaming, pushing his body up and back against the wall. "Jesus!" Light broke the darkness as Reed reached for the window and lifted the shade.

"Fuck..." Wiping the sweat from his brow, he noticed his drenched hair.

He looked at the clock on the nightstand. Noon. Reed slid back down in bed. Night shift at 8 p.m., a break from five to ten, day shift through to 6 p.m. Thirty-plus hours stretching out ahead of him. Sleeping until 5 would no longer happen, not with his nerves on edge as the horror of the dream hadn't left him. On his break, he would consider a power nap and run to re-energize. Regardless, being awake now wasn't good; he'd be dragging himself through the next 30 hours.

Reed stood and walked through the house to the foyer, where he opened the door. The cold air rushed in, needling his skin. He shut his eyes and breathed. Badge appeared at his side and sat.

Chapter 10

Prosser sat in his Explorer, looking back at the items he had taken from O'Reilly's home, and he weighed his options. Leave them in the vehicle and the spooks could swipe them without him knowing. Bring them inside the station; they could still pull bureaucratic bullshit to take her things, but at least he'd be there to put up a fight.

He walked the short distance to the front door, the box and laptop tucked under his left arm. Inside, he greeted the officer at the front desk and headed to the second floor. Rows of old metal desks filled the floor, the back wall broken up by a handful of offices. With only four desks occupied by various officers or detectives completing paperwork, he moved to his own at the back by Chief Oberman's office.

Prosser tucked Katherine's items in the bottom drawer. With one motion, he swiveled in his chair to face Oberman's office and leaned back. She was on the phone, and Prosser smiled as she glanced up.

"Detective!" LaFontaine appeared behind him, holding a small USB thumb drive. "Twenty-four hours of footage. More than I asked for."

"Excellent, officer."

"Security said they watched it, sped up, and that only O'Reilly entered that office."

Prosser took it and held it in a fist. "Any trouble acquiring it?"

"None. Security was helpful."

Prosser nodded. "Anything else happen? Talk to anyone? See anything?"

LaFontaine shifted his weight, eyes finding the floor.

"Officer?"

The cop shook his head and raised his shoulders. "Yeah, but you know, was probably nothing to sweat."

"What's not to sweat?" Prosser asked as he tucked the USB into his pants pocket.

"A couple guys, plain clothes, flashed badges real quick, so I didn't get a good look. They asked who was lead on this."

"You didn't get what agency they were with?"

"No, sorry."

Prosser leaned forward. "What did you tell them?"

LaFontaine shuffled in place again. "I said I wasn't at liberty to share any information at the time, and they should contact the Department with questions."

"Good job." The tactic wouldn't delay them much, but perhaps it bought him enough time to not already have Oberman breathing down his neck.

"Now," Prosser stood and shook the man's hand, "get back to work."

"Of course. And, hey, call if you need anything else, okay?"

"Sure thing, Officer."

Prosser sat back down and watched LaFontaine make his way to the stairs.

Secure the evidence and meet with family. The former he'd

do clandestinely, and would wait a day before bringing it to the department's IT team. The latter, he'd track down her boyfriend and family, as was standard procedure. That wouldn't raise any red flags.

Prosser swung the chair around to see Oberman at her desk. *Like nothing's going on,* he thought to himself. *Suicide, open and shut.* And while he believed that to be true, he wouldn't say anything that might threaten his ability to continue digging into the case. This was no longer about what happened to Katherine; she jumped. Not even why. This was about the Feds. What else was going on? Was there something else Dr. O'Reilly was doing to get their attention?

Oberman hung up the phone and motioned for Prosser. He stood with a smile and entered her office, not bothering to shut the door behind him. *No signs of secrets here.*

"What's going on? Dr. O'Reilly?" she asked.

Oberman was a strong woman. The Department's first female Chief, and the youngest in its history. Prosser knew she played rugby in college, and the fact that she could kick half the department's ass went a long way with the respect she garnered. Her brown hair was pulled back in a low ponytail, and as usual, she wore light makeup.

"Pretty clear at this point. Did you hear about the satellite?"

"I did." Her tone acknowledged the impact that must have had on Katherine.

Prosser sat on the brown leather couch facing the Chief and exhaled. "Yeah, awful, right? Her life's work. Just gone in a flash, and sounds like the cost meant doing it again wasn't going to happen. It devastated her. She even took down an image of dark matter from her wall. It was some important discovery of hers."

"So, suicide? That's it?" She dropped her hands to her desk.

The question pecked at him. *Why is she asking? Who was she just on the phone with?* There were messier cases than this she'd never once checked in on.

Prosser smiled at the Chief. He wouldn't show his cards, even if she had already shown hers. "Yeah, open and closed. But why do you ask?"

Oberman leaned back in her chair. "Shut the door."

The two remained silent as Prosser did as told, then he took one of the stiff armchairs closer to her desk.

"I'm getting calls. A lot of them," she said.

"About?"

Oberman drummed her fingers on the arm of her chair. "Closure. Hints that she was...mentally unhealthy. But to be honest, the way they were saying it made it sound like they were trying to convince me that was the case. They just want this to quietly go away."

"Who called?" Prosser tried his best to sound disinterested.

"Officials with high clearances that you don't find on LinkedIn. And the Governor."

This wasn't just some minor interest from spooks. *What the hell was she doing?*

Oberman squinted. Prosser knew that look, the one that remembered how he'd earned the nickname *Presser* interrogating a state senator for five straight hours. During that time, he painted the middle-aged man with a superiority complex into a corner until he broke down and admitted he had been giving high school girls cocaine at parties at his home. That relentless approach didn't seem to be what Oberman was after.

"Well, I can tell you it looks like suicide. I still need to complete my investigation, of course. Review security footage, talk to her family. But it appears she was alone in that room and jumped."

Prosser watched Oberman's eyes dart around his face for any hints of subversion. Then she nodded and leaned forward, her elbows pressed hard on her desk.

"I've known you a long time, John," she said.

He sat silently. A question would have to be asked; he wasn't about to give anything otherwise.

"And I've never known you to be so flippant about any case. You always have something to press."

"I'm not following."

"The fuck you aren't." She smiled. "What aren't you telling me?"

The calculations rolled in his head. He could admit to something now, but downplay it so as not to cause alarm. Or admit nothing and be in a heap of trouble later.

"Yeah, okay. There were Feds at the scene. But, God honest here, Lesley, it seems O'Reilly jumped."

She dropped her hands and tapped her fingers on the desk, her eyes locked on his. "Prosser, I fucking swear to you, you fuck up, and I'll hang you out in the street during the Fourth of July parade. The people calling me are not to be fucked with. You tell me everything and submit your report to me *before* filing."

"Hey, first, you got it. No problem. But this is what it is, Chief. I don't know why they are calling you, but it doesn't change what happened." Prosser dropped his palms onto his knees.

He told the truth, just not in its entirety. Walking from the case wouldn't happen. Not for anyone.

That seemed to put Oberman at ease, but she kept her eyes

on the detective. "Okay then. Okay."

"So, can I go?"

"What are you doing next?"

"Talk to the boyfriend, then her parents—both maybe tomorrow. I also have to watch the security footage to confirm no one was in there besides Katherine. Once that's all done, you'll have my report."

"Before you file."

"Before I file." He raised his right arm and stuck out his pinkie finger. "Swear it."

"K, get the fuck out of here."

Prosser stood and exited, returning to his desk. With his back to the Chief, he checked the drawer for his evidence.

Chapter 11

At 10 p.m., Reed sat in the cruiser, struggling to keep his eyes open. Tasked with patrol in northern Bridgewater again, he watched the occasional car pass and compared his estimation of the vehicle's speed to the radar on the dash.

A dispatcher's voice interrupted him, "Jacobs, we have a four-fifteen. Overlook Park. Group of teens having a party and making quite a bit of noise."

"On it."

Reed pulled his vehicle onto the road and turned around. Typically, the four-fifteens came later in the night. Considering the hour, he figured the group would be on the younger side.

Overlook Park was on a hill overlooking a sprawling upper-middle-class neighborhood. As Reed entered, he found it empty. He parked his cruiser and walked the stone-lined ridge to check for vandalism or litter, but found none. The semi-circular parking area hugged an inactive fountain. In summer, kids would make a wish and toss in a penny. Reed noticed something dark resting on the short granite wall that surrounded it. It took form as he got closer, and he picked it up. It had to be twenty pounds.

Reed held a lead mask, the proper size and shape for a person. It was thick, with two holes for eyes, a narrow slit for the mouth, and a space for the wearer's nose. It was dull and gray and didn't have any apparatus to attach it to someone's head. He brought it to his car and dropped it in the trunk. *Kids thinking they're cool,* he thought.

Returning to the ledge, he looked out again and found the nearest home. Off to the right, about forty yards, and down an embankment. A large house with its lights on. While the call may have come from there, Reed couldn't see anyone.

Dark, undulating clouds blanketed the region, blocking most of the moonlight. Reed looked forward to the warmer weather forecasted for next week. For early April, it was far too cold.

The crackling of the small radio on his shoulder fractured his thoughts. "Reed, car four-four. Reed, car four-four. Please respond."

"Reed. What's up?"

"Where the hell have you been? Is everything okay?" the voice rang through the radio.

"What do you mean? I just got to Overlook, no one's here."

The dispatcher seemed to calm. "That was over an hour ago."

"It's like ten o'clock. The call was maybe 10 minutes ago." He felt annoyed that he needed to defend himself. He hadn't taken a break or even stopped for coffee yet.

"Reed, it's 11:30."

He checked his watch. 11:30. Where had the hour gone? He arrived just minutes after the call, walked the perimeter, and found the mask...it had been fifteen minutes, tops. Reed pushed the button to speak to the dispatcher. "Guess I lost track of time out here."

"Thinking about old times at Overlook?" The dispatcher insinuated that Reed had used the park for the purpose it was known for among young lovers.

"I was too busy with football," Reed responded.

"Sure, bud. Get back to work. We were worried here and almost sent someone to check on things."

"Roger."

Reed watched the clouds roll across the sky as he attempted to figure out what had happened with that hour. But no answers came.

"I need a coffee."

The drive to Sally's pulled him deeper into rural Bridgewater. Pulling into the gas station, he parked at the side of the building to avoid being in the way of the pumps.

"Free coffee for first responders," Patch said as Reed entered.

Reed waved to the clerk as he turned toward the coffee before stopping in his tracks. "What's this?"

"What, no like?"

Reed stood staring at it.

"I don't know about you, Officer Jacobs, but when I think 'coffee creamer' I immediately think 'praying mantis.'"

The cardboard display stared back at Reed. A large green head of a praying mantis, with a horrible jaw that looked like it would rip him apart, and big, deep black eyes that examined his thoughts. The head floated above the circular rim of a black coffee mug, steam rising from it and enveloping the bug's head.

An uneasiness whorled within Reed. He contemplated not

getting coffee at all; he didn't want to get closer to the thing. But a cardboard bug wouldn't bully him. Then the lights inside the gas station flickered and went out with an audible static hiss.

Through the windows, Reed could see the pump lights still on, but he sensed a strange stillness. The clouds didn't move, the same for the tree branches, and the dusting of snow on the ground. Then the pump lights blinked twice before turning off. Only the dim moonlight from the clouds' dark filter offered any illumination.

"I guess the power is out," Reed said with his attention pulled away from the mantis. He turned to Patch.

The young man stood in his usual spot, both hands touching the counter. His long-sleeved uniform shirt rested on his thin frame. His eyes open, glassy and unblinking. An unnatural smile was left on his face with his lips apart, teeth clenched, and the edges of his mouth pointed slightly upwards. He looked positioned by someone, or something, who understood that humans smile, but had never seen one before. He stood motionless, frozen in place.

"Patch?" Reed asked, feeling in his bones that he wouldn't get a reply.

"Patch?"

Reed walked to the counter with deliberate steps. The clerk's teeth were clenched so tight Reed figured he'd have to be breathing through his nose, but not hearing anything; he had no indication Patch breathed at all.

Reed leaned closer, preparing himself for Patch to jump at him like a juvenile prank. A glimmer in Patch's eyes caught Reed's attention. He leaned on the counter to pull himself in for a better look. The reflection of a light in the store's corner shone white in his pupils. Reed turned his head to the front corner of the building but saw only shadow. There was nothing to cause the reflection.

After pushing away from the counter, he waved his hand in front of Patch's face. No reaction.

"What the fuck is going on?"

To check the outside again, he stepped to the doors. The world remained still. He grabbed the cold handles and tried to pull them open, but they wouldn't budge. Then, as if it had been waiting for Reed to realize his predicament, something rustled from his right, then abruptly stopped.

As Reed waited, the sound came again, like a mouse dragging a box. Reed moved to the coffee counter, a hand on his holster. Another step, and the sound of shifting paper came. The mantis display jittered. Not wanting to be too close, he took a wide angle.

The display, in the night's darkness, seemed alive. The mantis head partially protruded through the cardboard. Its disgusting mouth with pincers and fine hairs opened and closed in a struggle. The strange appendages reached for anything to pull into its jaws. Its head moved side to side, revealing each black eye. It strained to escape the fabricated reality of the coffee creamer's display.

"What the fuck?"

Reed stepped back, bumping into the shelves of potato chip bags, then moved to his left to get further away.

The head continued its impossible labor, stretching with each outward push. As it rotated its ugly head, the black eyes reflected the white light that didn't exist. Darkness covered anything that might have been hidden there.

"Fuck this." Reed shook his head.

He walked to the doors, set on escaping. Just as he was about to touch the metal of the handles, the world came back to life. The LED lights overhead and on the various signs lit, the radio station continued its nightly playlist over the speakers, and Patch jumped back in alarm.

The door opened from the outside as Reed reached for it, and before he could avoid the collision, a woman in a white sleeveless dress entered and bumped into him.

"Sorry," Reed said as he angled his body to sneak by her to the outside. He only managed a quick glance at her. She was slender, with straight black hair. Her eyes were set too far apart and high on her head. *A deformity*, he thought.

"The gas here is way too expensive," the woman said as she closed the door.

Reed ran around the building to his cruiser, started it, and hit the overheads. He looked over his shoulder as he pressed the accelerator and backed up, turning the wheel. Through the rear windscreen, he could now see the woman's car parked by the pumps. A white Tesla.

Quickly shifting the vehicle into *Drive*, Reed pushed it to its limits and skidded onto Route 4 and away from the gas station.

"Fuck fuck fuck..."

Pain shot through his arms as he gripped the wheel as tightly as he could.

"Fuck!" he yelled in a terrified anger.

Seeing the brightly lit but empty parking lot of the pet food store ahead, Reed yanked the wheel to the right and hit the brakes. The cruiser almost rolled as he pulled in. He stopped under a lamppost and turned off the car.

His breathing escalated. With deep breaths, he gripped and squeezed his thighs. Reed slowly let the air out, forcing a physical calm for his mind to follow.

After collecting himself, he played the events over in his mind, confirming that he had actually seen what he thought he had. *The power went out. The outside world froze, as did Patch. That...thing came to life. The reflection of something in both Patch and the mantis' eyes.*

And that woman?

What the fuck was up with her? She didn't look...human.

The thought struck him. *She didn't look human.*

And what was that she said? The gas was too expensive. She drove a Tesla!

It made no sense.

Reed rested his head on the side window, and the cold glass felt good against his skin. For the remainder of the night, he stayed within the steel cage of the cruiser.

* * *

Between shifts, Reed's sneakers pounded against the pavement for a quick jog, beating the previous night's events from his mind and reinvigorating his senses. Then, after a shower, he reclined in his car for some shut-eye.

At the start of his day shift, Reed circled blocks of Old Bridgewater and allowed only quick conversations. Staying mobile was the only way to fight off his rising exhaustion and to keep the thoughts of the previous night from tormenting him.

He passed the wood-fired pizza joint, its brick facade shaded by the black awning, and the bookstore no wider than a grocery aisle. "Good morning," he said to the mailman emptying the collection box, who nodded back.

Old Bridgewater was a favorite destination for many in the area. The centuries-old buildings were restored decades ago as part of a revitalization effort that turned the section into a hotbed of locally owned commerce.

Though cold, the sun began melting the snow-packs along the road and businesses, and puddles formed. As Reed's body settled into a rhythm, his strides getting longer, gunshots shattered the calm.

Pedestrians collapsed to their knees or darted into shops as drivers hit their accelerators and sped off. A white SUV's tires screeched as it careened around an old woman who held up her purse and shimmied across the street. Reed didn't flinch. He glimpsed a man in a black hoodie and red sweatpants, a gun in his hand, rounding the covered bus stop in front of Quarry Park. With his hood up, Reed couldn't get a good look at him. The man burst up a side street and out of sight.

Not seeing anyone injured from the gun, Reed launched into a sprint, crossing the street and turning to follow the man. He passed Quarry Park, the temperature still too cold for its fountain to be on, and its stretch of grass still covered in snow. Adrenaline rushed through him, forcing out all the fatigue. His pulse quickened. His eyes dilated. A smile came to Reed. *Finally, some action.*

Reed's hand brushed against his pistol as he ran. *Easy now*, he said to himself.

He hit the radio on his shoulder. "10-71 at Quarry Park. In pursuit. North on Wells."

The distance between them halved as the shooter zig-zagged between cars and around people. Reed saw him slip on a patch of ice and hit the ground, but the man hurriedly rose, tossed his hood back on, and continued running.

The perp turned down a street on his right, and as Reed took two more steps, he peeked his head around the corner. The man's arm rose to train his weapon on Reed.

Screams came again as the gunshot cracked the air and the bullet ricocheted off a store's sign as Reed jumped into a brick alcove.

Without hesitation, he dashed back out in pursuit, the perp already out of sight.

"Turning onto Morgan," he alerted dispatch as he took the corner at speed, pushing his hand against the wall of a bakery to keep his momentum.

Horns honking and brakes shrieking drew Reed's attention across the street, where the shooter dodged cars before rushing into an alley. Reed slid as he changed direction and jumped over the hood of a parked sedan. He followed the man. The heat from Reed's racing blood caused steam to rise from his skin and crowded out any sense he had for his own safety.

As he reached the alley, a metal door 50 feet in slowly began closing. It creaked as it did, echoing along the brick walls. He sprinted to it and grabbed the rusted handle. Another shot rang out, sending sparks flying from the metal.

He covered his head before glancing inside. The man's foot at the top of the dark stairwell pushed him into a hallway to the left.

Reed took the steps three at a time. "Bridgewater PD!"

Another shot hit the wall in front of Reed, halting him at the top.

"Bridgewater PD." He flipped the cover of his holster and drew his sidearm. "I'm not going to give you another warning. Slide your weapon over to me and lie face down."

"Come and get it!" the perp yelled before firing. The bullet nicked the corner of a wall.

Reed mapped the space fast. Three feet between the lighted hallway and the stairs behind him. A four-foot width of the hall, with unknown contents, and beyond that, the rest of the entranceway to a closed door. He needed to understand the space. How many potential exits did the man have? Were there any civilians?

After two quick breaths and pointing his feet across the hall, Reed swung across and glanced down at the perp, who rang off another failed shot.

One door, no bystanders. Hall twenty feet long. The guy looked about 35, going on 60, with a rough beard and weathered skin.

Reed heard the rattle of a doorknob, urgent, then desperate.

"There's nowhere for you to go. This is the last chance I'm giving you. Toss your weapon down to me." Reed said forcefully with his back to the wall.

Two more bullets exploded drywall inches from Reed's shoulder, spattering his face with the white dust.

Reed recognized the cloud settling over him, the rage that burned out reason, the animal need to close the distance and hit something until it stopped moving. On the other hand, he couldn't just start firing down the hall. A stray bullet through a door or wall could wound or kill someone. He re-holstered his pistol.

"Come on, pig!" the man called out.

Reed clenched his jaw and brought both fists up to his chest, squeezing until his knuckles ached, as if his hands had already found the man's throat.

"I said, come and get it, pig!"

Blood rushed to Reed's head, pushing out any last bit of concern. The anger took him over. He pivoted and stepped into the hall, his frame taking the bulk of the space.

The man raised his gun as his eyes widened. Then he smiled before...

clunk

His grin faded, and he looked at the weapon. "What the?"

In response, Reed took two large running steps.

clunk clunk

The man tried popping off two more shots, his face now a deer in headlights.

Reed ripped the gun from the aggressor's hand and pushed him back. He tossed the weapon down and raised his right fist. With his left arm, he held the man firmly against the wall. Reed's knuckles cracked as he stretched his fingers before resetting his fist. The perp closed his eyes and held his breath.

"Jacobs!" the voice called out from behind.

Reed turned his head to see Keyes approaching with his sidearm out. He looked back at the frightened man and snarled as he lowered his fist.

"I got him," Keyes said as he spun the man around and cuffed him.

Reed stepped back and took a breath.

Keyes dropped the man to the ground on his knees before gripping Reed's arm. "What the hell happened, man? You okay?"

"Yeah, yeah, just glad you got here when you did."

Keyes lowered his voice. "You do anything to him? Just tell me now, Jacobs, I don't want trouble for you."

Reed looked down at the handcuffed suspect, who threw himself onto his backside to stare up at Reed with a smile.

"No, didn't touch him." Reed felt his blood rushing upward again. "I gotta get some air." He walked down the stairs and moved deeper into the alley, where he ducked behind an old dumpster and punched it twice.

Reed rested his back against the brick wall and placed his hands on his head. *Get your shit together. That gun jammed, and if it didn't, God knows where you'd be right now. Don't end up dead like Pops.*

* * *

"You're so damn lucky." Chief Oberman stood behind her desk.

"I know," Reed said from the chair in front of his boss.

"No, you asshole. I don't mean you're lucky you didn't get killed. I mean, you're lucky he shot at you in the building and fired his weapon in the park. Otherwise, this conversation would be your last as an officer."

"That doesn't sound like luck. That sounds like me doing my job."

Oberman crossed her arms and looked down at him. "Bullrushing? Kamikazes are a liability, and goddammit, I know what you would have done if Keyes hadn't gotten there!"

Reed shrugged. "I had to take action. He was a threat."

"Jesus." Oberman moved behind her desk and sat. "You sound so much like your father."

"I'm not my father."

"Pff." Oberman cupped her hands on the desk. "I hear you're studying for the NDIT."

"Yes, ma'am."

"You're a smart guy. I'm sure you'll pass. But that doesn't mean you'll ever be a detective."

Reed went still.

"You have to apply. And unless you clean up your shit, I'm not promoting you. Is that clear?"

"Yes, ma'am."

"Talk to Detective Morello. He's young and smart. Bright future."

Reed's hands found the arms of the chair and held on.

Oberman's expression softened. Her shoulders dropped. "Look, I know you need the extra money right now, but I also don't need a reason to pull shifts. Focus on what you need to do. Okay?"

Reed nodded, understanding her message.

"Get out of here."

Chapter 12

"Where's Daddy?" Charlie skipped along the still brown grass in his family's backyard, clutching the soft football with both hands. His boots carried clumps of mud.

The dark-stained deck caught the last of the light, its swing set and slide stood quiet now that the cold had come. The two-story, yellow home in shadow.

The sky hinted at the dark night to come, and Sarah wanted Charlie to see his father before going to bed. "Work, honey," she said.

Charlie stopped and ran over to his mother, who sat on the edge of the wooden porch. He snuggled in between her knees and dropped his head to her chest. His dark brown hair smelled of shampoo. "I want to see him."

"I know, sweetie."

Sarah Prosser had Charlie late in life, at forty-four, feeling like she wasn't quite ready before then to be a mom. Now, at five years old, he brought a heightened sense of duty and wonder. Sarah had dark hair and kept her slender 5'6" figure. She wore sweatpants and a t-shirt, her typical after-work attire since having Charlie and doing too much laundry.

Sometimes she'd want to curse John for coming home late or missing some event. But she would remind herself of the work he did, often tracking down murderers or other serious criminals, and that he promised to retire when Charlie was ten. She'd be fifty-four then, and likely still working as a project manager for a company that made applications for educational institutions. At fifty-nine, John should still have enough energy to manage a budding teenager.

"Can I have a drink?"

"Yeah, come on." Sarah took Charlie's hand and led him inside, through the sliding glass door to the dining area of the open kitchen.

"Daddy!"

They entered to find John placing a laptop and a small black box on the dining table. He unbuttoned the top of his white shirt.

Sarah rounded the table to give her husband a kiss.

"Buddy!" John knelt down to embrace his son, giving him a big hug and a kiss on his cheek.

"Have you been good for Mom?"

"Mm-hmm."

"He's been great." Sarah tousled Charlie's hair, then walked to the adjoining kitchen to get a cup of water for her son.

"I played football with Mommy."

"Oh, yeah?" John sat at the table and pushed a chair out for Charlie while sliding Katherine's things out of reach.

"Yup, I throw good. Right, Mom?"

"You throw great, Charlie-P."

She put the plastic Spider-Man cup on the table in front of him. "Do you want something to eat?" Sarah asked her husband.

He shook his head.

"Work?" She motioned to the things John had in front of him. Sarah was used to evidence and papers associated with her husband's investigations, but typically the items had department tags or stickers on them.

"Yeah."

"That scientist?"

"Yup," he said with his attention still on Charlie.

"What scientist?"

The couple had been having to be more careful in their conversations around Charlie. His language skills were beyond what his teachers and pediatricians were used to.

"For work, buddy."

"Something bad?"

"Not anything to worry about."

Sarah sat next to her son.

"You get the bad people?" the boy asked as he rotated his cup.

John leaned over to nudge his son with his elbow. "That's right."

Seemingly reassured, Charlie took a sip of his water.

"What did you do today, buddy?" John asked as he poked Charlie.

"Used the digger."

"You use the digger every day."

Charlie shrugged. "I like it."

"Did you do anything else?" Sarah asked.

Charlie thought a moment and turned his head to look at his mom, his chin resting on the edge of the cup. "Patty went potty in his pants, and all the kids kept saying it." He turned back to his father as if for guidance on what was acceptable behavior.

Sarah leaned closer, her arms folded on the table. "What were they saying?"

Charlie raised his voice, mimicking the other children. "Patty potty. Patty potty. Patty potty."

"That's not nice," John said.

Charlie shook his head vigorously. "I didn't say it!"

Sarah rubbed his back. "You're a good boy."

"Yeah, you are."

"Are you about ready for bed?" Sarah asked Charlie. Given the news coverage, she surmised her husband would work late into the night and didn't see a need to keep the boy up any longer.

Charlie looked up at his father and brought his shoulders up to his ears. "Are you going?"

"No, buddy, I'm home for the night."

"Okay then."

Charlie popped out of his chair and brought his cup to the kitchen, where he slam-dunked his cup into the sink.

"Thank you for taking care of that. Say 'goodnight' to Dad."

"Night, Dad." Charlie embraced his father before Sarah led him to the front hall and up the stairs to his room.

* * *

From the recliner in his living room, Prosser took mental note of what he needed to do. *Review security footage. Check Katherine's laptop for anything I might find on Federal agencies. Plan tomorrow.*

He looked over at Sarah, who had settled into the beige couch with her Project Management book. Behind her and to her left, the windows to the backyard were closed and the blinds open. Across from them, the black television rested under the array of family photos.

Between him and Sarah, a round end table held the lamp that lit the room.

"You going to read?" he asked.

Sarah smiled and nodded.

With that, Prosser moved to the kitchen and grabbed Katherine's items. He passed the pale green countertops he knew his wife loathed to the short hallway behind the kitchen. He turned right to the home office with blue walls that he and Sarah shared. It held two desks, a closet, a bookcase, an armchair in the corner by the door, and a window on each outside wall. Sarah used the more modern white desk on the left, while John preferred the wooden one by the window, even though its drawers often stuck.

Prosser sat at his desk and contemplated the best place to hide the laptop and box.

"What happened to that woman?" Sarah asked as she appeared in the doorway.

He turned to see Sarah backlit by the bright ceiling light in the hall. "Book not interesting enough?"

She shook her head.

"Well," Prosser thumped his knees, "looks like she jumped from her window eight stories up."

"Jesus."

Prosser trusted Sarah. He shared non-public case details with her, knowing that she wouldn't tell anyone. This time, though, he kept the spooks bit to himself.

"Did you watch the news coverage?" Prosser asked, curious of how they reported the incident.

"Yeah."

"What did they say?"

Sarah sat on the armchair, her legs crossed and hands in her lap. "They said it wasn't suspicious, nothing that suggested foul play. Most seem to believe the explosion of the satellite sent her into a depression."

"They said that?" It surprised Prosser to hear the entire theory already laid out on the news before he had completed family interviews. *I wonder who told the press that...*

"Yeah, why?"

"It's odd timing." His eyes darted from his wife to the floor. "It's likely the truth, but to just say that before a case is closed is unethical."

"They sounded dismissive of the whole thing. It was a short piece, like thirty seconds."

"Hmm, okay."

"What's going on, John?" Sarah had her fingers intertwined on her belly, her elbows on the chair, and her gaze lasered in on him. He knew that look well, having been with her for over twenty years and since her college graduation. Sarah recognized his tells better than Oberman, and he knew it.

He smiled. "Oh, nothing. That is what happened. But being this respected scientist, there's more attention on the case."

"Anything to worry about?"

"Nope. Just need to dot my I's."

Sarah nodded, stood, and kissed her husband. "Don't be up too late."

"I'm afraid I have security footage to review. I may not be up until later."

"Want anything?" She gave his shoulder a gentle rub.

Prosser placed his hand on hers. "No. Love you."

"Love you." Sarah smiled at him before leaving the room.

Prosser unlocked the bottom drawer of his desk for Katherine's belongings. He then opened his personal laptop and pulled the USB stick from his pocket. The *Welcome* screen appeared, and after putting in his PIN, he inserted the drive. A window appeared with a singular file, titled *UoB-hall-0413.mp4*. He double-clicked, and the black-and-white video file played.

He noted the time, noon, April 12th. Using the settings, he set it to 4x speed and leaned back in the chair. Prosser recognized the hall and Katherine's office door. He settled in for a long night and kept his eyes trained.

After two cups of coffee and hours of footage review, Prosser confirmed Katherine had entered her office alone. She appeared calm, with a spring in her step. Only after her jump did anyone else enter.

He admitted the strangeness of it. Katherine's big day, the launching of her satellite, and she sat alone in her office streaming it on her laptop. Finding a free page in his notepad, he wrote a note to ask her boyfriend about the launch. Prosser wanted to know if this was out of character for her.

Prosser stood, stretched, and checked the time. One in the morning. He retired to the kitchen to find all the lights downstairs off. The house would have been pitch black if not for his neighbor's floodlight.

Lawrence had lived with his family next to the Prossers for a decade. Two years ago, he installed a light on the side of his home, pointed down toward his pool, supposedly to see if anyone snuck in to swim. Prosser, however, thought it was because of Lawrence's fear of swimming in the dark water at night, as it seemed rare for it even to be on. Nonetheless, with the cold April, the pool wasn't open.

Thankfully, the Prossers' bedrooms were at the other end of the house.

Light cut through the blinds in sharp white bars across the couch, the floor, the dark television screen. Somewhere in the walls, the Wi-Fi extender ticked an intermittent, static-like pulse.

"Damn thing." Prosser had someone network the home since all his new appliances were "smart", and the device, which he thought was a gimmick, sometimes made odd noises.

Since no one in his house was complaining about the light, Prosser retrieved a cup and filled it with water from the refrigerator. He turned and walked to the glass doors to the back and looked up out of curiosity, but couldn't see the light source, only the bright white light that seemed to encompass everything.

At that moment, it shut off, turning everything dark. Just then, Charlie's voice came from behind him.

"Daddy?"

Prosser spun, his free hand going to his hip in a flash from his patrol days. He set the water down.

Charlie stood in the doorway in his Iron Man pajamas, hugging Ducky Ducky against his chest, the stuffed duck so worn and loved that its fur had clumped.

"Hey. What is it, buddy?" Prosser stepped to him and picked

him up. "Why aren't you sleeping?"

"The monkeys won't leave me alone."

"The monkeys?"

"They're in my room."

"Oh, okay."

The Prossers had spoken to the pediatrician about Charlie's vivid dreams, and she had told them not to worry. Children's rapid brain development can lead to periodic nightmares or even night terrors that feel very real. The doctor advised them to reassure Charlie that he was safe. There was no benefit in arguing about whether it was just a dream.

"How about I bring you upstairs and make sure they're gone? I'll secure the window, check under your bed, and lie next to you for a while. Sound good?"

Charlie nodded and hugged Ducky Ducky.

Chapter 13

Reed drove home late in the day, the traffic bleeding past him unheard, the cold air unnoticed. The adrenaline from the shooting had burned off, and he steered on reflex, the road narrowing to a gray smear ahead of him. Reed entered his home and dropped his things at the door. "Babe, I'm home."

"In the dining room," Wendy called out.

He hauled himself to the table and dropped into the chair across from her, where a plate of spaghetti waited.

"Oh my god, thank you!" He twirled the pasta around the fork and began shoveling. Badge appeared at his side and rested his head on Reed's knee.

"Sorry, I didn't wait for you," Wendy said as she watched him eat. "I heard about the shooting."

"Was nothing."

"Nothing?"

"Seriously, don't make it a thing. I was behind a wall."

"Uh, they said you charged at him and his gun malfunctioned or something."

Reed forked the pasta into his mouth. He didn't like the conversation, but preferred it to one about the previous night's inexplicable terror.

"I'm sorry," he said through chewing. "I know you get worried and want to talk about it. It's just that I'm tired, and it wasn't dangerous."

"I want you to be smart and strong."

"I know." Reed looked up and Wendy, who now crossed her arms in the same tight fold Oberman used.

"Don't be like..."

Reed pounded the table. "Don't say it!"

Wendy pierced Reed with her eyes. "Then don't do that shit."

Reed took a deep breath and slid back, the meal crushed before him. "Okay, I'm sorry."

Wendy leaned forward and kissed him on the forehead.

"Tell me about your day, then." Reed changed the subject. "Are they using any more of your ideas?"

"Well, Elizabeth came to me about raising awareness around some new radiology equipment. I thought she was just going to hand me one of her handwritten pages of instructions, but she asked me for ideas. She said...Reed?"

Wendy stopped. She had apparently noticed Reed peering out the sliding glass door to the backyard. He stood pressed close enough for his breath to fog the glass. There was... something...on the ground.

"Reed?"

His eyes remained fixed as his brain attempted to interpret what he saw. Vague lines made of mud, snow, and patches of dead grass. "What's that?"

"What?" Wendy stood and moved to the door.

"That?"

She followed his gaze, scanning the extensive field and the

tree line two hundred yards away. "I don't see anything."

Reed raised his right hand and tapped the glass. "There, right fucking there!" The more he looked at it, the clearer the shape became.

"What? What?" the volume of her voice raised.

Reed turned his head to address her. "You don't see it?" He pushed his finger harder.

"See what?" She squinted and leaned forward with the question.

He needled the glass again. "That symbol on the ground." Circles, triangles, definitive swirls of shapes formed by earth combined into an intricate pattern.

Wendy's head lurched back. "Symbol?"

"In the snow."

"What are you talking about?"

Reed's voice grew louder and more pointed. "About fifty feet out. It's made out of patches of grass and snow. Some large symbol. It's geometric! It's fucking geometric!"

Wendy shook her head as her eyes frantically searched.

"Come here!" Reed grabbed her hand and hurried to the foyer, virtually dragging her up to the second floor. Badge pursued, excited, up the stairs.

"Reed, stop!"

Holding her tight, he pulled her into the cramped bathroom and up to its window. "Look down!"

She peered down at the yard.

The glass wobbled as Reed knocked on it. "It's huge! A giant circle with these little other circles and triangles. There are lines going from them to the big one. It's right there!"

Wendy eased herself down from Reed's arms and took his hands in her own. "I really think you need to rest."

"You don't see it?"

"No, and you need to cut this shit out." She released him.

Reed's eyes examined Wendy's expression for any hint of lying.

How could she not see it? It's right there. RIGHT THERE!

"You've been working a lot. I've been telling you that. Take time off. So what if it takes you longer to buy a home? We'll have more time for fun."

Reed turned and left the room, and Badge followed. The floorboards creaked as he walked down the hall to the bedroom, where he sat on the bed. With the shades down, it was dark.

Wendy appeared in the doorway.

"I'm sorry." His muscles tensed. *I'm not sorry at all. Not fucking at all.* "I guess I'm just tired." *I don't need sleep. I need to know what's fucking going on.* "You're right." *You're not fucking right!*

Wendy went to him and rubbed his shoulder. "Go to sleep. We'll talk more tomorrow."

"Yeah." Reed watched her leave before he shut the door. Pacing the gloomy room, he thought about the symbols. They pressed against the inside of his skull, and he shivered.

* * *

My hand on the trunk of the maple. Its bark carved deep with lines. I run my fingers down them. Rough.

I get lost in the peaks and valleys of the bark's texture.

Like looking down on a landscape.

Mountains and valleys with roads.

A river.

Trees.

There's an ant. Black. Small.

It walks between mountain ranges and up the tree.

Curious.

I place my thumb on it.

Hold it there.

Feel it wiggling under my skin.

A praying mantis lands next to my thumb.

It looks at me.

Curious.

I look at Sadie.

Mouth open.

Muscles tense.

Screaming.

Soundless.

I press my thumb hard.

There's a pulsing.

Through the atmosphere above.

A thumping.

Bass.

Heavy.

Boom...boom...boom...

Waves from the pulses soak into everything.

Into me.

Boom...boom...boom...

I can't look up.
It won't let me.
Whatever it is,
it's pressing me.

* * *

Reed threw the blankets off and lunged for the bedroom door, collapsing to the cold hardwood floor. His lungs strained, and his throat burned from his screams that shattered the peace of the early morning. His eyes grew wide. The pain from pressing his nails into the floor radiated up his arms and sent the pressure sensation from the dream away.

"Reed!" Wendy called out as if in shock before turning on her bedside lamp and rushing to his side. She placed a hand on his back. "What's going on? Are you okay?"

The cries turned to labored breaths, and he pushed his body to a sitting position.

"Dream," is all he could say.

"Holy shit."

Wendy stood upright and examined him like a judgmental schoolteacher. "What is going on? That's no dream!"

Reed caught his breath. "Awful. Just...an awful nightmare."

"Since when do you have nightmares?"

Reed didn't answer. Rhetorical question or not, he didn't

have a good one and knew where the conversation would go, regardless.

"This is enough scared BS. When do you work next?"

"Today." Reed scratched at his forehead and noticed the sweat that had beaded across his skin.

"Okay, listen to me. You're going to talk to Oberman today. No excuses. And you're going to tell her you're taking time off. A few days at least. Don't fucking argue with me."

"Fine." He licked his lips and bit his tongue, knowing damn well a vacation would do no good.

Standing, Reed spun around to look at the clock next to his side of the bed. Four in the morning.

"Shift starts at nine." The bed squeaked as he threw himself back on it. "Let me just try to rest until I have to get up."

"Are you going to tell me what that nightmare was about?" Wendy asked with her eyes trained on him as she got back into bed.

"I don't even remember." The lie stung.

Chapter 14

Charlie lay on his side, facing the wall, with the blankets up to his chest. He cupped Ducky Ducky under each flappy yellow wing and held the stuffed animal close to his face. Focusing on Ducky was the best thing to do. Daddy tucked him in and said he was safe, so he was safe. Daddy knew that sort of stuff because of his job. He made sure people were safe. And when they weren't, he'd find out why and make them safe.

So that meant Charlie was safe.

Even though the monkey was back.

He could look at Ducky, and Ducky could look at him. Together, they could stay in bed and wait to get tired enough to fall asleep. Wait until they couldn't be awake anymore. Until their eyes closed and they slept in the safe bed.

Daddy said Charlie was safe. Daddy doesn't lie.

Looking at Ducky Ducky was the easy part. Lying in bed was easy too.

What wasn't easy was not turning around. Not rolling over in bed to see the small pointed tent in the middle of his room, between his bed and dresser. The one he liked to play adventures in during the daytime. With the small astronaut nightlight on top of his dresser, he could see the tent's shadow on the wall—painted next to his framed picture of the ABCs. And that shadow was good. It helped. It told him that the monkey hadn't left the tent. Yet.

Charlie knew it wasn't easy not to look because of the eyes. Both his own and the monkey's. His ears caught the rustling in the blue tent, and his eyes wanted to follow. His eyes wanted to see what it was doing in there. But Charlie also knew he didn't want to look, too. His brain didn't want to roll over to those black eyes in the tent.

The ones that stole him away. Where he couldn't call for Mommy and Daddy.

* * *

In the kitchen, after seeing Charlie back to bed, Prosser dumped his water and placed the glass in the dishwasher. "So much for a quiet night," Prosser said to himself as the ticking Wi-Fi device and Lawrence's on-again floodlight made the downstairs feel like the target of psychological warfare.

He crossed the tile floor to the foyer, unbuttoning his shirt on the way upstairs. Under Charlie's closed door, through the backdrop of the dim nightlight, the shadows of Charlie's skinny legs moved about the room.

"Go to sleep, little man," Prosser sighed as he passed.

Chapter 15

Reed, already in full uniform, took two steps at a time up to the second floor of the Bridgewater Police Department. "Hi, Pops." He touched the photo of his father, then entered the office space and passed through the hustle of early morning activity without notice.

The wheels of his desk chair rolled back as he took his seat, and he pulled himself close to the computer. He logged in and opened the department's Incident Management System. Not bothering to take off his jacket, he typed with a focused frenzy in the IMS.

He pulled all reports from Sally's Gas on Route 4 as his right heel tapped against the floor. Reed could think of nothing else. He had to find Patch, had to hear it from him directly. Maybe after a conversation, he could then piece together what was happening to him. The dreams, the mantis, the pattern in his backyard. Perhaps Patch had seen something, anything, that could crack it open. Any bit of information might help.

He scanned for "Patch" in the records associated with Sally's. At some point, something must have happened at the gas station where the clerk was involved, even if only as a witness. From that, he could get a last name and track him down. The swirling icon noted the search in progress.

The screen flickered, displaying *No Results.*

"Shit," he said under his breath.

Patch, what would that be short for?

Reed moved the cursor to the system tray and opened a browser. In the search engine, he typed *Patch nickname* and hit *Enter.*

"Bingo." The search results provided the name, Patrick.

Returning to the IMS, he scanned again. *Patrick Cooper, witness, public urination.*

Reed grabbed a pen and sticky note and wrote Patch's address, an apartment in downtown Bridgewater. He didn't care that it wasn't in his area of responsibility for the day.

The desk chair rolled back and slammed against the desk behind him as he stood, causing the officer seated to look up and raise his hands to Reed as he paced away.

* * *

The rear of the apartment building held a large, rusted green dumpster, a collapsing, unused garage, and what may have been a chicken coop at one time. Patch's apartment was up the new and unstained stairs at the back. If a hurricane were to come through, the powder blue building would disintegrate around the sturdy stairs.

The undercarriage of Reed's cruiser slammed against the frozen hump in the concrete slab driveway as he pulled the vehicle to the back of the house. He hit the brakes, causing the tires to dig into the backyard soil.

He raced up the stairs to unit D. The thin metal of the screen door almost tore from the frame as he pulled it open. Reed tried opening the inner door. Locked.

"Patch!" Reed yelled as he pounded the wood with his fist. The flimsy glass, which presented a depressing view of the grimy yellow kitchen, rattled.

He knocked three more times. "Patch!"

The young man appeared in the threshold between his kitchen and living area, wrapping a burgundy robe around his thin frame.

Patch squinted at the window and opened the door. "Yo, man. Now's not really a good time."

Reed pushed Patch back and guided him into the living room.

"Whoa, dude!"

Magazines, video game discs, and empty energy drink cans scattered as Reed shoved Patch onto the ripped sofa. Reed stood over him, lit by the front windows. "I need you to tell me what happened the other night."

Patch seemed to search Reed for answers of his own. "Fuck if I know."

The kid's tone told Reed he fought back tears.

Reed pointed a finger at him."You saw it, right? You saw the mantis. Some light in the corner. Right? Why didn't you fucking move or say something?"

"Mantis?" Patch whimpered.

"The mantis, Patch, by the coffee."

Patch shook his head. "You're fucking insane."

Reed dropped his arm. “What? What did you just say?”

“You’re insane, man. You pull that shit, then come in here acting all crazy.” Patch shifted his weight to sit upright.

“I didn’t pull anything.”

“Fuck you! Just because you’re a cop doesn’t mean you can do this shit—including coming into my place like this. You can’t mess with people like that.”

Blood rushed to Reed’s face, and his voice exploded in volume. “Patch, you’re pissing me off! Tell me, right now, what you saw. The light in the corner.”

“Fuck you, dude!” Patch waved his arms as he spoke. “You fucking come in, go to the coffee, and then fucking stand there like you’re frozen. All the electricity shut off, and you pull some psycho bullshit to freak me out. Well, fuck you! You stood there staring at the coffee display, eyes all glazed and shit. The phones weren’t even working. Then that owl started moving.”

Patch’s tone quieted. “I had to watch that owl thing until the electricity came on, and then you started moving again. You freaked me out.”

“You’re saying I froze?”

Patch shrugged. “Yeah.”

“I didn’t freeze, you did,” Reed said.

“That’s not how it went down.”

Reed had been conscious every second of it. That wasn’t something a person got confused about. He was conscious the entire duration. It was Patch that wasn’t moving behind the counter. “No, no, you were behind the counter, not moving. I walked up to you, tried to get you to react. You wouldn’t budge.”

Patch shook his head. “That’s not what happened.”

Thoughts came faster than Reed could process. He scratched at his arm and took a deep breath. He needed to remain calm to get what information he could. "What do you mean 'owl'?"

"That fridge we have, with the beer from Owl Creek Brewing. Its got that big-eyed owl, like a Harpy or something, at the top. Backlit. It started moving, like coming out of the display."

"What about the lady?"

"That came in when you ran out?" Patch pushed some clutter aside and tucked one leg under the other.

"Yeah."

"She sus."

"What do you mean, *sus*?" The thought of the woman made Reed's skin itch.

Patch crossed his arms. "She looked weird, suspect. Like she was born with some disfigurement. And what the hell, she was in a little dress when it was like 20 degrees out."

"Yeah, I noticed that. What did she buy?"

He laughed. "She bought one of the hot dogs on the roller. Had been there all day. *Ick.*"

"That's it? She got a hot dog?"

"She didn't even use the paper holders we have, just palmed a dog and slapped a ten-spot on the counter. Walked out."

Reed's police instincts kicked in. "Did she say anything else?"

"Just a 'thank you.'"

"But she was still in there when I left. There must have been more."

Patch shook his head. "She stared at the hot dogs for like two minutes."

"Stared at them?"

"Yup. With those bug-eyes of hers."

Reed nodded. "Thanks, kid."

"I'd say 'anytime,' but I prefer our little chats over coffee."

Reed turned on his heels and raced to the open back door.

He knew what to do next.

* * *

"Officer Jacobs, respond. Repeat, 10-16 with your friends the Bombards," the sharp voice on the radio demanded an answer.

Reed pushed the accelerator harder, the tires kicking dirty slush up behind him. "I'm on something. Call someone else," Reed responded in annoyance.

"All officers are occupied. What are you on?"

"Following up on something from last night."

"You need to respond to the 10-16," the dispatcher said.

"Find someone else." Reed tightened his grip on the wheel, knowing full well he'd be catching hell back at the station for ignoring the call and being away from his territory.

The voice returned. "Oberman says to be in her office after your shift and to get back to your beat."

The cruiser slid into Sally's lot and bumped the curb by the front door. He flicked on the overheads, hoping whoever was working would see them. As he left the car, he turned the radio volume down. Reed didn't need anyone to hear him being bitched out by dispatch.

He entered the convenience store with long strides and moved to the register, thankful there wasn't a line and only one person poking around.

"Can I help you?" the short, blue-haired woman asked with a smile.

"Officer Jacobs. I need to see the security footage from two nights ago, starting at 11:30. Interior and exterior."

"Do you have a warrant?"

Fuck her, Reed thought. *There are no Sally's Gas secrets to protect.*

He looked at her name tag. "I don't, Elly, I only need to see a few minutes for an incident."

She nodded. "Patch was freaked out that morning and couldn't wait to get out of here. Didn't say what happened."

"Yes, so the footage would help." Reed knocked on the counter.

"No warrant," the woman said with a frown and a shrug.

"Is there a manager here?"

"Sure is. Me." Her growing smile wore the title proudly.

Reed knew he was already in trouble with the Department and took a deep breath. An amicable solution would need to be found.

He exhaled loud enough for her to hear, playing whatever sympathy she had for a tired cop or a rattled coworker. "Look, straight this time. Something did happen that night, something strange. I can't explain what, but it's why Patch is freaked out. But it's one of those late-night things that no police department would ever investigate. The only reason I want the footage is to help find something reasonable to tell Patch. You know, so he doesn't feel too frightened to work here at night any longer."

Reed added that last bit as the cherry on top—Elly wouldn't want to cover overnight shifts while looking for another clerk.

Elly pursed her lips before speaking. "How do I know you're not trying to cover up something you did?"

"You can keep a copy for yourself."

She stood silent a moment, her eyes locked on Reed. "Hundred bucks?"

"Deal."

Elly grabbed a package that included two USB drives and scanned it. "That'll be $32.27. And you want a hundred cash back, right?"

Relieved, Reed dug for his wallet and ran his card.

Chapter 16

The morning rain broke the warm spell. Large drops, thick from the cooling temperatures, thumped Prosser's windshield as he reached into the back of his Explorer for his messenger bag. Inside was Katherine's laptop and that mysterious box, items he still hadn't checked in with Evidence. He would get the laptop unlocked by IT—its contents may prove invaluable.

He ran from his designated parking spot at the back to the front door of the station.

The waiting area was quiet. Not one for pleasantries, he gave the duty officer a quick nod and moved toward the back of the first floor where IT kept its office.

Inside, he found Jeannie Templeton standing at the tall wooden utility desk, a computer gutted and its contents before her. The room was like that, a morgue of electronics. The small IT team handled requests from detectives to access hard drives or cell phones, and also managed the department's own equipment and network. Prosser sought the former.

Jeannie looked up from the equipment to see the detective approaching. "For the love of God, Prosser, you're all wet. Take off your coat before you splatter water all over." Jeannie flapped her arms at him. Her natural red hair was the brightest thing in the room. She had the focused hands of someone gifted with electronics and had clearly spent more time on her eyeliner than most detectives spent on their reports.

Prosser smiled as he slid his jacket off to hang it by the door. He retrieved the laptop from the messenger bag as he walked closer to the woman and placed it on the table in the only bare spot. "Hey, I need access to this."

"Good mornin' to you, too." She placed her hands on the tabletop, not yet touching the computer.

"Good morning, Jeannie." He smiled as his past performance reviews flashed before him—hearing various chiefs say *you're a nice person, but nobody knows it.*

The two remained motionless, staring at each other.

"It ain't tagged," Jeannie said.

"It will be, I promise."

Jeannie didn't budge. She stood like the immovable object in high school physics puzzles.

"Jeannie, I swear to you."

"It's not Sarah's, is it? I'm not getting into a marital quarrel."

"It's my case."

"The jumper?"

"Yes."

"Why isn't it tagged, Presser?"

He peeked at the door before turning back to Jeannie for effect. Time to sell it.

"Look, I've got people breathing down my fucking neck on this, and I just need to get it wrapped up as soon as possible. Because she's some famous scientist who discovered something, everyone from the University to the Governor's office wants it closed. The thing is, it's a suicide. The woman jumped. That's it. But before I can complete the report, I have to talk to her parents, her boyfriend...you know, I can't just file the case if I haven't done my job. But all that takes time, and it will be a lot faster for me if I can just get the damn thing tagged in later."

He leaned forward and let his weight settle onto the table.

Jeannie tilted her head. "Well, Billy is a fucktwit."

"Yeah, exactly." In actuality, Prosser had no idea what she meant. Billy did a good job managing evidence, if not taking the cues to end an already exhausted conversation.

"Fine."

With a swift motion, she swiped up the laptop and spun it around so the opening faced her. Jeannie was showing off, and it reminded Prosser of the Globetrotters. After lifting the lid and plugging in both a power cord and another wire to a USB port, she began typing.

"Standard Windows security. Not the first U of B computer I've had here."

"Okay, sounds promising."

Jeannie glanced up at him. "Doesn't matter, though."

"Oh, of course."

She typed a bit more.

"PIN?"

"I don't know."

"No." She looked at him again. "What do you want the PIN to be? Four numbers."

"Oh, one one one one."

"Password?"

"Password, all lowercase."

She closed the lid, unplugged the wires, and gave it a quick lift and fast spin before presenting it to Prosser.

"There you have it."

"Hey, thank you. Seriously." He took it before Jeannie could have second thoughts and placed it in his bag. "You're the best."

He was almost to the door when he remembered the box. He pulled it from the bag and held it up toward Jeannie.

"Any idea what this is?"

"Nope."

"K, well, thanks anyway."

Prosser started walking back to the door and grabbed his jacket.

"Presser, at least tell me if what I did wasn't legit so I know how to answer questions."

The two others in the room also looked at Prosser, who gripped the doorknob. "Everything I said was true, scout's honor."

She shook her head with a frown.

Prosser smiled and left, shutting the door behind him.

* * *

The office space buzzed more than it had the day prior, when the warmth had pulled everyone outside. LaFontaine sat at the far left wall, as far away as Oberman could get him, with his head down in some papers. A few of the younger cops he didn't recognize, but most Prosser knew from either interactions on the job or department events like the annual family barbecue.

He noticed Reed Jacobs sitting a couple of desks away from his own. The man looked tired, with his eyes half-closed. Prosser gave a quick nod as he passed, but got nothing in return and took his seat.

Reed had been an early and promising star when he first joined the force at 24. He studied hard, and at 6'4" with an athletic build, he was intimidating. His advancement slowed as he earned a reputation as a hothead, a label that reminded officers too much of Jacobs Senior. Prosser wasn't sure if it was deserved, but heard about some altercations between Reed and various hooligans that didn't end well with the brass.

Laying out Sharma's business card, his notepad, and the laptop, Prosser set himself to work. Pulling up Katherine's parents' contact information on his computer, he found them in Leicester—not far from Bridgewater. With any luck, he'd wrap this up today and start digging into the Fed connection on his own.

He started with President Sharma and dialed her on his cell.

"This is Manjusha."

"Good morning, Mrs. Sharma, this is Detective Prosser."

"Yes, how can I help you?"

"I'm completing some formalities and came across a photo at Katherine's house of her and a man, whom I thought I saw at the University. In the photo, they seemed quite close. Do you happen to know who that might have been?"

"Yes, I would assume that's Professor David Jarrow. Katherine's partner."

"Professor?"

"Of Philosophy, here at Bridgewater."

"Thank you. That's helpful. If it's no trouble, do you have contact information for Professor Jarrow?"

"One moment."

Prosser went to his pad, found the page with the note about the boyfriend, and prepared to write. After a moment, Sharma returned to dictate the number, and the two hung up.

Prosser looked at his watch, 8:45. If he met David at 10, give that maybe an hour, he could be in Leicester by one to meet the O'Reillys. To be safe, and give him time for lunch, he'd ask them to meet at three.

He tried Jarrow first. After a handful of rings, a man answered. He sounded in mourning, yet happy to talk. "Hello?"

"Hi, sorry for disturbing you. This is Detective Prosser with the Bridgewater Police Department. I'm looking for David Jarrow."

"Ah, well, you've reached him."

"Hi, Mr. Jarrow. First, I'm sorry for your loss. Katherine seemed like an extraordinary woman."

"Thank you."

"Am I right to say that you and she were close?" Prosser asked.

"Yes, we were dating."

"I'm hoping to connect with you today in person for a few questions. Would 10 work?"

"That's fine. I've canceled my classes."

"Appreciate that. Where would you like to meet?" Prosser placed his pen on his pad.

"My office. I'm here today to support the campus."

Prosser wrote the address for Jarrow's office and moved on to the O'Reillys. After only one ring, a gentleman answered with a rough and deep voice. "Hello?"

"Hi, sorry to disturb you. This is Detective John Prosser with the Bridgewater Police Department. First..."

Before he could finish, the man interrupted. "Ah, rightly fuck off, would you?"

The line disconnected.

Prosser looked at the phone. Not expecting the response he received, he double checked the number. Appearing correct, he turned to his desk computer to see if perhaps another number existed. But before he could unlock it, his cell vibrated with an incoming call. The number displayed was the very one that had hung up on him.

"Detective Prosser."

"Hello, Detective." This time, a friendly woman responded. "I'm sorry for my husband. He's never been an overly pleasant man."

"Hi, am I speaking to Louise O'Reilly?"

"You are. We were told to expect your call."

"My condolences."

"Thank you. We haven't quite been able to wrap our minds around what happened."

"I imagine."

"How can I help you?"

"Well, in situations like this, I need to meet those closest to the victim. Would you have time today? Perhaps at 3? I can go there if that works for you."

She confirmed the time and address, and they disconnected. *Success*, Prosser thought as the day ahead planned out.

He moved his attention to Katherine's laptop. It only took twenty minutes to get to campus, so he had some time to explore its contents. Typing in the pin, it unlocked and presented the familiar Hubble image background with a series of folders on the desktop.

Syllabi, *Exams*, *Rosters*, *Research*, *Publications*, *Elisha.*

She kept her files tidy.

He double-clicked into the *Elisha* folder. Hundreds of files appeared, of various types and many unknown to the detective. There didn't seem to be a system behind the order, and the file names meant little to him. Looking for anything specific to investigate further seemed futile. *Instead*, he thought, *I should just pick one and go from there.*

He found the recognizable blue icon for a Microsoft Word document and opened it.

"Ah shit," he said softly and looked up at Reed, who appeared asleep with his head down on his desk.

The screen displayed multiple equations, or perhaps a singular long one. Annotations appeared along the side, and he clicked to expand one.

Adjustment to Newtonian gravity, traditionally F = G * (m1 * m2) / r^2

He shook his head and opened another annotation.

Vlasov

"What the hell is Vlasov?"

He closed the file after two minutes of reading gibberish and leaned back in the chair. This isn't how to find a connection to the Feds. He was too in the weeds. He needed to clear his mind and return to the computer another time. With a couple of clicks, he shut it down.

Outside, the sound of a passing police car's siren whirled. Inside, Officer Jacobs slept.

Chapter 17

Oberman reached across her desk, finger leveled at Reed, who sat in the chair closest to the door. "This shit stops, now!" The desk shook under her hands. "You told me you weren't going to be like your father. That you wouldn't cause headaches. Then you pull some psycho shit on that shooter, and you completely ignore orders today? What the hell were you even doing?" Oberman dropped back in her chair.

"I needed to follow up on something."

"I don't see 'Detective' in your title. What were you doing?"

Reed exhaled and leaned forward, placing his elbows on his knees. The carpet was old Berber, ground down to a gray mat. The thought of telling Oberman what happened at Sally's, the freezing of time and the coffee display's animation, didn't settle well. Reed figured he'd be sent for evaluation, and likely ostracized and re-assigned to desk duty. He couldn't do that. Couldn't sit at a desk all day.

He needed something to take the heat off, a clean infraction, minor enough that Oberman's mind wouldn't drift back to his father.

He looked up at his boss. "Someone started something with

me outside of the gas station. Just an idiot drunk. I didn't want to make a big deal out of it as nothing came of it. He ran off. But it scared the clerk working, and I wanted to check in on him."

Oberman shook her head. "Where's your incident report?"

"I didn't file one."

She slid forward. "Someone attacks a uniformed police officer, runs away, and you don't file a report? You don't call it in?"

She bought it. His shoulders loosened. "Like you said, I promised no headaches."

"Not filing a report is a serious problem." Oberman's volume decreased.

"I'm sorry. It won't happen again."

"You file it now, then you're suspended. Two days." Oberman held up two fingers. "And when you're back, no more double duty."

Reed unclipped his badge, set his sidearm beside it, and slid them both across the desk.

Chapter 18

Ten seconds. That's all it took for Prosser to hate the man.

Goddamn stereotype, Prosser said to himself as David Jarrow sat behind his desk, twiddling a custom bobblehead of himself. *He's probably contemplating his place in the universe.*

"It makes you think," Jarrow said in a low and distant voice.

"Hmm, it does," Prosser replied.

The professor wore a sweater, dark blue and white yarns interwoven and frayed. Around his neck rested a thick wool scarf that had to itch like hell. His long salt and pepper hair draped behind him. He had a long face and hadn't shaved in days.

Jarrow placed the bobblehead on his desk and tapped his mini-me one last time before turning to Prosser. "Why does one end their life, you think?"

"I'm hoping you can help answer that question."

"Some in Philosophy laud suicide."

"Oh?"

"Schopenhauer viewed it as the ultimate expression of freedom. Denying your innate will to live for your freedom from suffering. Of course, he also viewed women as frivolous and childish. Interesting how we now explore the mind of a woman who has, so unfortunately, taken her life. And Schopenhauer, no doubt, would perform philosophical gymnastics to expunge any sense of contradiction between his views and our Katherine." Jarrow spoke with his shoulders, punching words with a raise, shift, or a drop.

Prosser wanted to punch him. Instead, he asked, "How long did you know Katherine for?"

"The better part of a decade. No less."

"Were you romantically involved long?"

Jarrow smiled. Prosser's jaw tightened at the thought of the man lecturing on his carnal pleasures.

"A few years."

"Did she tell you why she didn't attend the launch for the Elisha in person?" Prosser asked.

"She did. Katherine said she was too nervous. That didn't surprise me. Anything of significance surrounding her work made her tense."

"What about her state of mind? Did you get a sense she was depressed? Any mental health issues you were aware of?"

The Professor of Philosophy inhaled deeply through his nose. "I suppose in the traditional sense, no."

"What do you mean by that?" Prosser regretted asking the question.

"Hyperthymesia. That was Katherine."

"Hyperthymesia?" *Shut up, Prosser.*

"She recalled everything. Quite literally. Every moment from her life, everything she saw." His tone exaggerated his list. "Everything she read, did, studied. That's functionally profound and also, realistically, a disorder."

"Wow."

"It is why she accomplished so much. She made connections in various disciplines and opened us up to a daring new world within dark matter."

Prosser nodded.

"It was also her near damnation."

"Why do you say that?"

"She would clutch," he put his hands out in front of him and tightened them into shaking fists, "at subjects and wring them dry. Obsess. It filled her until she exhausted it. Note I did not state that it exhausted her." His shoulders dropped as his eyebrows raised at the last point.

"I noticed at her home she had a room..."

Jarrow interrupted, "Yes, go no further. Three years ago, that room was filled with material on plasma physics. Then it was swiftly cleaned out," he swiped his hand across his body, "and replaced by electronics. Peak Katherine."

"Why was she so interested in electronics?"

"No idea. None. She wasn't a tinkerer or traditionally interested in invention. Though she did invent, but that was a byproduct of her research or a necessity for it."

Prosser shifted in his chair. From taking a single Philosophy course in college, he recognized Jarrow's type and knew they couldn't resist words like *epistemology* and *existential.* He waited for their inevitable use.

"Okay, um." Prosser took a moment to scratch his forehead, hoping it wasn't obvious how annoyed he had become. "To get to the heart of it, Katherine's death. I hear that the explosion of the rocket, the destruction of her satellite, must have been very hard on her. Do you think that's what happened? That she felt she wouldn't be able to build another satellite, and so it was the end for her? Perhaps professionally, or just that she wouldn't achieve what she hoped for?"

Jarrow smiled that smile again, too happy to talk about something so terrible as long as he got to hear his own voice.

"You consider Schopenhauer." Jarrow's shoulders moved. "He's ultimately right in his conclusion of the elimination of suffering. And you consider Katherine, her epistemological..."

There it is.

"...approach to life, reality, and our universe, and I'm left with a singular conclusion."

Jarrow paused. Prosser nodded.

"Simply, death for Katherine, with all of its unknowns, was better than life."

Robbed. All that bullshit for *death was better than life*?

He stood and offered his hand. Jarrow followed and shook it.

"Thank you, David. I appreciate your time and enlightening me about Katherine."

"Of course."

"My condolences."

Chapter 19

After being chewed out and suspended by Oberman, Reed headed home to have time to view Sally's security footage before Wendy arrived. He changed into sweats so she wouldn't notice his missing gear, then brought his computer to the sparse living room and started a fire. Badge curled up on his bed next to it.

Reed sat on the couch, clutching the laptop and leaning close to its screen as the video file played. Its poor quality tinted the station's interior light blue, and movement was choppy. The camera's position offered a view of most of the floor space and the front of the register. It wasn't the best choice for the location, as it provided a clearer shot of the clerk's face than someone who might be at the check-out counter robbing the place. Reed watched a customer walking around the store, distorted and pixelated.

He dragged the progress bar ahead, the grainy timestamp advancing to 11:30, and there he let it play. After another two minutes, he saw himself enter from the front doors on the right of the screen.

Reed didn't blink and barely breathed.

He followed the brief interaction between Patch and himself

and stared as he pointed to the coffee creamer display, and Patch said something about the praying mantis. Then the screen stuttered. Thick, wavy bars ran vertically on the screen, shifting and tilting like old, damaged videotapes. Thin horizontal lines of pixels appeared.

The footage flickered and grew darker. Reed could only make out shadows and rudimentary shapes. He leaned back as the file continued to play. "Useless."

It fluttered back on, revealing the woman in the white dress standing in front of the rolling hot dog machine to the left of check-out. Patch, though difficult for Reed to make out, cowered in the front corner of the store, as far away from the woman as he might get while still being behind the register.

She stood, motionless, just as Patch had said. Her arms at her side, head straight, and hair flat down to her shoulder blades. She looked out of place with her white dress and matching heels.

She raised her left arm and retrieved a rolling hot dog without using the tongs. With a practiced turn, she went to the register and dropped the cash on the counter before walking out.

Patch stepped forward and followed the woman with his eyes as she left. He bent his body and arms, as if he were about to run.

The beams from the Tesla's headlights appeared in the window and scanned the interior of the store as the car pointed to the road and disappeared.

Patch slumped to the stool with his back arched and placed his hands on his head.

Reed sighed as he closed the file and navigated the mouse to the one labeled *Exterior*, and double-clicked. The video opened with a view from above the gas station's doors, and as before, he brought the bar to 11:30.

The lights from his patrol car emerged from the right, then disappeared at the side of the building. Reed brought his hands up to his mouth in an almost praying gesture as he watched.

He saw himself enter the store, and a strange light faded in from the top left of the screen, its source out of view. Positioned above the pumps, the light was at least fifty feet off the ground.

Then the familiar vertical bar appeared, and the horizontal interference followed. Reed sat in silence as the file played, offering nothing recognizable.

A few minutes passed, and the image blinked before restoring to the expected scene outside the store. Reed's eyes found the Tesla positioned at the pump, directly under the light, which suddenly shot off into the distance and disappeared.

The woman exited the car and entered the store from the bottom of the screen. Reed then appeared, blasting by her as he ran out of view to his cruiser.

Five more minutes passed before the glass door swung open and she rigidly walked, hot dog clutched, to the vehicle. She entered and drove off without incident.

Reed waited another moment, watching it play and hoping something else might occur. But with a huff, he shut down the laptop in dismay. Tossing it to the cushion, he placed his hands at the side of his head and stared at the dull wooden floor.

The scenes replayed in his mind. He could only claim one thing as new information. Something was in the sky. The rest remained obfuscated by interference. And plenty of questions remained on what actually happened in that gas station.

Interrupted by the door in the foyer opening, Reed looked through the wide threshold to see Wendy dropping her bag and taking off her heavy winter jacket and boots. Badge pounced up and trotted over to her.

"Hi, Wen."

"Hey," she said with that tone of expectation. A serious discussion was coming.

She walked to the couch, slid the laptop over to sit next to her boyfriend, and kissed him. "How was your day?" Badge jumped up to join them.

Reed smiled. He had decided not to share the news of his short suspension. "It was uneventful. You'll be happy, though. I have the next few days off."

Wendy's chest deflated. "Oh, that's so good. I took tomorrow off, hoping that would be the case. I thought we could go into town and have lunch. A nice, relaxing day for us."

As much as Reed wanted to figure out what the hell had been going on, a calm day free from stress sounded beneficial.

"Perfect."

Reed put an arm around her and pulled her closer. The fire crackled.

* * *

Reed felt refreshed after an uninterrupted sleep. A stillness settled within him. Maybe Wendy was right, he had been working too much. Sure, strange things had happened, but maybe some sleep and exercise would have him looking at those events differently.

After a late start to the day, the two ventured into Old Bridgewater. Walking down the cobblestone sidewalks, used as outdoor seating for restaurants in the warmer months, Reed and Wendy passed their favorite bakery, and the pizza shop where he had heard the gunshots days before.

There was also the classic toy store filled with harder-to-find items, a few apparel businesses, from dressy attire to business-casual, and the mystical emporium Reed didn't understand—through the window, everything appeared purple, dark, and uninviting.

They settled on Rossi's, an Italian bistro. The seating area inside held two tables by the front windows, another two along the left wall, and one at the center, just feet from the register that sat on the glass display of pastries. The white tile of the floor contrasted with the black furnishings.

"Take a chair wherever you want to sit," the waitress at the counter called out. With only one other table occupied and no other staff visible, Reed and Wendy claimed a table by the windows to enjoy the natural light.

"Haven't been here in a long time!" Wendy said excitedly.

"Stopped here for coffee a few weeks ago, was really good."

The waitress approached and handed them thick paper menus. She stood so close to the table that her apron brushed over it.

She was pale, with brown hair up in a tight bun. She had no makeup or jewelry, and her shirt had one button unclasped. He watched as the waitress turned her head toward Wendy.

Her eyes never moved.

"Could I interest you in something to drink? Perhaps some fried potatoes?" she said with a smiling confidence.

Reed tried to give Wendy a loaded glance—the drink suggestion was so odd, Reed was unsure if he'd heard her right. All he could see, though, was the back of the menu with Wendy lost somewhere behind it.

"I'll just start with water, thank you," she said.

"Same." Reed watched as the woman sidestepped to the front door, opened it, and exited to the wintry day. She continued down the street and out of sight.

Reed looked to his girlfriend, eyes wide, searching for any sign that Wendy had found the interaction abnormal. "What the hell was that?" he whispered.

Wendy placed the menu down on the table and smiled as if she hadn't heard him at all. "It all looks so good. I'm so hungry."

"You didn't find that odd?"

"What?"

"The waitress!"

A man in a black shirt and pants emerged from the swinging door behind the register and, seeing the new patrons, approached them with a pad ready.

He spoke with an Italian accent. "Hello, welcome to Rossi's. Would you care for a drink?"

Reed pivoted in his chair to face the man. "Your waitress just took our drink order and walked out."

"Waitress? Besides the cook, it is only I today," the short and balding man responded with a smile.

"Just a prank, I guess," Wendy said.

Reed sank into his chair.

"We only asked for water." Wendy's eyes traveled from the waiter to Reed, who stared at her.

"I will be back with those." The man tucked his notepad in his apron and returned to the kitchen.

"She asked if we wanted fried potatoes to drink!" Reed gripped the table.

"It's patate fritte, it's Italian. And it was a joke."

"You don't drink them! And how about how she moved?"

"What are you talking about?"

"Are you serious?"

Wendy sat upright and crossed her arms. "Can we just have a pleasant lunch?"

Reed stared at her. "Forget it." Causing the chair to scrape against the floor, Reed stood and grabbed his jacket, but left the restaurant without bothering to put it on.

He started his way back to the car, shaking his head and bouncing between thoughts of walking home and tracking down the odd waitress.

In less than a minute, he heard Wendy's voice. "Reed!" she called out from behind him. The sound of her fashionable boots against the wet sidewalk picked up speed. As she reached him, Wendy grabbed his arm and swung him around. "What the hell? Why did you storm out like that?"

"Because I'm not crazy, Wen. That wasn't normal."

"Okay, so what if it wasn't?"

"So something's going on, and I don't like it!"

"What? What's going on?" she asked as she slapped her thigh.

"I don't know."

She shook her head and narrowed her eyes at him.

"Things have been happening."

Wendy shook her head again. "You're embarrassing me. All these little things making you act crazy. Like a baby." She tucked her purse under her arm and walked ahead of him.

Reed bit the inside of his cheek and fell back twenty feet.

* * *

The snowy hills and leafless trees blurred past the RAV4 as Reed fumed in the passenger seat. Something was fucking with him, and that waitress was another example. Wendy seemed to think he was making it up. But the question he struggled to answer was what to do about it.

He decided to hit it head-on. The next person who messed with him would regret it. Everything else be damned, Reed would approach the situation with blunt force and get answers. Screw the consequences.

"I'm going to take a nap," Wendy said as she pulled her SUV into Reed's driveway.

"Okay, I'm going to go for a run."

"Suit yourself."

Wendy stomped up the stairs to their room while Reed pulled his running gear from the hall closet: long pants, an insulated shirt, and sneakers fitted with metal ice grips.

Shutting the front door behind him, Reed started with a brisk walk down the road. He didn't bother with his earbuds—

he wanted to think. As he reached the small culvert, he took a deep breath and picked up speed. His muscles told him to sprint until the world flinched.

The road disappeared. Reed turned inward, picking back through the weeks, hunting for the start of it.

Sally's and that praying mantis thing trying to breach its place on the display. The thing in the store's corner that could only be seen in the reflection of Patch's eyes.

No, it went back earlier. What was that mask? That heavy metal thing at Overlook I tossed in the cruiser? Shit, it's still there.

God dammit, that's not even the start. The Collins' farm and whatever was running around in the barn. I walked down there, nothing got by me, and it disappeared. No, it...teleported or something back to the front and ran out by old man Collins. He says he saw nothing, but he must be lying. Must be!

And what did he say?

Come back when you remember.

Remember what?

Something from when I was how old? Eleven? How would I remember some little thing with Sadie from almost twenty years ago? We played together all the time. I lived across the street after all!

But is that what I'm dreaming about? Must be. We're out by the tree, the big maple, on the other side of the house. Is that what I'm dreaming? Or did that old man just play me, and my mind is freaking out over nothing?

Was that the start of this? What's next? What now?

Get back to work. Okay, not as many shifts. I'll keep my schedule normal until I get this figured out. Then it's back to focusing on Reed. Getting that money saved, telling Mom to sell her dump so she can get her own place in Florida, and not have to rent.

As Reed's confidence grew, so did something else. A frequency that hummed a pulsing rhythm in his cells. It flowed like a conscious virus into his bloodstream. From there, the spread infiltrated bones, organs, muscles, and tissues. And finally, his mind.

Reed stopped running and looked around at the barren fields of snow and dirt. The clouds of water vapor escaped his lungs with every breath.

The pulsing grew from a subtle feeling to an obtrusive and loud threat. Like the Earth daring him, no...warning him. All of reality aimed at him.

Reed looked for the source of the noise. There was no commercial building with a malfunctioning heating system, an electrical transformer, or a dam holding strong against a current of ice. There was nothing. Just the usual rural landscape of his runs.

This is it, he thought, *this is where I fight back.*

"Fuck you!"

Reed pushed his ice grips into the ground and returned to running. The throbbing beat at him like a fly inside a Taiko drum. He gritted his teeth, picked up speed, and drove air through his nose. He willed the drumbeat faster and faster.

Chapter 20

Since the conversation with Jarrow didn't last as long as planned, Prosser stopped at a small diner halfway to Leicester and ate too much. With each bite of burger, fries, and corn on the cob, his annoyance with the man loosened its grip. He expected more reverence for Katherine and self-awareness from someone who taught philosophy.

He ate, finished a couple of coffees, and used the restroom before paying and getting back on course. The Ford's navigation system had him down a series of dirt roads before approaching the white farmhouse with a large front porch far off to his right. Gravel popped and scattered under the tires as the Explorer chugged down the quarter-mile driveway.

As he neared, he could see a man and a woman sitting on the porch in rocking chairs, their faces weathered by decades of farming. Liam and Louise.

Though the rain had stopped, the sky still held thick clouds. The air was chilly, so it surprised Prosser that the couple waited outside.

Prosser stopped the car next to a polished red Silverado and walked to the home with a friendly wave. Liam stood and glared at the detective. He wore old jeans and a wrinkled white button-down shirt. After a moment, he turned and entered the house through the glass storm door.

Prosser took the steps up to greet the woman. "Louise?"

"That's me," she said as she stood and shook Prosser's hand.

"Please, don't feel the need to get up."

"Oh, I'm old but spry." She smiled. "And don't mind Liam, he's grumpy on good days."

"It's alright. I know it's a hard time." Prosser raised a cordial hand to the screen door in case the man could see him.

"It is." Louise motioned to the vacated chair, and Prosser sat. She wore a traditional white Irish sweater and jeans. Her gray hair was permed and thinning.

"Again, my condolences. I have a son, obviously younger than Katherine, but I can't imagine what you're going through."

"Thank you. Katherine blessed us in life. What can I do for you?" she asked as if cutting to the chase.

"I'm trying to get a sense of her state of mind or anything pertinent happening in her life."

Louise rocked, her gaze drifting out across the property. Extensive fields surrounded the home, most now used only for hay, but from the large barn to the left, Prosser imagined it once grew various vegetables and housed plenty of farm animals.

"People like Katherine come once or twice a generation. And we, as I said, were blessed to have her. And I don't mean that lightly." She looked at the detective. "They come along and advance us. Evolve us. Push humanity forward." Her hand swept upward, a slow rocket climbing. "I didn't know until a Harvard professor told me about others from past generations."

"It's like they're born with knowledge," Louise continued. "You don't teach these people. You're placed there by powers we don't understand to help them along. Once, when Katherine was nine, the AM station went down. Don't ask me why, I never understood. But Liam drove her into town because she just wouldn't shut up about it. She waltzed in, this diminutive thing, and somehow convinced the radio folk to let her look at the equipment. Within an hour, she had rigged a new...whatever it was," she waved it off, "from generator and car parts."

"That's incredible."

Louise nodded.

"She was brilliant. Everyone I've talked to has said it," Prosser shared.

"She was. But here's the thing, Detective..."

"Please, call me John."

"John, people like Katherine are haunted."

"Haunted?"

"That's right. Now, mind you, they aren't haunted like the rest of us. Everyone's got their demons. Everyone's got those things attached to them. Katherine's brother has demons, one is alcohol. Her great-uncle it was anger. Some people you know their demons, others can hide them. They're more subtle. But they're there."

Prosser listened.

"People like Katherine," her eyes drifted somewhere above Prosser's shoulder, "their demons are different. You and I, we can talk about the meaning of life. We can have fun discussing why the universe exists, or whether it's infinite. We talk, and it's nice, then we go about our lives. Make dinner, go to work, watch television...whatever. But for people like Katherine, those questions eat at them. They can't sleep, they can't eat, they must *solve*. They have to know. Those are their demons."

"I see."

Louise looked at him, her head cocked to the side with a humorless smile on her face.

He smiled back. *Caught red-handed.*

"It's okay. Us regular types never get it."

"I apologize for the indelicate question, but from footage of her office, it's clear that no one was in the room with her. Why do you think she took her own life?" Prosser whispered after rocking forward.

Louise nodded slowly, her fingers working an invisible instrument in her lap.

Prosser continued. "Do you think she did because her satellite was destroyed? That she would never have those answers? Never solve for those demons of hers?"

To Prosser's surprise, she shook her head and looked at him. "No. No, that's not it. It's not not knowing. The demons are real, John. The demons are real. She didn't kill herself because the satellite blew up. She did it because the demons won't stop."

Prosser leaned back and allowed for a moment of silence. He spoke as Louise began slowly rocking. "You've been very kind. Thank you so much for meeting with me." Prosser stood.

"I'd invite you in, but Liam would make you miserable." The woman half turned, peering through the window at her husband, who had spread a cloth across the dining room table and bent over an engine like it was the only problem worth solving.

Chapter 21

Sadie looks at me.

Her mouth screaming.

Her eyes crying.

She isn't moving.

The corn is still. As the pollen in the air.

My thumb is on that ant and it's dead, I know it.

The mantis is looking at me.

Oscillations now from...something...vibrate through it all.

The air.

Corn.

My bones.

I feel my muscles rumble.

I drop my arm and that tiny insect falls to the ground.

Can't see it anymore.

There are impressions on the ground.

Like footsteps, but different.

They circle me. Surround Sadie.

I know I can look up.

I know something is there.

The pulses emanate from it.

The mantis flies up.

And I do.
I look up.
And oh God!
Oh God!
It's black, like an insatiable hunger.
Black like a wanting eye.
The maple branches stretch below and across it.
A triangle.
Perfect.

It's feasting.

* * *

Reed jumped out of bed and shot across the room like a man on fire. Wendy jolted up, swung her legs out of bed, and turned on the light.

"Fucking again!" she screamed.

Reed slammed his body against the heavy bedroom door and collapsed to the ground, eyes still fixed on something that wasn't there. His heart hammered for a world that wasn't this one.

"Reed!" Wendy stood and held both hands up in a stop gesture.

Reed's legs kicked at ghosts. "Frozen! She's frozen!" His

words came fragmented, jarring, between hurried breaths. "The ship. Mantis. Have me. Here."

"Reed?"

Reed closed his eyes and took a deep breath. He placed his palms on the cold floor to push himself up to a table position. "Shit," he said as his body shivered and his mind awakened to the realization he was in his bedroom.

Wendy lowered her arms. "What the fuck?"

Reed stood, his resolve to fight returning to him. "I remember."

"What? Remember what?"

He looked over at Wendy, afraid he'd already said too much. "The things I've been dealing with. I'm fine. Just freaked out."

"Uh, no. No way. You will not pull that bullshit line with me again. You need to tell me what's going on."

"No, I don't," he said like an answer to a math equation.

"Are you kidding me?"

"No, I'm not. You're going to have to extend your leash a bit on this one."

"What did you say? My leash? Jesus, fuck you very much!"

Wendy went to the chair by the window, slid into her jeans, and tossed on a sweatshirt. "That's it. I'm out of here until you figure some shit out. I've had enough babysitting you."

She swiped up her phone from the nightstand and turned to stare at him, seemingly a message for him to move from the door. Reed stepped aside and opened it with an exaggerated motion to approve of her exit.

"You figure your shit out and call me when you're not a scared little man anymore."

Wendy stormed out. Her heavy steps traveled down the stairs to the foyer, where the slamming of the front door quickly followed.

The tip-tapping of Badge's feet against wood informed of his approach. Reed sat on the bed, and the dog curled up next to him.

"Good boy." Reed placed a hand on Badge's head and took a deep breath.

* * *

After inhaling breakfast and letting out Badge, Reed barreled through the snow with his siren on. At 6:30 in the morning, its screech flew unnoticed.

Reed's heart pounded faster the closer he came to the Collins' farm. The excitement at having an answer to what he saw years ago boiled over into his anger over recent events. His limbs thumped against surfaces, fingers drummed, and his body rocked. Slithering beneath the horror was something more dangerous, a genuine fear that when he reached Collins, he might not stop himself.

Reed skidded into the old farm's driveway and punched the brakes. He pulled so hard at the cruiser's key that he almost broke it off in the ignition.

"Motherfucker," he swore as he exited the car and took hulking steps up the walkway. Reed's anger spilled over as he approached the porch. "Joseph!" He leaped up the stairs and pounded on the door. "Joseph!"

Reed placed his forehead against the window carved into the top of the wooden door and turned his head side to side to check the corners of the front room. Finding it empty and not hearing any noise within, he walked down to the lawn, his arms swinging, and rounded the side of the home.

Two hundred yards away, old man Collins rode his ancient tractor, pulling a bundle of tree branches to the border of the property. Closer, the maple tree. The one he and Sadie had played around as children. It stood there the way bad memories do, ordinary, immovable, and waiting. A monument to his nightmares.

"Sadie," he said to himself as his heart sank and slowed. His eyes moved to the ground as he thought. He exhaled. She was who he needed to talk to. Sadie was the one who experienced the event with him and who he ran from that day.

Reed hung his head as he returned to the cruiser with slow and short strides. He tucked his hands in his pockets until he reached his vehicle, then pulled out his cell as he dropped to the seat behind the wheel.

He opened Facebook on his mobile and searched for Sadie Collins. Thanks to the small community of mutual friends, she appeared at the top. Reed tapped the FaceTime button to call her. The app opened with Sadie's profile photo front and center. After several seconds, it closed, noting no answer. He tossed the phone to the dashboard and rubbed his temples. Then the phone rattled against the plastic and his hand was already reaching. Sadie.

He snatched up the phone and, after a deep breath, tapped to answer. Sadie appeared, her face close to the camera. Her eyes were dark and tired, matching the tone of her voice.

"Reed, did you call me?"

"Hey, Sades. Yeah, I did." Reed's eyes scanned his old friend and the space behind her. Her hair was a darker blond than he remembered, and her features stark. Over her shoulder, a glass door framed a slice of blue sky, the white walls burning with morning light.

"Jesus. It's only been what, ten years? Probably twenty since we really hung out?" Sadie asked, scratching her head.

"Something like that. How have you been?"

"Okay, I guess. You?"

"Been better."

She half smiled. "Yeah, I hear that. So, why did you call?"

"Well, how do I put this?" Reed glanced over the phone at her father's barn.

"Okay, look," Sadie rubbed her hand over her head, "Dad told me what happened. Told me about what he said to you, and that he wanted you to go back to talk to him."

"Oh."

"So, really, just cut to the chase." Sadie leaned back, and the recessed light washed out her image for a moment.

"I remember. I remember what happened."

She shrugged. "Good for you. And now you, like, want to talk about it or something?"

Reed nodded and squeezed his cell. "Yeah. I want to understand."

Sadie let out a short laugh, stretching like the question bored her.

"Things are happening, Sade. Happening to me." Reed pleaded.

"Damn, you just don't have a clue, do you?"

"What?"

She leaned closer to the camera. "You call because things are happening to YOU. Guess what? They've been happening to me for a long fucking time. But, hey, you suddenly remember something and want to talk about it. Let me get up at say," her gaze moved over the cell to something before returning to the camera, "six-fucking-forty-five in the morning to play therapist for you."

Reed shook his head. "Look, I'm..."

"No, you look. It's been twenty years. Twenty years since we actually spent time together. You weren't there for me. So you're not going to wake me up to be there for you. It has taken me a long time to get to where I am."

"I'm sorry. I had no idea."

Sadie scoffed. "Yeah, anyway. Maybe we'll talk again. Maybe not, I dunno. But I'm going back to bed." Sadie raised a finger, then stopped and leaned close to the screen. "Hey, where are you, anyway?"

"Parked outside your old house."

"The fuck you are." Her eyes grew wide.

"I was going to talk to your dad."

"Then you're dumber than I thought." Sadie's finger returned, and then the video call disconnected.

Reed sat staring at the black screen. Guilt and something colder moved through him, slow and unasked for.

The seat groaned as he pushed his back against it and placed a hand on his head. He stared at the cell for a minute before flipping it over and over as his mind worked on what Sadie had said. *They've been happening to me for a long fucking time,* echoed in his ears.

He sighed and moved his gaze over the steering wheel. Through the windshield and at the corner of the house, Collins stood glaring at him. The man's massive mud boots made him look rooted in place.

"Shit." Reed's hand dropped to his pocket with his keys, then he stopped. He tossed his cell to the passenger seat before opening the door and making his way to the old man.

Reed slugged over the mud, watching Collins, who remained motionless. The tractor idled by the maple, the branches it had been towing now gone. Reed smiled. "Hi, Mr. Collins."

"Reed," he said gruffly.

"I remember now. I remember what happened."

"Well, good for you." Collins stepped forward. He brushed Reed's shoulder as he passed.

Reed turned and watched the man ascend the steps to his front door. Stretching his arms out at his side, Reed called out, "Aren't you going to tell me what it was?"

Collins grabbed the screen door's handle and opened it, then kicked off his boots. "Nope," he said as he entered his home without looking back.

Reed dropped his arms. He stood with his mouth open, staring at the Collins' home. The weight of the revelation bore down on him. *The craft. A UFO. The unbelievable.* The words died in his mind with no one to listen.

II

Part Two

"For I know this, that after my departing shall grievous wolves enter in among you, not sparing the flock."
- Acts 20:29

Chapter 22

Prosser had hoped for something from his conversations that would have offered a new avenue to investigate. But they left him having to accept that he'd be closing the case with few clues to the Feds' interest in Katherine.

As he drove back to Bridgewater and his office, he took a mental inventory of next steps. *Research public history of the satellite. If it was as ground-breaking as suggested, there must have been anticipation, much like the lead-up to the James Webb's launch.*

Who did Katherine work with on the project?

Search her laptop for any references to the alphabet soup of government agencies.

Prosser pulled his vehicle into his usual spot at the station and called Sarah.

"Hey, honey."

"You working?" Sarah asked over the rummaging of toys in the background.

"I need to get this report done. I'll be home late. Just got back from the O'Reillys and am at the station now."

"Make sure you eat. Do you want to talk to Charlie?"

"Yeah, put him on."

The phone rustled.

"Hi, Daddy," the boy said over the dinging of a toy robot.

"Hey, Charlie-P, how was your day?" Prosser switched the cell to his other hand.

"I ate marshmallows."

"That sounds fun." Prosser smiled and looked out the windshield to the row of pine trees at the back of the lot.

"Are you coming home?"

"Yes, but it will be after you're asleep."

Charlie paused, and Prosser heard what sounded like stomping on the floor. "Can you wake me up?"

"I don't want to wake you, bud. But I'll come up and give you a kiss. Okay?"

For a moment, only Charlie's breathing came through the speaker. "But I want you to wake me up."

"I know. How about tomorrow, I'll bring you to that toy store you like? You can pick out a new airplane."

"Okay." The word came flat, hollow.

"Awesome. I love you. Put Mom back on."

"K."

The noise of the four-year-old jostling the phone ruffled the air until Sarah's voice steadied the clamor. "Hey."

"Hey, I'll spend some time with Char tomorrow. Thanks for covering."

"Of course. Love you."

"Love you, too."

As they ended the call, Prosser gathered his things and made his way through the drizzle to the station. Inside, he walked to his desk and dropped his bag on the floor.

For 6 p.m., the space was busy with officers milling about

between shifts—cops catching up, sharing stories of the day, or making plans. Prosser didn't bother with those kinds of conversations when he could avoid them. Not that he disliked anyone in particular, he just wanted to do his job.

The grumbling of his stomach reminded him to eat, so he pulled out his cell and opened the app for the sandwich shop around the corner. He ordered one turkey with the works, chips, and water. After alerting the officer on duty to expect the food delivery, he booted his computer.

Prosser retrieved various notepads and loose papers he'd need for his report and laid them out on his desk. Examining what he had, a lot of paper with little to show for it, he considered how to work in what Jarrow and Louise had told him.

After typing his password, his monitor displayed a photo of Sarah and Charlie at the river from last summer. Cluttered around it, and almost fully covering the screen, icon after icon of files and folders made a mess only Prosser could decipher. He right-clicked a Word document titled *template* and hit *Copy*. He navigated to his *Reports* folder, hit *Paste*, then renamed the file *Katherine-OReilly-0413*.

Opening it, he saw the familiar blank template—page after page of various fields for him to complete before sharing it with Oberman and filing. Before eating, he wanted to get in the basics: name, age, manner of death, address, etc.

Dinner arrived, and Prosser ate alone in the small department kitchen. He checked the news on his phone and saw no mention of Katherine. The world had moved on. There might not even be any follow-up coverage. Given the news already discussed the impact of the loss of the Elisha, perhaps that was the last anyone would hear of her.

For the first time, he wondered about Katherine as a person. To be so exceptional, master disciplines, accomplish so much, only to decide to end it all. Terrible. She seemed unique. The retro kitchen and various interests, from the sciences to electronics. What didn't Prosser learn about her? What was she like in a conversation? Did she ever relax?

Why the hell was she dating David Jarrow?

He finished his meal and tossed the garbage. Back in the office, Reed still slumped over his desk, asleep. Otherwise, the space was empty.

Prosser sat and tapped his PIN to unlock his computer. The fields appeared, and he worked his way down the report, not leaving one until addressed. Prosser detailed the series of events from the day: the satellite's launch, the call to President Sharma to alert her of Katherine's fall, his arrival...

The low din of the fluorescent lights pierced Prosser's nerves over the otherwise silence. He rubbed his eyes, then his ears, and looked at the time. Nine.

Not bad, he thought as he hit *Print.*

The office printer by the stairs clunked as it spat out paper, and he walked the line between desks to get his file. As he pulled the dozen pages from the tray, Reed snored.

Prosser snickered and returned to his desk. Frankly, it wasn't the first time someone slept in the office or even under their desk. Usually, it was due to long shifts, but a few years ago, old Wally Butler got in a big spat with his wife and stayed at the department for a week.

At his desk, he pounded in a staple and dropped the unsigned document on top of Oberman's keyboard. He'd be in the office to discuss with her in the morning, but this way she could read it if she arrived early.

Prosser hit the lights at the top of the stairs and descended, leaving Reed alone in the dark.

Chapter 23

Reed motioned for Wendy to sit on the living room couch and stood in front of her. At the end of his run, he knew he needed to talk the events out with someone. After being rejected by both Sadie and Joseph Collins, Wendy was the only person to share something so insane with. While her recent reactions left little promise, she was all he had.

"Thanks for coming over. I'm going to explain what's happening. I'm taking a big f'ing chance here."

"Okay," she said, squinting.

"Do I blurt out what's going on, or do I walk you through all the shit?" Reed asked as he stepped back.

Wendy put her knees together. "Can you just tell me? You're freaking me out."

Reed took a deep breath and blurted out with an expulsion of air. "I think aliens are fucking with me."

Wendy's jaw dropped.

Reed opened his hands and tilted his head.

"Uh, I'm sorry. What?" Wendy asked.

"Aliens. I think they are messing with me."

"Reed—"

He interrupted, "Look, I'm not working too much. That was never a problem, so don't go there. This isn't about how much sleep I'm getting or work stress. I'm putting myself out there right now."

"I don't even get what you're saying. Aliens?"

"Yeah."

"Whatever." She made a brushing motion with her right hand. "Tell me why you think that."

"Alright. So, first, I started seeing this praying mantis, but it was too cold. I saw him more than once, in different places. On my car, on a call. Always staring right at me."

Wendy didn't blink.

"Then, at Sally's, time froze. Everything stopped. And a mantis started coming out of a coffee display, like a cardboard cutout thing. It tried to come out, but was stuck or something. Only here's the thing: the guy who works there says *I* was the one who was frozen. Then there was this woman, who didn't even make sense. Like it was weird, out of place. And I got the security footage. It went haywire, but something was going on."

Reed pointed at Wendy. "And that symbol in the backyard and the waitress at Rossi's who wasn't a waitress, and she didn't make sense either."

He stopped and placed his hands on his hips.

Wendy clasped hers together. "So what makes any of that aliens?"

Reed shrugged his shoulders. "The triangles."

"Uh, my earrings?"

"The triangle that was in the sky when I was eleven. Their ship."

"Triangle in the sky? When you were eleven?"

"That's right. With Sadie Collins."

Wendy's eyes examined his. "You saw a...UFO?"

Reed nodded.

Wendy rubbed her eyes. "I can't believe this." She gestured for Reed to continue talking. "Like, how does seeing a UFO in the sky when you were eleven have anything to do with this?"

"Because it all started with farmer Collins."

"Farmer Collins?"

"Sadie's grandfather. I was at his house. Oh, that's another thing! When I was there, there was something in his barn, but I couldn't get it. Anyway, he said that when I was eleven, I was there and ran home scared. He told me to think about that day and to go back to him when I remembered. And I did."

"And?"

"That's when all this started. At least I think that's when it started."

Wendy pushed her butt closer to the back of the couch. "Did you go back to Collins to tell him you remembered, like he asked?"

"Yeah, I was pissed. But I ended up calling Sadie first."

Wendy nodded. "Oh, you called Sadie." She crossed her arms.

Reed looked at her, his eyes raised.

"I gotta be honest. I don't know what to do with that. Why are you calling an old girlfriend?" Wendy asked as she tightened her grasp on her arms.

Reed's shoulders dropped. "Are you kidding?"

Wendy stretched her back to sit upright. "No, I'm not."

"Sadie was never a girlfriend. What are you, jealous?"

"Look," Wendy released her grip, "there's no need to go telling other people and looking foolish. I just don't know what to do with this."

"Yeah, join the fucking club." He shrugged.

"You realize how it sounds, right?"

The blood drained from Reed's face. "Don't."

"It sounds crazy."

"I'm not crazy, Wen."

"Fine. You're not. What did she say then?"

"Nothing, she hung up on me." Reed looked down.

"And her grandfather? Did you talk to him?"

"He was no help."

She put her head between her hands and stared at the floor for a moment. "Alright." Wendy looked back up. "So, you are, or were, the most stable person I'd ever met. So, what are you going to do?"

Reed shook his head. "I'm still figuring that out."

"K, you're going to have to get help. Talk to a therapist. The department has resources you can use."

"Oh, right, like I'm going to spill this to anyone at work. I'd be off the force!" Reed threw out his arms.

"A private therapist, then. They can't tell anyone anything."

"I'm not seeing a therapist. Nothing's wrong with me."

"Reed!" She slapped her knees.

"I'm not."

Wendy looked away. "The way you've been hasn't been the strong man that I fell in love with. You've changed. You're different."

"No, I'm not."

* * *

The day folded into night. They set the conversation aside by unspoken agreement — the gym, a movie, an early retirement, filling the hours with motion rather than words. The two settled into bed, Badge in his in the living room. Outside, clouds smothered the stars. Sleep came fast.

Then Reed woke to sulfur searing his nose and the taste of metal eating his tongue.

The room glowed in a bright light that blurred objects and added a sheen around their edges. From every corner, under each piece of furniture, and behind the curtains, the white light permeated.

Reed squinted and raised his hand. "The hell?"

The numbers on the bedside digital clock raced like a time machine.

Beside him, Wendy lay still.

"Babe?" He shook her.

"Wen?"

No response.

He dragged his legs out from the covers. As he stood, he noticed the warm floor under his feet. The deep winter threaded itself into the house like mycelium, it should have taken weeks of warmth to push it back.

The thick dust in the air twinkled in the light. Small particles shifted in slow waves, drawn and released by a deep pulse that Reed couldn't name but somehow recognized. He stretched a hand out into the mass and turned it over. The lifelike sprinkles drifted between his fingers and around his arm.

He looked down to see the hairs on his bare legs dancing to the oscillations.

Reed stepped to the window to investigate the light source. A noise interrupted, tactile, wrong, scratching at his skin rather than his ears. Like giant fists wringing rubber, punctuated by the sporadic crack of old wood under weight. It came from the hall.

From under the closed door, a shadow swayed. Reed's heart pounded. Wendy still lay unconscious.

Reed grabbed his personal firearm from the bedside table and moved to the door without a sound. He placed an ear against it. Another sound now accompanied the heavy squeezing of the rubber. A low and ongoing inhalation never followed by the expulsion of breath.

Reed gripped the doorknob and leaned his weight back. He bounced on his heels once, twice, the old cop ritual of committing before the breach. He swung the door open and threw himself through it, arm rising to point the gun, and found himself standing in the middle of his front yard. It stretched empty between him and the road. Snow packed and cold, marked here and there with Badge's yellow spots. Stars. A sliver of moon balanced on the horizon. He lowered his hands.

"Reed?"

He turned to see Wendy running to him in slippers and her heavy robe.

"What the hell are you doing?" Wendy reached out and grabbed Reed's hand, which held the gun. "You're freezing! How long have you been out here?"

Reed shook his head. "I don't know. Seconds."

"Come on, get inside." She slid the weapon from his loose grip.

With hurried steps, Wendy led him inside, where she pulled off her robe and threw it over his shoulders. They stood in the entryway, and Wendy rubbed his chest for heat.

"Why were you out there?"

"I wasn't."

"Uh, no, you were outside. I just brought you in."

Reed shook his head, his eyes unblinking.

"Why did you have your gun?" she asked.

"Gun?" Reed's brow furrowed.

She lifted it, showing him the butt end of the weapon.

"Because of the thing in the hall," the memory faded back.

"What thing?"

"It was in the hall."

Wendy threw her arms out. "What? What was in the hall?"

"I don't know. I opened the door and was outside."

"You followed it out?"

Reed shook his head again. "No, the door opened to the outside."

"Come on." She grabbed his arm, but Reed didn't move.

"Wen?"

"What?"

Reed's eyes opened wide. "Where's Badge?"

Through the foyer, the couple looked at the empty dog bed next to the cold fireplace.

Chapter 24

After finding Badge in the basement, tail tucked and panting in sharp, shallow bursts, Reed fell into bed and scraped together a couple of hours of sleep. At 10 a.m., he white-knuckled the urge to run and dragged himself into the Bridgewater Public Library, a century-old stone building that sat two blocks from the central street of Old Bridgewater.

He paused as he entered, clutching the small notepad and pen he had brought, and looked around for where to begin. The ground floor housed a large area of old tables to his left, each crowded with students on laptops or with thick textbooks, along with the circulation desk. To the right, book stacks spread in even rows, with an elevator and staircase tucked beyond them.

"Welcome. Can I help you?" The friendly voice came from Reed's immediate left. A middle-aged woman in an Irish sweater and glasses stood behind the circulation desk.

"Yes, thanks." Reed looked around again. "Um, it's been a while since I've been in a library."

"That's okay. I can show you how to use our digital card catalog, or point you in any direction."

"Yeah, if you could show me how to find some books, that would be great."

"Sure, follow me."

She circled the desk and led him to four connected stations, each monitor glowing with the library's catalog interface.

"Sit." She pulled the chair for Reed. "Pretty self-explanatory, but I'll walk you through, and you can always track one of us down if you're having trouble. You can type in the title or author and get the search results along with the Dewey number, which will help you find the book on the shelves." She pointed to the row of long book stacks to their right. "You can see the numbers at the end of each section that correspond to the Dewey. The map over here," the librarian pointed to the wall, "will show you where each of those main classes, or the first number of the Dewey, can be found."

Reed nodded.

"Is there something I can help you find?" she asked with a smile.

"If I only have a topic, what do I do?"

"Ah, a researcher! Yes, just type that in the search box, and you'll get results. You'll see the Dewey numbers along with our classification, like fiction, non-fiction, history, religion, et cetera, and you'll notice the similarities. So you'll know which Dewey numbers correspond. If I'm making any sense." She winked.

"Sure."

"Want to give it a shot?"

"Actually, I'm good. I appreciate your help. I can take it from here." Reed grabbed the keyboard and mouse.

"Great. Reach out if you have troubles."

The librarian returned to the circulation desk, and Reed

looked around for any prying eyes. He typed in the search box.

aliens

A series of results appeared, from fictionalized versions of the Ridley Scott film to modern-day studies of immigration and books on missing time, UFOs, and abductions.

After a few minutes, he found his way to the third floor, a deserted area with countless book stacks that smelled of old paper. There, toward the back, were shelves of books about extraterrestrials. With no background on the topic to start from, he piled a few into his arms from authors who had more than one publication. His collection included material from J. Allen Hynek, Jacques Vallée, and Budd Hopkins.

He dumped them on a table alongside his pad and pen and sat. The titles heightened his anxiety surrounding his experiences. *Missing Time: A Documented Study of UFO Abductions. Intruders: The Incredible Visitations at Copley Woods. Confrontations. Night Siege: The Hudson Valley UFO Sightings.*

The floor was almost silent. Only the whirring of the heating system kept Reed company. Along his left, the rows of books concealed him from the elevators and stairs, and to his right, more shelves that separated Reed from a series of small privacy rooms that lay in darkness. He worked through the books, scanning the chapters for whatever might suggest a way to escape what now tormented him. But as nothing presented itself as a solution, he returned the books and grabbed more. This time, he selected by shock value. *Operation Trojan Horse*, *Walking Among Us*, *Encounters*, among others.

After another couple of hours unsuccessfully scouring through the material, Reed leaned back and slumped in the chair. He pushed a slow breath through his teeth. *Am I supposed to just accept this? Can I? How do I keep my job, my self-respect, with this hanging over everything?*

He checked his cell for any messages, none. He looked around the space for any people. Empty. Reed's eyes darted between shelves and books for any movement or signs of life as a shiver raced up his spine. With walls of books stretched to each side, he couldn't keep the entire space in his view. Reed looked to his left. *There are eyes on my back.* He turned to the right. *Someone's behind me.* He turned his head from side to side as his breathing quickened and he felt eyes on him from everywhere and nowhere.

Unlocking his phone, he stood and walked the length of the aisle. At the end, he found a privacy room ten yards to his left. He tapped the button to call Sadie as he walked to it.

"Hey, Sade," he said louder than he had intended when she answered. He ducked into the cramped room that held only a small tabletop screwed to the wall and a chair. He shut the door.

"Hey." Sadie smiled. She appeared to be in the same room when he had last spoken to her. This time, her hair was nicely done, and her eyes held more life. "I'm glad you called."

"Oh?" Reed's gaze darted from the slender window that provided an obscured view of the interior of the library to his cell phone.

"I was...a bitch. I'm sorry."

Reed pulled the metal chair out from the desk and sat. "No, Sadie, I'm sorry. I should have been there for you."

"Yes, that would have been nice. But we were both kids. We're not now, and I'm sorry for what I said. Especially the dumb part. You're not dumb."

"Can you tell me then? Can you tell me what happened?"

She shook her head. "We're not there yet. It has been a long time. But I hope you keep calling, and don't be a stranger."

"Thanks, I will. I kinda needed to hear a voice. Freaked out there a moment."

Sadie snorted. "Reed? Scared?"

He blinked and shook his head. "Shut up."

She smiled and rested her head on her hand. "And you chose to call me."

The hair on the back of Reed's neck tingled as if excited by electrostatic. He stood and went to the window, where he leaned close and tilted his head to look up and down the space. Nothing.

Reed stepped back, brought the cell up to his face, and opened his mouth to talk.

Then the library's lights went out.

He looked up, and his left hand found the doorknob. He held it tightly.

"Reed?" Sadie gasped.

He remained inches away from the window, out of which he saw nothing but the hints of angular shelves.

"What's going on?"

Reed shook his head. "The lights went out."

"What? Where are you?" Sadie asked, her tone concerned.

"A privacy room at the library," he whispered.

"Library?"

"Hold on." He turned the cell around so the screen's glow might illuminate the larger space, but he only saw its reflection in the glass.

"This is creeping me out. What are you doing?"

"Sorry," Reed turned the camera back to himself, "just trying to see what's out there."

"Probably books."

"Very funny."

"Just go out there. Keep me on, though."

Reed turned the knob, sending small metallic creaking sounds into the air, and paused. After a moment, he slowly opened the door.

"Turn the phone. Let me see."

Reed did, and the glare only penetrated a few feet of the darkness and barely lit any surfaces. He stepped out of the room and looked to the left, where the hall continued with more rooms and racks on the right. Down one of those was the desk he had been sitting at. At the far end, he could see the red glow of an exit sign on the ceiling.

He turned to the right to see more rows fading into shadow.

"Just get out of there," Sadie's tinny voice came from the small speakerphone.

"Yeah. I need to get my notes."

"K."

Reed made his way along the hall, holding the cell up to light his way. He looked down the rows for his desk. When he came upon familiar books, he stopped. "I think I was down here." The metal shelving felt cold as Reed placed a hand on one and turned, taking slow, methodical steps.

His eyes went from checking other rows from between the shelves to the strip of brown carpet that disappeared into darkness ahead. The air continued to cool as he walked down the aisle.

"Reed, stop."

He did. "What?"

"What's that?"

Reed kept the phone pointed to where he thought the table would be. The books went on as if forever, dissolving to the black abyss of the powerless library. He squinted but could see nothing else.

Sadie's tone hushed, "Reed, look at me."

He tightened his grip on the phone and took a deep breath as he rotated the screen. "What?"

"Run. Run back." Sadie's eyes were big. She leaned toward the camera and the fingers of her free hand tore at her shirt. "Back the way you came. Go to that room and shut the door, okay?"

"What? Why?"

"Just do it. Do what I say. Please!" Tears appeared, reflecting the light of her room.

Reed shook his head. "No, I'm not running."

"Reed, listen..."

"No."

He looked up into the blackness of the space and slowly spun the phone. He held his breath. The shiny covers of some books glowed, while others seemed to drink the dim light.

As the phone pointed straight ahead, he saw what he had before—the stretch into pitch black.

He took a step, and then another.

"Reed?"

"Shhh."

One more step, and he saw a vague shape. A small bit of white, then a space, and another small section below it, like a colon hovering off the ground.

Another step, then another, and he could see. A woman in a white dress sat in a chair, her back to him. Her black hair seemed to be part of the surrounding darkness.

"Reed, I don't like this."

"Hello?" he said softly to the woman, but she didn't respond or move.

Now in the open space between the long rows of book stacks, he sidestepped to his right, rounding the woman.

"Hey, you okay?" he asked.

Reed saw the side of her head. Her skin was only a shade darker than her pristine dress. The woman's hair looked combed down, without a strand out of place. Her hands lay flat on the table.

He maneuvered its side and placed his fingertips on the wooden tabletop.

"Reed, you need to run," Sadie's hushed voice announced.

The woman turned her head to Reed. The screen struggled to provide enough illumination. Reed saw her face dimly glow in the darkness. Her eyes were too far apart and too high on her face.

The woman from Sally's. The same one he saw after time stopped.

"Sit," she said as she raised her right hand. Her voice was precise.

Reed noticed her middle finger draped over the lower two, as if free of bones.

Suddenly, Reed's cell went dark, and he turned it around to see *Disconnected* displayed on the otherwise black screen.

"Shit!" He fumbled through the menu to turn on the flashlight and whirled it around at the woman, who sat there with her hand out, pointing at the seat across from her. Like a thick wet noodle, her finger hung.

She smiled.

"Um, okay." Reed moved to the chair opposite her and kept her in his sight as he sat.

With the brighter light she came into focus. The skin

beneath her eyes hung in loose flaps, and beneath that wasn't the red of exposed muscle, but the blackness of something sheathed in deceit. Her lower lip also hung from her face, revealing gray flesh underneath.

She lowered her hand to the table, trapping the flaccid digit under her palm.

"Who are you?" Reed asked.

"You need not concern yourself with that."

"That was you at Sally's. You had something to do with that, didn't you?" Reed's hand moved to where his pistol would be when in uniform.

"I've been sent to share certain information with you." She tilted her head as she looked at him, unblinking. "Perhaps it will put you at ease."

Reed shook his head. "What information?"

As she spoke, her lips drooped. "That you need not worry."

"Because you'll leave me alone?"

"Because your usage of the concept of 'me' is shallow. An individual is nothing. It is only the whole that is of concern."

As she talked, her skin shifted not from muscle moving, but something else, something with no connection to what lay above. Her shell hung loose, a bag draped over the wrong shape.

"I bring this to you as a gift. Knowledge of the greater whole that we cultivate through the propagation."

"The hell are you talking about?"

She smiled again and dragged her hands to her lap. "Find that insight satisfactory."

With a heavy electric *thump* that shook the building, the lights powered on. Reed turned his attention to the elevators two dozen yards away, and then back to the empty seat in front of him.

* * *

The glass door of the library shuddered on its frame as Reed shoved through it and broke into a run across the parking lot. Entering his Wrangler, he flung his notepad to the back seat and locked the door. He gritted his teeth and squeezed the wheel, then shook it so violently he heard a cracking from under the dash.

"Fuck!" Reed sat back and ran his hands through his hair. "One, two, three, four..." he counted as his breathing and pulse slowed. Reed shivered, but not from the cold cabin.

He grabbed his cell and initiated a video call to Sadie. When it connected, Sadie sat with her knees up to her chin. Behind her, a bright white surface claimed the remainder of the screen. It looked like she was crouching by her bathtub. She rubbed her red eyes.

"What was that?" Reed asked.

Sadie punctuated her yells with her free hand. "I TOLD you to run!" Her words broke through sobs. "Next time you DO what I say! There's NO reason to talk to them, you get it? NO REASON!"

Reed watched as Sadie looked up, seemingly to calm herself. She huffed and dropped her face to her knees. "Christ," she whispered. Sadie raised her head again. "Just don't, okay? You run the other way."

"Who was she?"

Sadie wiped the last of her tears with her shirt. "Them. She was them. One of the types."

"Yeah, I kinda got that feeling." Reed made a fist. "You were scared like you knew her."

Sadie pressed her tongue against her lip for a moment before speaking. "She's not a 'her' or a 'she'. I don't know what they are. I've never seen...that one, but others like it."

"You've seen them?"

"Yeah." She looked down and messaged a temple. "See them."

"As in, you *still* see them?" Reed waited for a response, but Sadie's gaze seemed to be lost somewhere else. "What are they?"

"Don't know. Never will."

"She said something about...about the individual not mattering. The whole is what's important. She said it like she was doing me a favor." Reed watched Sadie bite her lips like she didn't want to talk anymore. He broke the silence. "I can't get Little Red Riding Hood out of my mind."

"What?" Sadie looked at the screen.

"Little Red Riding Hood." He looked out the window at the handful of people walking across the green, ordinary and unbothered. "She goes to see her grandmother—she had flowers or food, or something. She goes in, and it's a wolf that wants to eat her, disguised as the old woman. Like it wore her grandmother's skin."

The two sat in silence for a moment.

The scene behind Sadie jostled as she shifted. "Yeah, that's pretty much what they are."

"Wolves," Reed said. "They're wolves." He clutched the emergency brake.

Chapter 25

When Prosser arrived home, he found Sarah sitting in her recliner in the living room, reading a thick spiral-bound book with a chart on the cover. The lamp on the side table next to her offered the only light. A Bluetooth speaker played instrumental acid jazz at a low volume.

Prosser threw off his shoes, then tossed his bag on the island between the dining table and kitchen. "Hey, honey." He bent to kiss her before plopping onto the couch.

"Hey. Long day?" she asked.

"Long. A lot of driving."

"Everything okay?" She kept the book on her page but turned it over.

Prosser stared at nothing for a moment. The image of the energy-sucking man hit him. "Oh yeah. David fucking Jarrow."

"Who's that?" Sarah chuckled.

Prosser slid up to correct his posture. "Katherine's boyfriend. I spent a year with him this morning."

"That bad?" Sarah groaned.

"Worse."

"Want anything? Did you eat?"

Prosser adjusted his waistband. "I'm good, but thank you. How are you? How was Charlie?"

"He misses you."

"I know." The image of Charlie playing without him tugged at Prosser's heart.

"You said you'd take him to the toy store tomorrow."

"I will. I placed my report on Oberman's desk. Tomorrow will be light."

"Good. He'll like the time with you. He talked about it a lot."

Prosser turned again to Sarah. "Thank you for doing so much."

She smiled. "No problem, I get it."

"Maybe we can get a sitter for a while. Or your mom comes over and watches him. Then we can spend a day, just the two of us."

"That sounds nice, but another time. I think something with the three of us would be better right now."

He nodded in agreement. "You're right."

Sarah closed her book and placed it on the side table. "I'm going to bed. You staying up?"

"Only for a little while. Going to unwind."

"K, love you," she said as she stood and kissed him before going upstairs.

Prosser didn't move for several minutes. Though the day was not physically challenging, he still needed to catch his breath. Days on the road did that to him.

As he stood, the neighbor's floodlight illuminated and lit the space as it had done the night before. "Jesus, Lawrence," Prosser said aloud to himself as he walked to the kitchen and retrieved a mineral water from the refrigerator. He took a big sip before returning to the living room and shutting off the lamp. "Don't need you now."

The couch squeaked as he lay down. He grabbed the remote from the table and turned on the television. Seeing the obvious cop drama, he changed the channel. Cycling through channels until he found baseball, he resigned to watch a few innings before heading to bed.

The batter sent a ground ball streaking into center field before a strange and inconsistent interference covered the television's screen. Vertical lines twisted like a wave pattern, tilted 90 degrees, and reflected in the small color pixels. Prosser changed the channel. Jagged lines bled across the screen in waves while the popular psychic Clausen Carey sat with an elderly woman. The pattern came and went.

He clicked back to baseball.

*One...two...three...*Prosser counted between each pulse of the twisting lines.

Every three seconds.

Prosser considered turning off the television and going to bed, or pushing through the interference. Then the Wi-Fi device hissed static again. It just wasn't worth it. He clicked off the TV.

Standing with a grunt, he grabbed his drink and walked to the kitchen. At the sink, he guzzled down the last of the lime-flavored bubbly water. Without a sound, the neighbor's light turned off.

"Quick dip."

Prosser almost expected to hear his son call for him, as he had the previous night, but the house remained silent. He tossed the glass container into the recycling bin and headed to the stairs.

As he turned into the foyer, Charlie was standing there, arms hanging empty at his side.

"Oh, buddy. What are you doing up?"

The little boy, this time in his Superman pajamas, remained quiet. Prosser picked him up, and Charlie rested his head on his dad's shoulder, exhausted.

"You okay, little man? You want anything?"

"No." His voice was quiet, distant.

"Where's Ducky Ducky?"

"I can't get him."

"Oh."

Prosser started up the front stairs, hugging Charlie tight and rubbing his back. He took a left at the top, where the hall overlooked the foyer. Straight ahead was Charlie's room.

Passing through the open doorway, he entered the dark room, where he gently returned his son to bed and covered him with a blanket. In the room, Prosser scanned for Charlie's most treasured stuffed animal.

"Where is it, Charlie-P?" he whispered.

"It's in there."

Charlie pointed to the tent.

"Oh, you could have got him."

Prosser walked over and got on his knees to reach into the dark tent. In the dark, he fumbled around until he found the stuffed animal and pulled it out. "Here you go." He handed Ducky Ducky back to Charlie, who tucked it under the blanket in an embrace.

Prosser sat next to him. "Love you, dude."

"Love you, Dad."

"I'm excited for tomorrow. I get to spend time with you."

He placed a hand on his son's shoulder.

Charlie looked at his father. "You said the toy store. You said."

"I know. I said." Prosser tousled Charlie's hair and stood. Making his way to the door, he paused to gaze back at his son.

Charlie rolled over to face the wall.

Chapter 26

The weather had finally turned. After a long winter, the sunshine and warmth felt good on Reed's skin as he walked to the door of Bridgewater PD. He nodded to officers as he passed, shaking hands on autopilot, the wolf from the library crouching at the edge of every exchange. He kept his eyes moving, never settling too long on any face.

"Hi, Pops." Reed tapped the plaque as he headed up the stairs to complete the return to duty paperwork and collect his badge and weapon. Routine. Normalcy. And maybe, eventually, optimism. Reaching the top of the steps, he noticed a group of five male cops laughing and talking together. The desks were mostly empty, but Oberman sat in her office talking into her phone.

"Yo, Reed!" Matheson, a rookie, called him over.

"What's up, guys?"

"Enjoy your vacation?" Keyes asked as he approached.

"Nope," Reed responded. "Hey, where is everyone?"

"You didn't hear?" Matheson asked excitedly.

"No, what's up?"

"Jumper. Some scientist lady. Guess it's a big deal."

Keyes interjected with a more professional tone. "Katherine

O'Reilly. My wife followed her work, armchair scientist that she is. O'Reilly taught Cosmology at U of B. She was a celebrity. The real deal. Like Einstein."

"Holy shit." A case like that, that was the kind to live for. His feet tapped against the floor.

"Check it out." Matheson changed the subject and handed Reed his cell phone.

On it, Reed saw a photograph of a naked woman, Peyton Lynton, an actress famous for dramatic roles. Green palm trees sprouted behind her, and an inviting blue pool waited at her side.

"Dude, it's Peyton Lynton!" Matheson said as he patted Reed's shoulder.

"Uh-huh. What's wrong with the photo?" Reed squinted as he examined more closely. The woman's glassy eyes had no life behind them. Her skin had a faint, sourceless sheen, not quite lit, not quite real. The angles of her fingers were wrong in a way he couldn't name.

"It's A.I., bro!" Matheson said excitedly.

"A.I.?" Reed kept his gaze on the eyes of the woman.

"You burning that image into your brain?" Keyes asked with a laugh.

Reed shook his head. "Her eyes, man. They're dead."

"Yeah, like I said, it's A.I." Matheson snatched his phone back. "You're ruining the fun."

"A computer made that?" Reed asked.

Matheson turned off the screen. "A program trained on images of her."

Reed looked at the cop but spoke to himself. "A.I. That's why it's off."

"Dude!" Matheson threw his arms up.

"Guys, I have to get the forms done to get back on duty." With a nod, Reed turned and walked to his desk.

"Later, man," Keyes called out.

A.I. A.I. A.I. Reed repeated to himself.

Maybe that's what's going on. Maybe that's what they are! It's why everything is so...weird. Why that woman looked strange. Why the things they say don't make sense. Because it's just some A.I. trained on human interaction, but they don't understand it.

Reed sat, but his hands gripped the chair, ready to push forward. The impulse itched at him. He wanted to run to Collins to tell him, to call Sadie about his revelation. But he leaned forward and placed his elbows on his knees.

Wait, what am I doing? Who would I tell about this A.I. theory? Why? So what if I'm right?

Reed pulled himself to the desk.

Even if I am, there's nothing I can do about it. It doesn't help me stop them. I need to let it go...

He completed the paperwork in twenty minutes, had the short required conversation with Oberman, and walked out with his shield and his gun.

Chapter 27

After getting his gear, Reed drove home to an excited Badge and a quiet Wendy. They ate in silence, the scraping of forks the loudest thing in the room. She scrolled her phone while Reed laced up for a run. Later, he fell asleep with his duty belt already laid out on the dresser.

In the middle of the night, he awoke to the room being engulfed in that light. Reed raised an open hand to shield his eyes. As he sat up, he groaned and squinted. The lamps were off. The intruding glow pumped through the bedroom's windows. It made the imperfections of the wood floors and plaster walls more pronounced.

"Oh, fuck," he blurted as the memory of this light came to him.

The grinding of the bedside table drawer echoed through the room as he opened it and retrieved his pistol. The reverberating sound made the space seem larger.

He stood and pointed the weapon at the window to his left. Drawing the shade to the side blinded him, and he returned it. The light pressed against him like being chest-deep in water.

"Wen, wake up."

Reed moved to the window at the far side of the room.

Peeking behind its curtain proved just as fruitless as before.

"Wen."

The glow even found its way from under the door. This time, no shadows or sounds came from behind it.

"Wendy!"

Reed turned to their bed. Empty.

"Fuck!"

Reed ran to the door and thrust it open. Before stepping out into the hall, he paused to ensure it wasn't his yard. Finding the hall normal, he hurried to the stairs and descended them.

"Wendy?" he yelled.

With no response, he moved to the kitchen, then to the living area.

"Wendy?"

Reed ran to the front door and opened it. Unlike the house, it was a dark night outside. Without bothering to put on shoes, Reed walked over the remaining ice, snow, and muck to his driveway. Behind him, the house somehow showed no illumination. He turned to the field at the side of his home. Fifty yards ahead, the leafless forest waited. The trees' spindly branches reached out in all directions. Between Reed and the woods, Badge stood snapping his jaws. His teeth bit at air. Spit splattered from his mouth as he made a barking motion. But no sound came from the dog. The world was muted.

Just before and above the treeline, the black craft loomed. Silent. Motionless. Easily two hundred feet across.

A colossal pyramid, black as a void, hovered without sound or tremor. Its edges were so sharp they seemed to cut the fabric of the night sky open. Clouds parted around it. Its finish swallowed moonlight whole, no gleam, no reflection, just an absence where something massive should have been. The craft from his childhood.

At eleven years old, he only saw one side—a triangle. Now the ominous craft unveiled itself. As if in a demonstration of its will, the place at which the four triangular sides came together pointed at his house.

And then he saw Wendy suspended under it, just feet off the ground. She hung like a rag doll in the darkness. Limp. Her hair draped over her face. Wendy's body, with her pristine white nightshirt, rotated like an object in a display case.

Reed dove to a full sprint, his bare feet crunching snow. "Wendy!"

He passed Badge, who continued the soundless barking. The distance between Reed and the UFO quickly shortened, but to Reed it felt like he only got further away. The landscape lengthened as he ran. A hallway of trees and dirt and sky that seemed to go on forever, with the pyramid at its center. His lungs pumped oxygen to his muscles. Reed's legs propelled him forward.

Approaching the shade of the vessel, Reed pulled his body back. The world went crashing forward as his legs dug into the frozen ground. Reed stopped just short of the UFO's shadow.

Below the craft, under its dark skin, the terrain seemed to have vanished. A black hole. Reed looked out at Wendy; her eyes were closed. He turned his attention back to the land and stretched a foot out to feel for a surface. The cold earth pricked at his skin. The ground was there, but somehow the ship consumed the light. Except, Reed realized, it allowed him to see Wendy. Like it wanted him to.

Reed broke back into a sprint, entering the blackness. An electric wave washed over him, causing the hair on his body to rise. Reaching his girlfriend, Reed wrapped his arms around her legs. As he did, Wendy dropped to his shoulder. Whatever had held her, let her go.

Reed stepped back and looked up. Pure darkness broke the already sunless sky, like a tear in the cosmos that presented hell. He raised his pistol and pointed it at the craft. Reed pulled the trigger.

clunk

Nothing.

The pulsing came. Boomed throughout his body and sent shock waves through his system. Reed looked down and shook his head to fight off a sudden vertigo.

He turned and ran. Pushing his legs to their maximum effect, he stumbled as he made his way through its inky shadow.

As the visible turf returned, Reed found his footing and passed his dog. "Come on, Badge."

Badge followed. The pulsing continued. It pounded his mind.

They reached the house. Reed slammed the door behind them and locked the deadbolt. With the home now dark, he carried Wendy to the living room and gently placed her down on the couch. He flipped on the lamp and brushed Wendy's hair from her face. Reed found her eyes still closed.

The pulsing stopped.

"Wendy?"

Badge trembled next to them. The couch creaked as Reed stood and returned to the door. He unlocked it, swung it open, and stepped outside again to look toward the woods. Gone. The night sky appeared as it should have.

Returning to Wendy, he knelt on one knee and tucked his sidearm under the sofa. "Wendy?"

Reed rubbed her shoulder. She grunted and opened her eyes.

"What? What?" Wendy pushed herself up to a seated position and looked around the room. "Why am I down here?"

Badge licked Wendy's arm. The red and swollen flesh of Reed's feet burned and throbbed with each heartbeat.

"Um..." Reed looked around the room as he shifted his weight to ease the burning. Then he sat on the couch.

Wendy's eyes grew wide and red as she covered her mouth. "No."

"I'm sorry."

"You're not going to say..." She raised her knees and clutched them to her chest.

Reed reached to place a hand on her shoulder. "I found you outside."

Wendy's gaze remained locked forward. Her eyes on his.

"I woke up, and you weren't in bed. I found you outside," Reed explained.

The muscles of Wendy's jaw tightened as she slapped her knees. "Bullshit!" she yelled.

"What?" Reed retracted his hand.

"What'd you do? Hmm? Carry me down here and wake me up as some sort of ploy to get me to think all this is real?"

Reed stood.

Wendy's face flushed a dark red. "How fucking dare you." The words came out harsh and pointed.

"I'm not lying." Reed pointed to the door. "I found you outside, hovering under the ship. They were taking you! I brought you back in!"

"Jesus, you expect me to believe this shit?" She swung her legs over the cushions and to the floor. "If I was outside, why am I not cold? Hmm? Or dirty?"

Reed shook his head. "I don't know. Maybe they..."

Wendy cut him off. "Exactly. You can stop the game now."

"I'm not making it up. Look at Badge!" Reed pointed to the dog two feet away, who was shaking and panting.

"Really? *Your dog?*"

"Badge was outside, too. He was barking, except I couldn't hear him. Look, his paws are all dirty. So are my feet!" He lifted one.

Wendy stood and stepped close to Reed. She looked up at him. "Give it up."

"I'm telling you the truth."

She turned and made her way to the stairs. "I'm getting my stuff. I'm out of here. You call me when you get your shit together."

"Go. I'll call you every day. My shit's together."

"Whatever."

* * *

From his front stoop, in gray sweats and with Badge at his side, Reed watched Wendy drive past where the large craft broke the sky just hours earlier. The clouds warned of rain.

"Come on, Badge."

Reed entered the home and closed the door. Taking gentle steps with reddened feet, he continued to the kitchen where he dumped ground beans into his coffee machine.

Badge growled as a knock came at the door.

"Coming." Having been only a minute, and not seeing another car along the open stretch of road as she drove away, Reed assumed Wendy had turned around.

Badge growled again. "Buddy, stop."

The dog trailed behind Reed as he approached the front door. He opened it to find three men, each sharply dressed in black suits and fedoras. One had stark blond hair, and they all stood tall, with strong, straight postures. "Can I help you?"

A pristine black 1970 Ford LTD waited in his driveway.

"Yes, we'd like to talk to you for a minute," the blond man said with a deep voice.

"Sure, what can I help you with?"

"May we come in?" Another asked from behind.

"Depends. What's it about?" Reed braced a foot behind the door.

"This morning."

Badge bumped Reed's knee. "Um, yeah. Okay then."

He stepped back and motioned the men to enter. As if knowing the house's layout, they moved to the living room and sat on the couch. Reed took the stiff wooden chair in the corner, and his dog sat at attention next to him.

The blond man spoke again. "We understand you may have seen something. Something unusual."

"Maybe. What's your name?"

"Of course, I'm Agent Sanders, and this is Agent Duplessis and Agent Vitally."

"And you're with what agency?"

"That's not important, Mr. Jacobs. What is important is what you think you saw." Agent Sanders said.

"What I *think* I saw?"

"That's right. In the early hours this morning. But in fact, you didn't. It was just a normal morning for you and your girlfriend."

"Ah. Well, Mr. Sanders..."

"Agent."

"Sure, why not, *Agent* Sanders. My girlfriend and I did experience something this morning." Reed placed a hand on Badge's side and petted him.

"No, you didn't, Reed. Nor did Wendy Joyner. Nor did Badge here. In fact, you had a restful sleep and a pleasant morning. Perhaps you admired the sunrise, excited about the new day. Maybe you and your lady fucked. Or made breakfast together and planned for a hike now that the weather has improved."

"But you didn't witness anything," one of the other men added.

Reed examined the men. They sat with their hands on their laps.

"What agency did you say you were with?" Reed asked again.

"We didn't. We have a simple message to deliver. Then, once we're all in agreement, we'll be on our way, and you'll never hear from us again."

The men sat motionless.

Reed squeezed the arm of his chair. "Yeah, well, let's cut the shit then. What are you saying?"

"We've already said it, Mr. Jacobs. You had a delightful morning. With nothing worth discussing with anyone."

"And if I do?"

The blond man continued with a straight expression. "You will disappear, as will Wendy and Badge. Reports will be that you took her and that investigators believe the stress of your job got the better of you. The three of you will never be seen again. Then your mother will drown off Panama City Beach."

Reed's face flushed, and his nails now dug into the wood of the chair.

The man smiled. "Good. Glad we could clear the air." He stood, and the other men followed unprompted. They went to the front door and opened it.

Reed followed, keeping a safe distance.

"Take care, Mr. Jacobs," Sanders said as they exited.

The men walked to their vehicle, with Reed now at the door watching. The LTD's engine roared as it started. Badge snarled.

Reed looked down at his running shoes. "Fuck it." He slid them on his throbbing feet.

"Come on, buddy."

Badge barked and followed his owner out to the Wrangler. Reed opened the driver's door, and Badge jumped into the passenger's seat. The LTD pulled onto the street.

Reed smiled, started the engine, and looked at his dog. "Just a little adventure, Badge. Let's see where these assholes go."

The Wrangler growled as Reed pushed the accelerator. The Ford continued at the same steady pace, neither slowing nor pulling away.

The agents went three miles before the first light, where they stopped at a red. The thin traffic at the intersection passed before the indicator turned green, and the vehicles moved forward.

The Ford LTD turned onto an on-ramp for a connector to the heart of Bridgewater, and Reed followed. Something didn't sit right with him. "Why are they not trying to lose me?" he asked Badge, whose gaze remained out the windshield. "It's clear I'm following."

The car continued at an even pace. As they approached the densely populated region of Bridgewater, the vehicle stopped at another red light with the Wrangler directly behind. Large raindrops started pattering the windshield, then hammered as the sky opened.

Reed leaned forward and looked through the agents' rear windshield, his view distorted by the sheet of water. The three men sat with their heads forward and still. "Do they not care?"

Badge growled.

The light turned green, and traffic continued. The Ford navigated through the streets at posted speed limits and turned right with a blinker after another two blocks.

"What the fuck? What are they doing?"

The Ford flashed to turn left onto Main Street, and Reed did the same. They merged onto a busy four-lane road that funneled toward the tunnel beneath Elm River, the low concrete throat that emptied out into Springfield.

"Where are you going, guys? Springfield's a dump."

Badge barked.

They approached the darkness of the tunnel. The black Ford passed into the shadow, disappearing in the darkness. Two seconds later, Reed's Wrangler entered the underpass. The sound of the beating rain ceased.

"What the fuck?"

Badge barked again, clawing the cloth seat.

"What the hell!"

In front of Reed, an old red Volvo wagon drove along.

"They're gone!"

Reed scanned both sides. Concrete walls, pillars, a solid stream of cars. No Ford LTD. No gap, no turn-off, no explanation.

"Where did they go?"

The Wrangler emerged from the tunnel, the thumping of the rain returned, and Reed parked in a gas station's lot. He looked back and around, knowing the Ford was gone. He pressed his palms against his eyes and held them there.

"Jesus, Badge," Reed said to the dog, who now lowered himself to the seat. "I'm sorry, buddy." Reed leaned back and massaged the scruff around Badge's neck. "I gotta get some sleep. Somewhere safe. That means you're going to the kennel. It'll be the best place for you."

Chapter 28

The sound of the tent's plastic rubbing against something called for Charlie's attention. But he held Ducky Ducky and kept his gaze locked on his friend. Charlie hoped that the dragging noise was from a supporting pole sliding across a wall, and not a monkey's foot exiting the confined space.

Charlie squeezed his eyes shut, his mouth too, every muscle in his face pulled tight, silently telling the monkey to go away. He opened his eyes. The monkey's shadow stood perfectly still. Its head was a stretched egg balanced on a stick of a neck, set above shoulders almost too narrow to hold it.

As he gripped Ducky, he caressed its soft belly with his thumbs. He wanted Ducky with him, to remind him of home, of his parents, of all the things that loved Charlie. He needed those reminders most when they came. But he also knew that wasn't how these things went. He didn't always get what he wanted.

The shadow shuffled. He felt the creature's fingers run along his cheek. They reached for his stuffed animal.

Its flesh gave like Play-Doh, cold and tacky, nothing hard beneath it, no bones at all. Just like the snakes he'd roll out of the clay.

The appendages crossed Charlie's vision. The three gray and skinny fingers extended forward to wrap around Ducky. Charlie winced at the smell. It reminded him of that spray bottle in the bathroom with a lemon on it, but with something super gross, too.

Charlie didn't resist as it pulled Ducky from his hands. Nor did he fight as his body rose. He knew better than to do any of that. It made no difference. They'd take him away anyway.

Chapter 29

After dropping Badge off at a kennel, Reed drove to the police station—perhaps the only safe place to sleep.

He entered the lobby, where Officer Carpenter was behind the safety glass, compiling sheets of paper. "I thought you started back tomorrow?" she asked.

"Yep," the word stretched from Reed's lips as he pulled his shoulders back to open up his lungs.

"You look beat." She watched Reed enter the hall as she buzzed him in.

Reed took the stairs to the office space, pushing against the railing with his arm to reduce the weight on his feet. "Hi, Pops."

At the top, he waved to his peers and sat at his desk.

He stared at the keyboard, mouth slack, with lethargic breaths. Prosser walked by, but Reed didn't acknowledge him. The detective was probably busy with that scientist who jumped.

Reed lowered his head to his crossed arms.

* * *

With the ceiling lights out, the LEDs of the office equipment pricked the space like stars. Reed woke at his desk to an empty station and a splatter of drool under his chin, which he wiped away. As he sat up, his joints cracked. He stood and stretched. "Ugh." The desk chair, government-issued, had left his bones aching.

Sitting back down, he rubbed his eyes and turned on his computer. He slugged through emails and some basic prep for the next day. Once done, he turned off the machine and swiped up his jacket as he stood.

More bones cracked as Reed walked to the conference room at the front and shut himself inside. Steeped in darkness, he kicked off his shoes and ducked under the table. He rolled his jacket into a pillow and lay down. *Goodnight,* he typed and sent to Wendy before placing his phone face down.

* * *

A breeze through his hair yanked Reed awake. He opened his eyes to the night sky encroaching on him. Bridgewater's skyline glowed in the distance.

"What the...?"

His hands reached behind him. No bed. No floor. Nothing. Just the brisk night air. He kicked on instinct.

A low rumbling pulled his attention to the sky above. Against the deep blues of the atmosphere, the darker pyramid emerged. It ruled the sky and commanded the surrounding thin clouds.

"Oh, fuck." The shape grew larger as Reed realized he was rising toward it. "Oh, God!"

A jolt of electricity struck Reed, and his body stiffened against his will, locking his muscles. He attempted to move, to flail, only to be denied access to his own body.

As Reed watched, a shallow circular indentation appeared, at first subtly. It grew as if being sucked into the object. A hundred feet across, its center moved inward. Ten, twenty, fifty feet, the diaphragm deepened until Reed passed the rim of the concave shape. Then the bladder shot downward. It rushed at him like a freight train. It swallowed him.

Reed tried to scream, but no noises came.

Now, in a bright light without Bridgewater as a reference, he could only tell his body moved by the swaying of his hair.

The lights began dimming as his body came to a stop. A cold surface pressed on his back. The space grew darker. Reed saw blurry shadows, spindly ones, crossing his field of vision. They completed unknown tasks, seemingly preparing for something Reed didn't care to know about.

Oh, God! The wolves!

The lights went out. Reed found himself still unable to move and now in profound darkness. He couldn't even see his own nose.

Numerous invisible things touched his skin. He wanted to

kick, to shudder, but his body remained unresponsive. They felt like dead flesh. Clammy. They searched his body.

Reed tried to scream, *Stop touching me!* But only the reverberations of the words through his mind came.

The wolves' caress ran from Reed's eyes to his mouth. They turned him and pressed on his back as if to count vertebrae. They inserted what felt like a needle into his navel. Reed's hate pooled with him on that table. Soaked him. Drowned him. He fought his ancient reptilian brain from allowing him to lose himself in panic.

We won't hurt you, came a dispassionate voice into his thoughts. *Relax, and you will be fine.*

Let me go! Reed said from his mind.

We will let you go when we are completed.

Let me go, now!

We cannot.

Why are you doing this? he asked in desperation.

It is our right, it replied.

They continued their explorations of all that made Reed. He repulsed with each touch. But his body and mind remained available to them like a wilted lotus.

Reed sensed another presence. Something different. Its touch was hard, not like the flesh from before—more like a cold and unforgiving armor. Like bone. It sent Reed's heart racing. He frantically messaged his limbs, but received no response.

Jesus, God! Reed wanted to fight. His fists needed to hit something.

Calm now, a new icy voice came.

Fuck you. Leave me alone! Reed demanded.

We will not. You will endure.

Fucking right. Then fucking shoot you, motherfucker!

Meaningless expression of your fear. Pointless fear.

Fuck you.

You are ours to do as our will demands it, the voice said to Reed.

A smell came first. Citrus smeared over rot and ammonia. Three fingers and a thumb, all gray and slender, rested on his face. He could see them. Somehow, he could now see into the darkness, if only a short distance.

The digits spread, leaving space for Reed's eyes. These were the soft fingers that had examined him earlier, not whatever the harder appendages were. Reed understood they were not from the icy voice, and that this thing had been dispatched to him from a being in control. He didn't know how he knew, but he knew it like he knew his bones.

The rancid smell would have gagged him if he could. Instead, it infiltrated his throat like an infection.

Something else approached, close to the hand that rested on his face. Two black eyes, bigger than softballs and pointed like almonds. Centimeters away. Reed felt his psyche being penetrated by them. He put everything into a scream that never came. The eyes entered Reed's mind. They left it empty.

* * *

Reed woke with a jump, his head slamming into the underside of the conference table. He covered it as the pain radiated around his skull. "Ow...shit."

He got to his knees to peek into the office space. The early morning light softened the room, which was occupied only by LaFontaine. Turning and leaning against the wall, Reed's heart thumped in his chest.

A sharp itch appeared on his arm, and he scratched at it. Reed pulled up the sleeve of his sweatshirt and found three bright red dots in a triangle pattern in the crook of his elbow. He pressed a finger to the mark. The memories detonated. The black pyramid. The darkness. The things touching his skin. The eyes.

Reed grabbed either side of his shaking head and stifled a scream. Spittle ejected from between his clenched teeth. Looking up at the ceiling, he took a deep breath. *On duty means to get your shit together.*

He forced another breath before grabbing his stuff and heading to the basement for a quick shower. By the time he returned to the second floor, officers and detectives were standing and talking.

"Something happened last night."

"Yeah, everything's fucked."

Reed weaved between the groups to his desk and sat. Turning on his computer to get to his timesheet, the monitor flickered between static and a white screen.

"Hey, you doing okay, Reed?" Prosser asked as he walked by.

"Yeah, fine."

Reed watched Prosser continue to Oberman's office, then returned his attention to his computer, the monitor still acting up.

"Great." He looked down and rubbed his temples. *Push it all away, Reed. Be a machine again.*

The rambling voices of the room cluttered the few minutes of his focused breathing. As he felt a calm energy return, someone shattered whatever peace he had manifested.

"Maybe you did it, Reed." Jeannie stood over him with a Cheshire Cat grin on her face.

"Did what?" Reed asked with a sigh.

"Something. Not nothing."

The old chair creaked as he swiveled around to face her. "Why do you think this has anything to do with me?"

"Well, shit, could be anyone, Reedsy. Security cameras all went down. Maybe you had a party here."

"Fuck you, Jeannie. I'm too tired for your shit."

"Whoa, whoa, whoa! *Inbreed* is a little sensitive this morning!" She bellowed to the room.

A crowd gathered around Reed's desk.

"The fuck you call me?"

"Look, your Wrangler was here when I left yesterday and was still here this morning. Same spot. And now my system's fried."

Reed stood and stepped to the woman. He looked down and pointed a finger at her face. "If you're saying I did something, then say it, Jeannie."

"You don't intimidate me," she breathed.

Reed clenched his jaw and stepped closer. The surrounding officers jumped between the two, chanting for them to calm down.

"Fuck you, Jeannie!"

"Back at you!"

Chief Oberman appeared at her door, with Prosser behind.

"What the hell is going on out here?"

Jeannie pointed at Reed. "He attacked me."

"Reed?"

"All good, Chief," he responded as he stepped back.

"Fuck you are. What happened?" Oberman asked the room.

"I was just checking with everyone about their computers, because something happened last night that took out our systems, and Reed's all up my ass about it."

"What?"

"It's my fault, Chief. I just...didn't get much sleep. I was here all night, and I took it as blame. But I had nothing to do with it, swear."

Reed offered his hand to Jeannie, and she shook it.

"You've lost it," she said.

Chapter 30

Prosser walked lighter knowing the rain had finally moved through, the temperature climbing enough that his coat felt unnecessary. Plus, he'd be picking up Charlie from school to bring him into town for a little toy shopping. Walking between the desks to Oberman's office, he saw others in high spirits as well.

He came to Reed's desk, where he sat filling out a form. "Hey, you doing okay, Reed?"

The man looked up, surprised. "Yeah, fine."

Prosser continued to the Chief's office and entered the room with a smile, which Oberman returned. She placed her cell down and grabbed Prosser's report from a pile at the side of her desk. "Clean. Thank you."

Prosser shrugged it off. It's the reaction he wanted, but the trick would be to get any other details from Oberman on the phone calls she had received on the case. He closed the door and sat on the couch under the stretch of windows that offered a view of the larger office.

Oberman continued, "You didn't sign it, though."

"Not until I get the coroner's report. If it's clean, which I suspect it is, then it's just the formality of including it and signing off."

"K." Oberman looked at him with squinted eyes. "Something on your mind?"

Shit. Should have kept the door open.

"Thought we could chat," Prosser said.

"Okay, chat." She placed the papers down.

"Like you said, clean. Suicide. Her life was science, and there seems to be no hope of rebuilding that satellite. Too expensive."

"How did the conversations go yesterday with her family?"

"Fine. Nothing out of the ordinary."

Oberman nodded, her eyes locked on the detective.

He leaned forward, elbows on his knees, fingers laced. "So, who were these people calling you?"

She shook her head. "Leave it."

"I'm not a dog, Chief."

"No, but I'll put you in the fucking dog house."

"Look, she was straight as an arrow. Everything in my report is true. She jumped. There wasn't anyone even in that room with her. So why the interest from the alphabet soup?"

"Who cares, John. She worked on a high-profile project. Lots of technology, lots of geeky knowledge. Maybe they just considered her an asset to the country."

"Aren't you curious?"

"Sure, but the reason's mundane. Whatever it is. And not worth rustling feathers over." She returned to her cell.

"You ever get calls like that for anyone else?"

"Anyone in the public sphere dies, I get those calls." She began tapping. "The damn computers are down."

Prosser shook his head.

Screaming from the office area drew their attention: two

people yelling at each other, with officers trying to break it up. Reed's and Jeannie's voices dominated the commotion.

They stood and looked out the window at the open office area. A crowd of people had gathered at Reed's desk and were holding him back from Jeannie, who stood with a big smile on her face and making a *come here* gesture with her hands.

"Fuck you, Jeannie! "

"Back at you!"

The Chief led the way into the open space, and Prosser followed.

"What the hell is going on out here?" Oberman sounded shocked more than pissed. Both Reed and Jeannie looked like they could wreck people, so the thought of them fighting seemed dangerous.

Reed tightened his lips, forcing himself to keep his mouth shut.

Jeannie raised her hand to her aggressor. "He attacked me."

"Reed?" Oberman turned to the man, whose fists were clenched and who had a half-dozen others holding him back.

"All good, Chief." He swayed as if every ounce of energy went to sounding calm.

"Fuck you are. What happened?" Oberman asked the room and not anyone in particular.

"I was just checking with everyone about their computers," Jeannie said, gesturing animatedly. "Because something happened last night that took out our systems, and Reed's all up my ass about it."

"What?" Oberman asked.

It made no sense to Prosser. There's no reason for Reed's anger over Jeannie doing her job. Something was going on with him.

"It's my fault, Chief. I just..." Reed seemed to search for something, "didn't get much sleep. I was here all night, and I took it as blame. But I had nothing to do with it, swear."

He reached between two officers to offer Jeannie a hand, and she shook it.

"You've lost it." She turned and headed back to the stairs down to her office.

The others relaxed and returned to their desks.

Oberman turned to Prosser. "Get out of here. I'll find another case for you soon."

"Sure thing."

Prosser glanced over at Reed. He'd returned to his desk, head dropping into his hands.

Chapter 31

The purple-and-black storefront gave Reed the creeps. Two energy drinks buzzing through him, the high of finishing his first shift post-suspension still sharp, he pushed inside. The smell hit him like a wall and he pulled up short, breath locked in his chest. Sage, something darker and resinous, and a sweetness he couldn't name thickened the air. Two other patrons explored various items and walked about the space. The ornate ceiling in the two-hundred-year-old building fit the room's mood well. The cash register at the back rested on a natural-edge table, and a black curtain separated the store from what was likely storage.

Standing in the doorway in jeans and a t-shirt, his sunglasses tucked into his shirt's neck, he suddenly felt like an impostor.

"Can I help you?"

Reed looked over to the voice. *Of course, blue hair.* She stood five feet tall and wore a crocheted purple-and-blue shawl over a black dress. Her hair was the exact blue of those sugar-coated gummies he'd hoard as a kid.

"I'm not sure." Reed looked around at the shelves of books, oddities, and other unfamiliar knick-knacks. With what seemed like a mess of clutter, he didn't know where to begin.

"Okay, is there something that you're looking for?" She clasped her hands in front of her body.

"I don't know. Maybe this was a mistake." Reed turned to exit.

The woman leaned forward. "People come in all the time dealing with things that they think there are no answers for."

Her friendly and non-judgmental tone made Reed stop. "Really?"

"Every day." She smiled.

Reed returned his attention to her. "What if you're not sure what's going on? Like a friend tells you he's seeing things. Experiencing strange...creatures and you want to help."

"Ah, that's a tough thing to be living with." Her black dress swirled as she spun around and went to a display at the back of the store. Two wide, rough-hewn wooden cases held the kind of objects Reed had no names for. Driftwood crosses, leather-bound books, crystal skulls lined up by size, all of it staring back like it knew something he didn't.

"Two things." She grabbed a small white object hanging from a thin leather rope. "First, you'll, er, your friend will want this talisman for protection. They should wear it at all times."

The woman handed it to Reed. The coin-like metal had a six-pointed star on it and unknown, rudimentary shapes within and surrounding it. A rough punch hole allowed it to hang from the black leather.

She moved to a taller shelf dedicated only to books and retrieved a small, dark red one, which she also gave to Reed. Its cover featured no graphics or design, just the words "The Lesser Key of Solomon."

"This grimoire should be read and understood. Studied. From this, they can craft a banishing spell. Great care needs to be taken. But the result would be complete banishment of the demons."

"Demons?" Reed's gaze shot from the book to the woman.

"It can be tough to say or admit. Is there anything else that I can help with?"

Reed took a moment to digest what she had said. "Um, anything to help someone sleep?

"Yeah, Valerian root." With a sudden spring in her step, she walked to the center of the shop where she took a glass canister from a display. "Make it in a tea before bed."

"Thanks."

"Anything else today?"

Reed held up the items. "No, I guess this is it."

"Great. Let's check you out over here." She waved Reed to the register.

After paying and thanking her, Reed rolled the store's paper bag tight and held it closed as he walked back to his Wrangler. *Demons. Yeah, why not? They do terrible things, cause pain and torture, and don't seem to care at all. That sounds like demons to me.*

The thought sent sensations of crawling insects up and down Reed's arms. His eyes darted from one person to another on the crowded street. *Were they looking at me? Why are they looking at me? Do they know? Can they tell something's not right? Do I look crazy?*

Reed slid his sunglasses from his shirt and put them on. *Stop acting paranoid.*

He took a left onto a side street, where his Wrangler waited in a public parking lot. Being out of the crowd allowed him to take deeper breaths, and his body calmed. Reed unlocked the door and tossed the bag onto the passenger seat. The day was dying. He pressed the accelerator and didn't look back.

Chapter 32

Clark's Toys sat on a street dotted with mom-and-pop stores in Old Bridgewater, where the buildings of aged brick circled a small community green. Prosser followed Charlie around the cramped store. Besides the mainstays like Legos and big-name board games, the store's shelves were filled with curated wooden toys, realistic dinosaurs, and other fun objects. It was Charlie's favorite place.

In one hand, the young boy held a die-cast medieval knight with a black surcoat and menacing spiked helmet. With the other, he touched a variety of colored sea creatures along a shelf.

"Those are pretty cool too, bud."

"That's an octopus," Charlie stated as he pointed to the reddish-orange bulb with eight tentacles that hung over the display.

Prosser knelt down. "Yeah, he's awesome."

Charlie held the knight up to the Octopus, the two locked in a child's combat. He looked at his father with big eyes. "Can I get them both?"

"Hmm, only one today. We need a reason to come back

again."

"Okay."

Charlie pressed his lips to one side, staring hard at the shelf. "Well, I like the knight."

"Sounds good, little man. Let's do this."

Prosser stood and led Charlie to the register, where he paid and handed the toy back to his son. "There you go."

"Thanks, Daddy."

"You're welcome."

With a few steps, they reached the front of the store, where a large glass window looked out onto the busy street. Prosser stopped and put a hand on Charlie as he saw three of the spooks from Katherine's office stroll by. The man with the blond hair walked closest to the glass. They seemed focused on something, or someone, ahead.

Khaki shorts, no brand tees and hats, sunglasses...

"I'll be damned," he mumbled. Prosser hustled to scoop up Charlie and exited the store, its bell ringing as he did. He turned left to see them continuing down the street.

The men walked stiffly and shoulder to shoulder. They didn't appear to be talking to each other and did a poor job of blending in among the natural pedestrians.

"What are we doing, Dad?"

"You hang tight." Prosser held his son in his left arm and placed his right on the boy's chest. "Secret mission."

"Cool!"

Prosser searched for details and clues about who they were but found none. He wondered if they were wearing the same clothes as the other day. *Who do they work for? Who are they following?*

"What do we do on a mission?" Charlie asked.

"We have to be quiet and alert."

Charlie nodded and looked around as he gripped his new toy.

They continued a block, past an old stone bank that had been converted to a museum on Bridgewater's history. Then Prosser noticed someone ahead, Reed Jacobs. He wore sunglasses and kept glancing to his side, seemingly unaware of who was following.

Prosser considered interrupting the tail, making some excuse to run the twenty yards ahead to talk to the men and distract them, so Reed could get away. But he continued to follow. He'd rather confirm their target and see what might happen.

"Shit." Prosser realized he had almost forgotten to take photos. He retrieved his cell from his pocket and, awkwardly with one hand, zoomed in on the men. He clicked the shutter button repeatedly, dodging the other pedestrians and not caring about what they might think.

A few of the frames would be solid; each man had turned his head at least once to check a side street.

"Who are you taking pictures of?"

"That's the mission," Prosser said to not cause any alarm. "To get photos of my police officer coworkers when not in uniform."

"That's silly." Charlie didn't sound impressed.

They continued another block with Charlie's attention on his new toy. Reed then turned left toward a parking lot, and the spooks followed. Prosser did as well, and when he saw Reed getting into a Wrangler and the Feds into a black Suburban, he ducked into a pharmacy's vestibule and watched.

"Are you still on a mission?" Charlie asked.

"No, buddy. Was having fun." Prosser didn't want Charlie spilling the beans to his mom that he might have been doing police work with his five-year-old son. "Are you ready to go home?" He lowered Charlie to the ground.

"Yeah."

"Okay, one sec, little dude." Prosser watched the white Wrangler drive by the pharmacy. A moment later, the large black Chevy Suburban of the Feds passed. Charlie had his knight jumping from a rack of brochures of local attractions.

They are following Reed, he thought. *Why?*

This could be a break, a new thread to pull on. He moved to the door, keeping a hand on Charlie, and glimpsed the license plate just in time to catch the digits.

He wanted to drop Charlie off at home and run back out to continue investigating, but he knew he'd catch hell for that after promising the rest of the day to him. Prosser would need to wait.

But the trail was hot.

III

Part Three

"Raging storms, evil gods are they
Ruthless demons, who in heaven's vault were created, are they,
Workers of evil are they,
...From city to city darkness work they"
- Sixteenth tablet of the Evil Demon Series. The Devils and Evil Spirits of Babylonia, London, 1903. Translated by R.C. Thompson.

Chapter 33

Charlie brought his new knight into the corner play space of their living room, where he introduced the toy to Iron Man. Prosser went to the kitchen, grabbed a dirty plate from the sink, and started scrubbing. A bird crossed the window and he tracked it without seeing it, his mind turning over the events of the past few days like evidence on a table.

"I can tell when something's on your mind," Sarah said from the kitchen island.

He turned to see her sitting on a stool and staring at him. "Remember when I told you there were Feds at U of B?"

"No."

"Oh, right. Well, there were Feds at the scene after Katherine died."

"For what?"

"That's the thing, I have no idea. But get this, I saw some of them following Officer Jacobs today."

"The same Feds?" Sarah raised her brows.

"Yup. Walking out of Clark's, they passed right by." Prosser rinsed the plate.

Sarah lowered her voice. "Do you think Jacobs had something to do with her death?"

"No. I saw footage from when she entered her office to the first officer's arrival. No one was in there."

"You didn't talk to them?"

"No. That wouldn't have been anything but trouble. They were also in civvies, so I don't think they wanted to be noticed."

Sarah nodded. "So something unrelated?"

With the dish still in his hand, he leaned against the sink and crossed his arms. "What would be the odds? The same spooks looking into Katherine's death are following Jacobs, for different reasons? In peaceful Bridgewater? I doubt it."

"Then what?" She mirrored her husband and crossed her arms.

"I don't know. Not yet, at least."

"You have that look."

"Yeah."

Sarah exhaled slowly and dropped her elbows to the counter. "You won't let this go, will you?"

Prosser shook his head.

"Talk to Jacobs."

He placed the plate on a towel next to the sink. "He's suspended, I think. Not sure when he's back."

"What? For what?"

"Went off the rails one day. He'll be fine." He moved to the island and faced Sarah.

"Did he hurt someone?"

"No."

"Go to his home," she said.

"Can't." Prosser rounded the counter and took the stool next to Sarah, then swiveled to watch Charlie play in the other room. "If I go there, and he's still under surveillance, then they're on to me. There's no other reason for me to visit. Shit, they could be in his cell phone."

Sarah slapped the counter. "Wendy Joyner."

"What?"

The stool squeaked as she quarter-turned to face her husband. "You get to Wendy Joyner."

"Who's Wendy Joyner?"

"His girlfriend. You met her last year at the department barbecue."

"Jesus, do you remember everyone?" Prosser smiled with the question and looked at her.

"The question is, why do you remember everything from your cases, and nothing about your coworkers?"

"I focus on the job."

Sarah placed a hand on his shoulder. "It wouldn't kill you to be friendly."

"I am friendly."

"I don't mean be nice when someone happens to talk to you. I mean, actually go out of your way to talk to others."

"Hmph."

Sarah pulled out her phone and tapped it. "She works at the med center. Marketing. That's close to my office. Give me a note. I'll swing by her work and tell her to give it to Reed."

Prosser thought a moment. "Can I give you a package?"

"Package?"

"Yeah, I have to be steps ahead here. They don't know I'm aware yet, and I need to find out who they are. Let's face it, Reed doesn't know he's being surveilled or who these people are. Or who they work for."

"Right." Sarah nodded excitedly.

"I have to figure that out before I can meet with Reed. I'll get a couple of burner phones, one for me too, just in case. You give that and a note to Wendy. I'll put the note in a sealed envelope, only for Reed."

"Good idea."

"I need to go to J-Mart to get phones." Prosser stood upright.

"It'll be open tomorrow. Spend time with Charlie."

Prosser stopped, and the couple looked at their son, who was playing out an adventure with his toys.

* * *

Reed opened the door to find Wendy on the stoop, a small cardboard box in one hand and an expression that made clear she hadn't volunteered for this.

She outstretched the item with one hand. "I promised Sarah Prosser I would bring this to you."

"Sarah Prosser?" Reed asked, eyeballing the small box.

"Yeah, remember her?" The box rattled as Wendy jostled it.

Reed took it and flipped it over to check for any labels indicating what might be inside. "John's wife."

"She stopped by my office. Of course, Elizabeth was all like 'Why are you getting visitors?' Sarah was super nice, but she really only came by to pass that along."

"She didn't tell you what's in it?" Reed looked out at her.

"Nope. She said it was important that only you opened it because it was work-related, but that John couldn't give it to you in person. She stressed 'only' and definitely wanted me to remember that John couldn't give it to you."

"Why not?"

Wendy shrugged. "She said once you open it, you'll understand."

"Oh. Want to come in?" Reed opened the door more.

Wendy shook her head. "No. Where's Badge?" Her gaze moved about the place.

"I boarded him."

"Why?" She seemed surprised.

"He's safer there until I figure out what's going on."

"Oh." Reed heard the disapproval in her tone. "I guess I'm going to go now. Maybe we'll talk soon. I hope you...figure it all out." She turned and took steps toward her car.

"Yeah. See ya."

Reed watched her drive away before turning his attention to the box. "What are you?" he asked as he shut the door.

Returning to the living room, he sat on the couch and dug his pocketknife out from his jeans. With a quick slice, he opened the box along the top. "What the hell?" Reed removed the envelope to reveal the cell phone package beneath. "A burner?"

Flipping the white envelope around, Reed didn't see anything on the outside. He ran his finger under the glued flap. Inside, he found a single sheet of paper with a typed letter.

Reed, I hope you're doing well, and you return to duty soon.

This letter, no doubt, comes as a surprise. Please read it carefully. On April 13th, I investigated the death of Dr. Katherine

O'Reilly. During that investigation, it became apparent that Federal authorities were interested in her and her demise. I saw four of them outside of her office, in plain clothes, among the crowd. While there's little doubt her death was a suicide, it's still curious that they were there clandestinely.

So, what does this have to do with you? I saw three of the same agents tailing you on the 15th. They followed you through Old Bridgewater to your Wrangler, then got into a black Suburban and continued to follow.

I'm reaching out this way because I want to determine why they are interested in both you and O'Reilly. Right now, we have one advantage—that they're unaware of my seeing them tail you. I want to keep it that way for now.

Use the burner phone here to communicate with me. I wrote the number to my burner inside. Be careful when and where you do this. Your house and car are likely bugged. As is your personal cell.

Here's what I want you to do first.

Chapter 34

The top level of the parking garage afforded a view of downtown Bridgewater and radiated the heat from the day's sun. Prosser stood by the cement half-wall, looking down at the garage's exit to Main Street. Below, he saw the line of high-end shops, national bank chains, and pedestrians carrying their bags.

His burner cell buzzed, and he read Reed's message.

Level 2.

Prosser peered back over the ledge to see Reed emerge on foot, and within thirty seconds, two spooks hustled behind.

Prosser hit the heavy metal door at his right and took the staircase down two steps at a time to the second level. There he walked the lines of cars, checking each. Not seeing it, he turned up the ramp. There, he found the black Suburban with plates that matched his memory. Prosser slowed his pace and looked around the garage. Only the sounds of a distant car suggested anyone was around. He knelt, pretended to tie his shoe, and scanned under the vehicle. Seeing nothing strange, he stood and stepped closer. Prosser raised a hand and fixed his hair in the reflection of the back glass.

No one was inside it. Prosser got to work.

With his personal cell, he took photos of the plate and the VIN on the dashboard through the windshield. He dug in his jacket for a small black box and reached under the SUV. With a forceful snap, the magnet clasped it to the frame.

Prosser fast-stepped back to the stairs and rushed to the top level and his own car.

Done, he messaged Reed.

He tucked the cell away and lowered himself into the seat. Prosser drummed on the steering wheel, a grin spreading slow and wide.

* * *

Reed purchased a new pair of jeans and got a black coffee from the shop nestled within a bookstore. He then perused the selection, staying in the sections he typically browsed—*Criminal Justice*, *Thrillers*, and *Exercise*. Along the way, he caught glimpses of two men following him and, more than once, tightened his fist to be ready to take them on.

An hour after getting Prosser's text, Reed wrapped up his diversion and headed back to the parking garage with his new pants and a novel about a haunted young woman.

The uneventful drive didn't help Reed's anxiety. He frequently checked the cell for any missed messages from Prosser and glanced at his rearview mirror for his tail. He stopped for gas at Sally's, where the Suburban passed the store and headed toward his home.

"Gas is too expensive here," a voice called out to Reed.

Reed looked at the old man at the pump across from him. He wore a blue windbreaker and hunched over as he got gas. "What did you say?"

The man pulled at his belt. "I remember when it was a dollar! I remember when it was less than even that!"

Reed nodded before turning away to watch the machine tally up his usage.

He said it. He said, 'Gas is too expensive here.' Why those specific words? He's just some old guy who doesn't seem weird at all?

The questions wouldn't leave Reed alone. "Why did you say that?" he asked as the old man replaced the nozzle.

"What's that?" The man looked back.

"Why did you say 'gas is too expensive here'?"

"Well, I guess because it is." The man placed the cap on his tank.

"Did someone tell you to say that?" Reed's hand squeezed the pump hard enough to send pain shooting up his arm.

"No, sir. Was making small talk. Have a good day now." The stranger kept his eyes on Reed as he shuffled to the car door and got in.

He drove away with a friendly wave. Reed stood there, the pump still running, unable to move.

* * *

Prosser lowered the shades of his home office and turned on the desk lamp. He placed the burner down with its screen and speakerphone on. In front of him, the laptop displayed a map with a pulsing red dot situated by a gray box.

"I'm heading into work soon. Where are they now?" Reed asked through the phone.

"Parked at CIA regional offices in Hartford."

"CIA. No shit."

"It's behind the security gate. Hasn't moved in hours. Definitely spooks."

"Learn anything else?"

"Hold on. Where are you, Reed?" Prosser looked at the cell.

"Come on, man, give me some credit. I'm on a trail that goes through miles of woods behind my house. They didn't bug the forest."

"Okay, just checking."

"So?"

Prosser returned his attention to the map. "Whoever is driving seems to live in Manchester. It's been there nights. Doesn't move."

"Manchester."

"That means something to you?" Prosser asked.

"What? Oh, no. Hey, how long are you going to watch them? We need to be doing something. I can't just keep sitting around."

"Let's give it one more day. I'm going to head out to scope his home. I want to put a face to that driver. After that, we can get together, and I can research the VIN. I have to wait on that so I don't set off any alarms."

"That makes sense."

Prosser sat back and crossed his arms. "Have you thought

any more about why they are following you?"

"I don't know."

"There's a reason. You must have some idea."

"Sorry, I've got nothing."

Prosser looked at the phone and scratched his head. The silence from Reed's end said more than his words. Something wasn't being said. He let the moment pass and changed the subject. "In case you're curious, the coroner's report came back on Katherine. Blood work was clean. I signed my report confirming it as a suicide."

"Hmm."

Prosser felt he could see Reed's shrugging through the phone. Something else was going on with him.

* * *

After hanging up with Prosser, Reed jogged back home, jumping over downed limbs and blankets of wet leaves from the winter. He entered through the sliding glass back door and went to the living room, intending to head upstairs to change. Instinctively, he looked for Badge. But the mystical book, the tea, and the talisman resting on the coffee table caught his attention.

He grabbed the book. "The Lesser Key of Solomon."

Flipping through pages of odd symbols and words he had

never seen before, he laughed to himself. "Horseshit." He snatched up the Valerian root and threw it and the book in the fireplace. After examining the necklace for another moment, he tossed it around his neck.

Reed moved to his bedroom where he changed for duty.

* * *

Reed sat in his cruiser, chewing on his thumbnail and pounding the center console. Patience smiles at a ticking time bomb, only to be blasted by shrapnel. It watches a punch to its face. Reed was never very good at it.

Figuring the CIA had a tracker on his patrol car and his phone bugged, and that Prosser was right to want to wait before meeting, ate at him. He had no outlet, no means of action or information whenever he wanted it. His instincts screamed to push the accelerator and turn the wheel to Manchester, where he could rip apart the agent in the Suburban.

"Car Four-Four-Zero, we've got cows wandering around the road out on the Collins' farm," the voice came from Reed's radio.

"On it."

Finally, a distraction. Reed pulled his cruiser onto the road and flashed his overheads. Collins, in his old age, must have forgotten to lock the gate. Herding cows will help the time pass, so Reed welcomed the unusual call.

As he approached, the Holsteins meandered along the road and adjoining fields, with one stationed at the door of his childhood home. He maneuvered around them to enter the driveway to the Collins' farm. Reed exited his vehicle and looked out at the dozens of cows walking aimlessly. A periodic *moo* rolled along the landscape.

Walking to the barn, unsure with the warming weather if he was stepping in mud or cow shit, Reed called out, "Collins?"

"Joseph?" Reed entered the barn and, with a quick look, found it empty. The livestock ignored him as he turned for the house. He approached the side door first, knocked, and looked through the screen door to the kitchen. Empty.

"Hey, Joseph, you here?" After a moment of silence, Reed slipped his boots off and left them by the door before entering. "It's Reed Jacobs. Your cows are loose. I'm coming in."

The kitchen offered no suggestion of disturbance, so Reed passed through the dining room and into the front living space. "Joseph? You home?" Reed called out and looked to the stairs to the second floor. "Joseph?" The aged, cracked steps creaked as he remembered from twenty years back. Light from the adjoining rooms' windows penetrated the center hall.

"Joseph? It's Reed. You here?" He moved to Joseph's bedroom. The sparse room was decorated with a Christian cross over the headboard and a family photo, framed and dusty, by the window. No sign of the man.

He turned to Sadie's old room. The twin bed rested along the windowless wall, seemingly untouched for years. Her short dresser across from it had knick-knacks cluttering its top. He picked up a CD of the Beastie Boys, then tossed it back down. Glancing around the room, he saw only the mundane remnants of a childhood.

A honking outside brought Reed's attention back to the purpose of the call. He ran downstairs to the side door, where he exited and slid into his boots. Reed saw a Toyota rounding the large animal and continuing down the road as two more cruisers arrived.

The officers pulled behind Reed's cruiser. After a quick conversation, they began directing the cows back to the barn as Reed called Sadie. She answered after the first ring.

"Hey, I'm at your dad's. All the cows are loose. Do you know where he is?"

"He's not there?" she asked.

"No."

"I haven't talked to him all day. Is his truck there?" Her voice sounded upset.

"Yeah."

"Then he's got to be there. He has no friends."

"We're rounding up the animals. I'll take another look after."

"Call me, please. I'm worried."

"I will." Reed disconnected.

After mucking through the sludge to get the herd back in the barn, Reed made another pass through the house. With acres of property, he wouldn't be able to complete a thorough search, so he checked the fields he knew Joseph tended to.

The pasture and what would be a pumpkin patch offered no clues, so he continued on to the freshly tilled cornfield. The turned soil stretched out before him. He remembered planting season. The early mornings Sadie would complain about as she helped with farm chores, and the sounds and smells that would permeate the area.

Reed stopped to think. Joseph could be unconscious or, worse, under some piece of farm equipment. Or something as simple as a neighbor needing help with their car pulled him away from home. But why were the cows roaming free? Joseph diligently cared for his farm, and Reed recalled nothing like it happening before.

The tilling had cut grooves into the ground, creating rows of what would become tall corn stalks. But they were not quite uniform. A deep shadow stretched out through the field diagonally to his right, like a wound along the fresh dirt.

His eyes followed it from twenty yards in front of him to another 70 beyond. Then it stretched along the horizon to a point before turning again. He followed the line until it converged to the spot ahead of him. A square.

Reed rushed forward into the field, stopping with his feet on either side of where the lines came to a point. From here he took it in. Two hundred feet across, a defined square. At its center, a circular mound of earth where an indentation must have been in the...UFO. The thing must have looked like a pyramid had been transported from Egypt to the Collins farm.

No. No way! Why land?

Reed's mind raced.

They didn't seem to land to take me. And, it hovered in the sky when I woke to find Wendy levitating below it. Why would it land? Why?

While Reed's questions screamed across his consciousness, an answer came to him from somewhere. *They did it to mock me.*

The realization sank into Reed's gut. He looked at his cell. *Should I tell Sadie?* The thought settled like hot coals in water.

Chapter 35

The knock came and, anticipating Reed's arrival, Prosser answered the door. Sarah and Charlie converged behind him to greet their guest. Reed wore jeans, a t-shirt, and a Red Sox cap.

"Come on in." Prosser motioned Reed to enter and closed the door. "My wife, Sarah, and little man, Charlie."

"Yeah, I remember you from the barbecue." They shook hands, and Reed knelt to talk to Charlie. "You still like construction equipment?"

With a sheepish nod, Charlie ducked behind his mother.

"Good memory." Sarah raised her eyebrows to Prosser, the message clear—other people reserve mental bandwidth for their co-workers.

"Well, look what I have." One by one, Reed released a finger from his fist to reveal a small metal forklift. "This was mine when I was your age. I don't play with it much anymore, so why don't you take care of it?"

Charlie smiled and snatched up the toy. Reed chuckled and stood.

"That was sweet. Thank you, Reed," Sarah said, patting Charlie's back.

Prosser turned away before his wife could give him the look again. He changed the subject. "Kick off your shoes and come back to our little office. We'll get to work."

"Have fun, guys." Sarah led her son into the living area.

The men walked through the kitchen to the home office. "Here, have a seat." Prosser pulled a chair out for Reed at his desk and opened his laptop to the map he had created. Now multiple red dots appeared, one in Manchester, another in Hartford, and the third in Bridgewater. Red trails zig-zagged through the map to mark the vehicle's travel.

Prosser pointed at each. "His home, CIA regional, and just down from your house. That's where he goes."

Reed nodded, unblinking. "Who owns that house?" The screen warped as he placed his finger on the indicator in Manchester.

"Ethan Boyd."

"Who is he?"

Prosser stood upright. "Don't know. He's not in NCIC. Can't find anything."

"Fuck." Reed crossed his arms. "Where is he now?"

Prosser moved the mouse to bring up the live view. "Around the corner. That's my home." He pointed to a gray square close to the red dot.

The revelation seemed to spark Reed. "Let's fucking go get him!"

"Then what?"

Reed thought for a moment. "Who cares? We'll see what happens."

Prosser leaned on the desk. "We need some cool heads here. There are questions we have that he's not going to answer."

"Fine. Did you look up the VIN?"

"VIN and plate came back with nothing."

"That's not possible."

"They're blocked."

"CIA." Reed huffed.

"Yup. Here, check this out." Prosser retrieved his cell and swiped until he found what he needed. In it, a blond man emerged from the Suburban in a residential driveway. As if presenting evidence in court, Prosser placed it down on the table for Reed to see. "Ethan Boyd, at his home."

With a shot, Reed jumped to his feet and stepped back, almost tripping over the chair. "That's him!"

"Who? You know him?" Prosser stood. Grabbing the cell, he held up the image.

Reed took a deep breath, and his shoulders lowered. "Yeah. But he said his name was Sanders, not Boyd."

"Okay, tell me more."

Reed paced, cracking his knuckles. "Give me a minute, all right?"

"Yeah, sure. You okay?" Prosser's eyes followed Reed. The energy in the room changed. This seemed personal for the man.

"Just give me a minute." He circled the small room. "K, so...so I haven't been entirely honest, but I didn't think these things connected."

"What things?"

Reed stopped and locked his eyes on Prosser. "I've been seeing things. No, more than that, experiencing."

"What do you mean?"

"Like...like aliens." Reed threw his arms out in surrender.

"Aliens?" Skepticism peppered Prosser's tone.

"Yup! Well, a UFO at least. I've seen their ship and have

seen glimpses of them. They've been messing with me and Wendy. They fucking...they fucking took me, man."

"Took you?"

"Yeah, fucking abduction. Alien abduction, Close Encounters. The whole thing." Reed placed his hands on his hips. "I call them 'wolves' after Little Red Riding Hood. It's like they disguise themselves as people, poorly, like the wolf did. But they're hunters. They're hunting. I can feel it."

"You're kidding."

"Don't fucking do that." He pointed at Prosser.

"What? Do what?"

"Don't fucking doubt me, Prosser. I'm telling you the craziest shit, and it's tied to *that* guy." Reed redirected to point at the cell. "So don't doubt me."

"Fine." Prosser crossed his arms. "But how is Boyd involved?"

"After I saw the ship, a giant pyramid by the way, him and two other guys appeared at my door. Sanders, *er*, Boyd, threatened to kill me and everyone I care about if I said anything."

Lines appeared across Prosser's forehead.

"Then I followed them, and their car disappeared."

"Disappeared?" Prosser gestured for Reed to keep talking.

"Under the tunnel, to Springfield. Went into the darkness and then was gone."

"That's not possible."

"Right?" Reed's eyes grew wide as he said it. He adjusted his hat.

Prosser leaned on the desk. "So what does this have to do with O'Reilly?"

"Yeah, bud. I don't know, but I'd sure like to."

"He's one I saw at the scene. And now he's following you. And you're seeing aliens." The lines on the laptop's screen teased Prosser.

"Experiencing. They stop time. They show up and say weird things, looking like people. At least that's what I think those people are. I dunno."

Prosser shook his head. After a moment, he stood to take his turn pacing the room.

"So what now, Detective? You don't want to drag that spook out of his car. What do we do?"

Prosser stopped and spoke as if reciting from memory. "We take inventory. Collect all evidence and determine the next step based on that."

"We've got fuck-all for evidence."

"Not quite."

With a smile, Prosser opened the closet and moved aside a few boxes. From the back, he pulled out the black box from Katherine's home and placed it on a desk. "We've got this. And..." He reached into one of the closet's corners. "We've got her laptop."

"John, this stuff should have been returned by now."

"Clerical error."

Reed pointed to a security sticker on the computer. "That's the University's?"

"Those large organizations are terrible at inventory."

"Almost as bad as the Bridgewater PD," Reed said, looking at it.

"Like I said, clerical error."

"So what's this?" Reed pointed to the modest black box.

"Don't know. She had it on a workbench. Her home office had all these electronics everywhere. This seems to be what she was building. A hobby for all I know. Like meteorology. Warned of a coming storm or something."

Reed turned the object over in his hand, then flicked the silver antennae before placing it back down. "What's on her laptop?"

Sliding the computer onto a desk, Prosser sat and placed a hand on it. "She's got tons of dense documents. Stuff I don't understand."

"It may have nothing to do with her death."

Prosser tapped it. "I think it does."

"Why?" Reed asked.

"Because there was a picture in her office that she obviously had taken off the wall and hidden. I read about it. It was an achievement for her, for humanity. The first image of dark matter."

"So?"

"So why did she hide it? The rocket explodes, taking any hope for furthering her research, and then she hides this image and kills herself?" Prosser asked rhetorically.

"You think it's a clue?"

"I think it's a message. That we would all be better off forgetting about it."

Reed sat at the other desk. "Yeah, I can see that. There are things I'd like to forget, too."

* * *

"Daddy, you tell the best stories." Charlie hugged Ducky Ducky as he nestled into his pillow.

"Thanks, buddy. I love you. Sleep good," Prosser said as he kissed Charlie on the forehead and pulled up his blanket.

"Love you."

After a moment rubbing his son's back, Prosser stood and crossed the room. He turned off the light and glanced at Charlie before shutting the door and continuing downstairs.

Sitting on their beige couch, Sarah's project management book was closed on her lap, her eyes waiting for Prosser, her face in a shallow smile. A sure sign she wanted to talk.

"How's the book?" Prosser asked.

"Boring. How was your guys' day with Reed?"

Prosser opened his eyes wide to exaggerate the experience. But, perhaps, there was no way to magnify the unbelievable claims Reed had made.

"What? What happened?"

Prosser sat next to Sarah and huffed as he ran his hands through his hair. "He says he's being visited by aliens."

"What?" Sarah pushed herself back.

Prosser placed a hand on her knee. "He says he sees aliens. Has these odd experiences and that they've, well, taken him on a ship. A UFO."

"Space aliens?" Her tone was flat, like she repeated her grandmother's lasagna recipe.

"Yup."

The table thumped as Sarah placed her thick book on it. She turned to face Prosser. "He's having encounters?"

"You sound like a nurse right now." Prosser chuckled.

"What did he say? Exactly."

Prosser recounted the ridiculous events as described by

Reed: the man's terror, the odd occurrences, and the supposed interactions with his dog and girlfriend.

"Holy shit."

"Sarah, Jesus. You're not buying the bullshit?" Prosser looked over his glasses.

"You don't think it's possible?"

Prosser rolled his head. He knew how the conversation would go. He'd dig in, and she'd take advantage of his stubborn position by relentlessly poking holes until he surrendered. So Prosser skipped to the end.

"Sure, it's possible. Lots of things are possible."

"I don't see why he would lie. What would he be getting out of it? If anything, he risks losing all credibility. And Reed's a macho guy. He would never admit to it if it were not true."

Prosser took a long, deep breath in. "Fine, but that doesn't make it true, either."

"How would this connect to the CIA?"

Prosser pursed his lips and crossed his arms. "It isn't. It's all bunk."

"They're following him," she reminded her husband.

"Yup, I just don't know why."

Sarah put one arm up on the top of the couch. "You once told me a good detective is like a scientist."

"That's right. Name a scientist who believes this crap!" Prosser nodded.

"It's not about belief. It's about where the evidence takes you."

"Tell that to all the scientists that debunk this shit."

Sarah shook her head. "I'm not convinced. They risk their credibility admitting there might be anything to it. But, there is such a thing as bad science."

Prosser shrugged. “Yeah, okay.” He turned away and grabbed the remote to search for a ball game.

Chapter 36

The men each sat at a desk in the Prosser family's home office for another day of research. Prosser picked at Katherine's laptop, scouring her documents for dark matter research. Reed was at his own, doing the same with a folder of files they migrated from her computer. The two open windows offered plenty of light, which didn't help them translate the dense material to plain English.

Reed threw his hands in the air and looked over at Prosser. "This is bullshit, John. A total waste of time."

"Come on, keep at it." The outburst didn't move Prosser's attention.

"For what? What do you think we're going to get out of this? I haven't understood a single sentence in any of these documents, and don't sit there trying to impress me like you have."

"I've learned a few things."

"Yeah, right. Like what?" Reed crossed his legs.

Prosser swiveled in the chair. "Like Katherine believed dark matter held a small electrical charge."

Reed barked out a laugh. "So what? How does that help us at all?"

"I don't know yet. I'm looking for something, anything, that will start making sense."

"Well, I quit. I'm doing something else." Reed turned back to his laptop.

"What?"

"I'm going to check out the video of the rocket launch," Reed said as he closed the files.

"For what?"

"Anything. Just like you."

"Fine." Prosser returned to the documents.

Reed pulled up a web browser, happy to feel like he was doing something he'd at least understand. A quick search for *elisha rocket launch* produced a long list of results from the major news outlets with headlines like *Rocket Lost at Launch* and *Satellite Explodes on Takeoff*. Each had the same thumbnail of a blue sky and a cloud of white smoke.

He scrolled for anything that might stand out, but they all reflected the same few pieces of information—within thirty seconds of launch the rocket had erupted, and shortly after its creator took her own life. Reed clicked on a video that took him to YouTube, and the large image of the sky with a white rocket blurred from haze appeared.

Clicking the large *Play* button sent the rocket in motion. The shaky camera followed as it passed through a cloud. Its white booster reflected the sun and roared.

Then a bright flash, no longer than a blink, and it broke into pieces. The booster veered violently off the screen, and the camera panned out to witness the priceless parts fall under the newly formed thick mist.

The video stopped.

Unsure what he should have even expected, Reed sat back

in the chair with his hand still tight on the mouse. He scrolled down the page, mindlessly. The comments expressed sorrow and dismay over the lost knowledge.

UFO takes out Elisha

The blue link caught Reed's attention as it emerged from the bottom of the screen. "What the..."

He brought himself close to the monitor and clicked the link. The video played with the audio muted. It started the same as the last one, the rocket pushing upward. The zoom and haze distortions degraded the quality. Then the flash came, and the rocket disintegrated.

After a moment, the video reversed. The pieces came back together to form the projectile that held the Elisha. Time stopped with it hanging in the air. Reed's hands rose slowly to his mouth, fingertips pressed together.

The frames clicked forward, one by achingly slow one, until three white dots appeared—two at the right of the screen and one at the far left. Another frame forward, and the three orbs surrounded the missile. A third frame and white beams streaked the space between the unidentifiable objects and the rocket.

The next frame showed only the white blast of flash before the object blew apart. Reed brought his hands to his head. "Holy shit."

"You find something?"

"You're not going to believe it, but I fucking told you so!" Reed slapped the desk. "I fucking told you so!"

"What?" Prosser turned to see Reed dragging the video progress bar back and resizing it to be full screen.

He rotated it to face Prosser and motioned him to come closer. "Watch this."

Prosser stood and approached the screen as Reed hit *Play*. The scene unfolded. The Elisha powering through the atmosphere until explosion, the rewind, and the slow-motion playback to reveal the apparent destruction by UFOs.

They stood in silence for a moment before Reed played the video again.

"Let me think a minute," Prosser said as he turned his eyes away.

"Yeah, you think on it, Chief." Reed's tapping of his fingers punctuated his sarcasm.

"Can you find an original video? One from some official source or from one of the news outlets, and slow that down? I don't want to assume this is...what it seems to be if it's some nut in his mom's basement making a video for followers."

"Damn. Yeah, I can do that." Reed clicked back and scrolled through the list of videos. He dragged the mouse to the first listing he saw from a reputable source and clicked to start it.

The video began as expected. Reed hit pause as the screen flashed from the explosion and hit the back arrow until getting to the frames with the unidentified objects. "There. There you go. Happy?"

Prosser scratched an eyebrow as he looked at the orbs.

"Cat got your tongue?"

"I don't know what to do with that, Reed."

"Yeah, well, imagine a hovering pyramid in your backyard sucking your girlfriend up." Reed smiled, and his heart beat faster.

"Look, let's say UFOs destroyed it..."

"They did." Reed jabbed the screen.

"What does that mean for us?"

"I bet you she saw it. I bet you, with whatever is going on, after it blew up Katherine watched it again. She saw what happened. She knew."

"So she jumped out the window because..." Prosser raised his shoulders.

"Because they got to her satellite."

Prosser sat again and spun the chair around to face Reed. "That doesn't add up."

"She saw the video and jumped!"

"She didn't kill herself because her satellite blew up. I've established that through her parents and boyfriend."

"She did it because aliens destroyed it."

Prosser shook his head. "No, I don't buy it."

"Jesus, Prosser." The chair rattled as Reed shot out of it. He walked in a small circle.

"What? You believe just because it was aliens, she jumped?"

"Fuck you!"

Prosser reached with a leg and pushed Reed's chair in. "It's evidence. I'm not saying it's not. But it's not enough to form a conclusion. Let's just note it, okay?"

"Note it. Right. Noted, Chief."

"Stop calling me that."

"So what's next, Detective?" Reed stopped and trained his eyes on Prosser.

"Well, you're also right about not getting anywhere with her material."

"Surprise."

Prosser swung to Katherine's laptop. "Let's track someone down who worked with Katherine on the project. We'll ask about her work, say it's just a part of our investigation."

"Yeah, sounds like a plan."

Reed pulled the chair over and sat. He leaned as far back as it would let him and stared at the white ceiling. Closing his eyes now, he sank further into the cushion. Something about a family's home suddenly made Reed feel at ease.

"Reed."

Prosser's voice shattered the peaceful moment that had snuck up on him. "Yeah, what?" Reed sat up and looked over his shoulder at the detective.

"I've got a name from an article on her work. Donald 'Dobbie' Whitmire. Dobbie owns Advanced Dynamics Engineering in Millbrook, about an hour north. I'm calling him."

Reed slunk back down. "You do that." He closed his eyes and listened to his breathing. The sounds of the suburbs also flowed to him. Outside, a lawnmower did its job, and inside, the dishwasher ran.

* * *

The fireplace crackled in the dark night, causing shadows to dance in corners. Badge's dog bed sat empty and still positioned to capture heat.

In sweats, with his hood up, Reed sat on the couch. His hands rested on his pistol, the safety on. If they appeared, and he had any physical capabilities at his disposal, he'd shoot them without hesitation. Come in peace or not.

Seeing the video earlier in the day of the orbs taking out the

Elisha motivated Reed to try. He felt like he was protecting more than his own home. Now, he had to protect and serve all of humanity.

Reed's cell buzzed to notify him of a text. He picked it up, thinking he'd received a response from Wendy to his *goodnight* message. Instead, Sadie's name appeared. *Arriving tomorrow morning. Let me know if you hear anything and let's catch up.*

Reed focused on his breathing and walked through what he knew. Harassed by beings. Some taking a human form. Maybe others little insects. They took out a satellite destined to bring knowledge of dark matter.

Then there were the questions. Who were they? Where were they from? Why were they interested in him? Did they kill Katherine or make her jump?

He sat alone with his questions and a pistol, waiting for the extraterrestrials.

He tapped a reply to Sadie. *Text me the time. I'll pick u up.*

9:30, she responded.

Reed checked his watch, 11 p.m.

With a grunt, Reed stood and fed the fire another log. It flared and sparked as he jabbed it with the poker. The scraping sound it made as he leaned it against the brick sent shivers down his spine.

He returned to the sofa and sank deep enough to rest his head on the back. Sleep called, and he resisted, only allowing his eyes to briefly close.

Reed pushed against the growing fatigue, but something pressed back. It closed in. Distinct. Veiled. Creeping through the vacuum of space, invisible. It settled over his body like a wetsuit. His eyes shut as the fire dissipated. Just before 2 a.m., he fell asleep.

* * *

Reed opened his eyes and stared. Surrounded by unending blackness. *Am I awake?*

Something distinct alerted him, signaling his conscious state. Those fingers, slick and spongy. Thin ones. They wrapped around his feet, legs, and arms.

Reed tried to push his body up, but it didn't budge. He moved his gaze toward his toes. He couldn't see anything. Just like the last time.

Off to his left, something different emerged. A set of two elongated orbs with pointy ends, even blacker than the surrounding space. They absorbed everything, like black holes. Two more appeared on his right. He turned from one pair to the other, and then, inches from his face, a third set opened. His pulse raced. The dark pools pulled at his psyche. He'd fall in. He'd never return.

They blinked.

Fuuuuck!

Reed's nervous system signaled his muscles to move in an outburst of fury and madness. With no response from his body and no outlet for the fear, his mind searched for an escape. None came.

Fuuuuck! Nooo!

The smell arrived and burned Reed's nose. He managed to press his mouth shut as the sulfur taste struck his tongue.

Reed heard whispers in his mind. Foreign words that ripped at his psyche. They made him want to thrash out in a mindless, terrifying rage again. His eyes jerked from corner to corner, searching for any exit. Tears ran down the side of his head.

Absent of visual information, a message came to his mind. *Subsist.*

The fingers retreated. As did the taste, smell, and the black holes. Reed held his breath. He looked one way and then another, anticipating their return or the presence of something new. Surely they wouldn't just leave him to lie there.

As a minute passed, he breathed again. He moved his focus from sense to sense. Listening, he heard nothing but his beating heart. Feeling, nothing came but the cold slab under him.

He settled himself. Steadied his breathing to try to relax.

Reed waited, possibly for hours, in the void of wherever he was—the belly of an unknowable monster. When would they return? What would they do? What about Wendy? *I'll be strong. I'll be strong. Wendy won't need to know about this.* Reed forced a slow breath through his nose, held it, let it go.

Hey, let me go! You hear me? Let me go. Now!

Reed lay on the slab, listening. Nothing came back.

Sadie, he thought. *Did she go through this? Did they do this to her? Make her lie here, wondering what came next?*

LET ME GO!

No response.

I have to pick up Sadie and go with John to talk to the Dobbie guy, too. I don't know what the hell he's going to offer, but I guess it's the next logical thing to do. Prosser doesn't seem like such a bad guy; he could loosen up a bit, though.

Are they going to let me go? Will I still be here when Sadie needs me?

Reed looked around. The darkness hadn't changed.

How long are they going to keep me here? Forever?

LET ME GO! JUST LET ME GO!

What do you want? I don't have much besides my dog, Wendy, and my Jeep. You can have the Jeep!

Reed's eyes searched.

Nothing.

Hours of it passed. Of nothing.

You want something else? You need me to do something? What then? What do you need me to do? Do you want DNA? Take it! How about my memories? An organ? What?

Reed tried screaming, but no sound came. He commanded his limbs to move, to punch, kick against the surface under him, or to sit him up. Though he didn't move, his muscles ached.

What do you want? Please, just tell me. Just tell me what it is. Whatever it is, maybe we can work something out. Please...

...say something.

The thought came to him clearly—an answer that there would be no answer. They would do nothing. Not tonight. They did nothing as a torment, a taunting. They told him they could do anything by doing nothing at all. Whether a message or a recital for what might come didn't matter. Reed resolved to face the oblivion.

Chapter 37

Reed woke at 8 a.m. to his bedside alarm. It screamed the way something inside him couldn't. He found himself on top of the comforter.

As it blared the annoying and repetitive beep, Reed sat and looked around the bedroom. The sun warmed the floorboards as a fresh breeze ruffled the curtains. His heart pounded. Reed shivered, and he slapped the clock.

Wasn't I on the couch?

He shifted forward as something pressed against his foot. His left sock was upside-down. The patch for the heel rested on the crook of his ankle. He huffed as he pulled it around.

Standing, he noted his neatly made bed. A memory scratched at him, then hid from his searching mind.

Reed headed down the stairs to find a cold fireplace and a pile of ashes, almost begging him to tend to it like he typically did before bed. The thought of his pistol came as he glanced at his sofa. He'd have to find it. *It was there, I'm sure of it,* he thought in a daze.

In the kitchen, Reed opened the refrigerator and grabbed the jug of milk. He poured himself a glass and took a swig. As he pulled it from his mouth, he noticed the white liquid coating the inside of the cup. It slid down the glass. His eyes lingered, watching it. Through the glass, his fingers emerged from behind the milk, slightly parted. Between his fingers, slices of the dark kitchen took shape, then morphed into their own slender digits as if locked with his own in a tender embrace.

Then they moved. The space between his fingers moved like fingers themselves. Writhed and wiggled.

"Fuck!" Reed threw the glass. It shattered against the oven. The shards glistened as they fell to the floor. Reed looked at his hand. He expected to see something unwanted. But found only his sweaty palm.

He left the mess, returning the way he came, and walked back up the stairs to his bedroom. Perhaps a shower would wake him.

Reed stopped as he entered his bedroom. On his pillow, his pistol waited. The weapon hadn't been there moments ago, couldn't have been, as he would have felt it under his head. The weight of the metal made a soft indentation in the cotton. It sat like a present saying 'hello'.

* * *

The morning rush of air travelers buzzed past Reed. Some hustled, dragging wheeled luggage behind. Others talked on their phones as they strolled by with stuffed backpacks.

Everyone seemed to smile.

Reed stood a dozen feet from the wall of windows and revolving doors behind him. The foot traffic flowed through. As did the sun, which lit the tiled floor. Across from him, a line of ticket counters stretched for what seemed like miles. Between him and them, a maze of velvet ropes guided the airlines' customers. A hundred feet above all that, another row of windows.

Are these people in the same world I am? This place is enormous. It's too big. I don't like it.

Reed's heart beat faster. The squeaking sounds of his shoes grinding against the floor flew unnoticed. He found himself spun around and staring out at the road.

Maybe I should leave. Is something looking at my back? Something's looking at my back.

"Reed!"

He turned to his right to see Sadie Collins jogging toward him. She wore faded jeans with frayed edges, a white buttoned shirt, white sneakers, and round sunglasses. A small brown handbag hung from her shoulder. Her ponytail swayed behind her thin frame.

Reed smiled and wrapped one arm around her as he snatched her duffel bag with the other. The warm press of her lips against his cheek loosened something knotted behind his ribs.

"It's so good to see you," Reed said as he released his hug and guided Sadie to the doors.

"You in a hurry?" Sadie's eyebrows raised above her shades.

"Oh, sorry." Reed checked himself and slowed. "Do you need anything before we go? Do you have more luggage?"

She shook her head. "No, just the bag and my purse." Sadie took Reed's hand and squeezed it to stop him. "Hey, are you okay?"

Time stopped, but not like before. Sadie's soft voice and genuine concern caught him. He couldn't remember the last time he felt like someone cared. The muscles in Reed's face relaxed. "Yeah. Yeah, thanks." He smiled and rubbed the back of Sadie's hand with his thumb.

"If you say so. Let's go then." Sadie released her grip. Fresh air swept over them as she opened a door.

"This way." Reed guided her across the street and through the parking garage to his Jeep, with small talk about Sadie's flight.

He tossed the bag in the back and opened the passenger door.

"A Wrangler. I could have guessed." Sadie smiled as she climbed in.

The car door shutting echoed through the concrete space. Reed circled the back to the driver's side. He entered, started the engine, and, after a few minutes, navigated to the main road; they were on their way to the farm.

Sadie lowered the visor to look in the mirror and pulled the tie from her hair. "My aunt and uncle are going to come by later. We'll take their ATVs around the property. I know a lot of it has been searched, but I have to try."

A lump formed in Reed's throat as the vision of the impression in Collins' field came to him. "Where do you think he is?"

She flipped the visor back up. "I don't know. This isn't like him. Something happened. He's always so quick to respond to my calls or messages."

Reed's eyes darted from the road to Sadie. She tousled her hair and brushed it down. "How are you doing?" he asked as he turned his attention back to the highway.

Sadie exhaled and pressed both hands over her face. A thin sound escaped between her fingers.

"Maybe I shouldn't have asked."

"No, it's okay." She shook her head and cleared her throat. "I keep checking myself, you know? Like, he's gone. I know it. I've cried my eyes out. He's an old man, and this doesn't happen. If he was okay, I would have heard. If not from him, then from some neighbor or church person. No one's seen him."

Sadie dried her hands on her jeans and continued. "So, that's it. That's it, and it's fine. He did everything he wanted to do in life." She chuckled. "Which was farming, but whatever, he loved it. And I know he was proud that he could sell off that land a long time ago. You know, to help me. Make life a little easier for his daughter. Then I check myself. He's gone, but I've got my shit to do for him. I've got to do him right and search. I'll put in a few days of that and go back home. I do some work for a group that helps disadvantaged children, and have some things to take care of. Then, I'll return to the farm to search again."

Reed's thumb traced a slow arc down the steering wheel. "You know, Sade, I really want to help search. Seriously. But I have to talk to you about this case. It might help."

Sadie cocked her head. "What?"

"I'm helping a detective at work. He had the Katherine O'Reilly case. Did you hear about her?"

"Yeah, the dark matter lady."

"Right. Well...there were some CIA agents at her death. This got Detective Prosser all worked up and thinking something more was going on with her. Then he saw the same CIA douchebags following me one day."

"What?" Sadie gasped.

"Yup. At least one of them was in my home, right after I saw the UFO pyramid thing outside my house. They threatened me. Said not to tell anyone, or they'd kill me and everyone I was close to."

Sadie's eyes grew large. "Don't mess with them."

Reed ignored her demand. "But get this, UFOs shot down her rocket."

Sadie clutched the handle above the door. "You gotta give this up."

"What do you mean? Something is going on here, and those guys are involved. Katherine, too. She may have figured something out. Who knows what she was on to."

She shook her head. "You're chasing ghosts. Nothing good comes of this, don't you see? Nothing good! Just leave it alone, Reed. It'll chew you up inside and spit you out. Just cope. It's all you can do. Fucking cope! You think you're this big, strong man to take it on, but strength is one foot in front of the other. Strength is living your life the way you want to without those evil fuckers changing you."

The two rode in silence as exit signs passed. Sadie retrieved her phone and started messaging. Reed pulled the car to the ramp and onto Route 4. After a few more minutes, they arrived at the farm.

Reed turned to Sadie. "I'm not going to cope. You can do that. Go about things like you have to. I don't blame you. But maybe I can do something. Maybe I can stop it. Stop it from hurting me and you."

Sadie reached across the car and placed a hand on Reed's cheek. He closed his eyes. She was so warm.

Chapter 38

Dobbie Whitmire led Prosser and Reed through the tight hall between the front office and the warehouse at the back of the building. Light burst into the dim hallway when Dobbie opened the door to the massive space.

"I don't let people back here, but Katherine was special," Dobbie said as he closed and locked the door behind them.

The words slipped past Prosser and Reed as they gawked at the imposing tank in the middle of the spotless hangar. The vehicle's shielding had sharp corners and was painted matte black. It juxtaposed the gleaming silver frame of the Advanced Dynamics Engineering building.

The men had spent the hour in the car largely silent, with the radio tuned to the local classic rock station. With their senses dulled from the drive, the stark vehicle raised their pulses.

"We just got it in," Dobbie shared. "State-of-the-art. I'm not at liberty to tell you much about it, but we're contracted to make...certain improvements."

"That's really cool." Reed didn't blink.

"Stealth?" Prosser asked.

Dobbie shook his head. "No, something else."

Prosser refocused his attention on the engineer. "Is there somewhere we can talk for a few minutes?"

"Yes, this way. My office."

The men crossed the long, polished floor to a small enclosed space by the hangar door.

"This place is impressive," Prosser said as they entered the cramped office.

"Thank you. I'm proud of where we've come. Please, sit." Dobbie motioned to the seats as he closed the thin metal door and shimmied behind his desk. Behind him, hanging shelves held books and models of advanced airplanes or fighter jets. Paper and electronics cluttered his desk. "I'm curious how you think I could be of any help here."

Prosser spoke, and Reed turned his attention to the detective. "We're hoping you can help shed light on Katherine and her work on Elisha. It will help us paint a clearer picture and answer questions we are getting from the community. We want to do that respectfully, of course."

"Of course. Katherine was remarkable. Met no one like her."

"How so?"

"Her mind. She absorbed information, but she truly understood the material. She made connections. Saw interrelationships. Would theorize on the fly. It was stunning to watch."

"We've heard that about her, that she was brilliant. Can you talk about what you were working on with her?" Prosser asked.

"Of course, the Elisha. Her brainchild, but she needed someone to build it. That's where A.D.E. came in. We're not a typical manufacturer; we aren't pumping out widgets. We specialize in more unique and exotic work. High technology. Often government or university contracts. Some prototyping."

"So you built the satellite?" Prosser continued.

"We did."

"What was the Elisha supposed to do?"

Dobbie took a deep breath. "Katherine imaged dark matter. Elisha would both improve the imaging quality and allow for detailed measurements of dark matter." He shrugged. "There's a lot for science to learn from measurement. If you can't measure it, you don't know it."

Prosser crossed his legs. "And was there anything you felt strange about Katherine or the work?"

"Strange? Like what?" Dobbie shook his head and squinted his eyes.

Prosser looked up to the corner of the room, his brow furrowed.

"Like any odd characters that may have hung around," Reed interrupted. "Or that you found had an interest in her or Elisha?"

Dobbie offered a slow and knowing nod. "There were the usual folks we'd see around projects like this, which some would call 'odd'. In large government contracts like these, there are people interested in the outcomes. And others in protecting the intellectual property. I always called them 'the suits.' Sometimes the Chinese poke around and the U.S. Government would help move them along."

"Suits, sunglasses, strong build?" Reed asked.

"Yes, that type. With the vehicle we have now, you might even see some when you leave." Dobbie snickered.

Prosser interjected. "You said 'government contract'."

"That's right. Katherine formed a company just for Elisha, and a government contract to realize it. Well, I say 'government', it was the Department of Defense."

"And she hired you?"

"Sub-contracted out the manufacturing." Dobbie grabbed a pen and tapped the desk.

"And this was all to what? Get some data on dark matter? Was there anything else?"

Dobbie tossed the pen and rested his hands on his desk. "I didn't understand it all. I've got three PhDs, two dozen patents, and Katherine was so far beyond me. I was a school kid next to her."

"So, what were you doing? What was this?" Reed motioned to the large workspace through the wall behind them.

"Like I said, manufacturing. I took direction from Katherine. She told me what it needed to do, we engineered it. And, maybe this sounds crazy, but I often questioned whether certain aspects would even work. She would tell me to trust her, and I did."

"What did you think wouldn't work?"

"Well, some of it was my ignorance of dark matter. Like she knew how to target. But some things had me worried." Dobbie placed his elbows on his desk. "She planned functionality that required immense amounts of power. I explained I could provide materials to withstand the energy, but no way of storing or generating those scales."

Prosser smiled. He'd been waiting for a foothold. "I read she believed that dark matter holds a small electrical charge."

"She did. I think this was related to that. It seemed like she wanted to..." Dobbie seemed to check himself. He sat back in the chair. "Like she wanted to shock dark matter."

"Shock it?"

"Poor wording, perhaps. That never made sense to me, but

she said it was a part of the measuring process. The energy source we couldn't solve. She said that WIMP was the key."

"WIMP?"

"Oh, sorry. Weakly Interacting Massive Particles. A part of her theory on dark matter. Well, not just her theory. Many physicists have hypothesized about WIMPs."

Prosser shook his head. "I don't get it. It sounds like you're saying she was going to get energy from dark matter and pump it back in."

"She suggested the energy source was WIMP. And she hinted at large-scale energy direction toward dark matter. Those were separate mechanisms."

"And WIMPs are dark matter?"

"Theoretical particles that could be a part of the makeup of dark matter, yes. But, please, I'm not an expert on it."

Reed interrupted. "Before you said the DoD paid her?"

"That's right."

"Why would the DoD be interested in this?"

"Or fund it? Must have been expensive." Prosser asked Reed.

Dobbie's eyes went back and forth between the men. "Exorbitantly. The Government funds several scientific endeavors. Frankly, without government funding, science wouldn't be where it is today. No Hubble. No James Webb."

"But the DoD?"

"Yeah, that is curious." Dobbie knocked on his desk.

"Do you have any material from Elisha here? Like spare parts?"

Dobbie crossed his arms. "All right, what's going on here?"

Reed and Prosser looked at each other and shrugged. "What do you mean?"

"You said you were here to learn about Katherine to help with the questions you're getting. Now you're asking about spare parts? Are you podcasters? Because let me tell you, there are ways to de-platform you."

Prosser pointed at himself and Reed. "Do we look like the podcast type?"

"Look, we're grabbing at straws here," Reed interjected. "Katherine killed herself, and that's a shame. But we don't buy that she jumped because the satellite exploded. There's something else going on, and we just want to know what. It matters to us, and it matters to her family that we try to get to the truth. So will seeing stuff from the Elisha help? No fucking idea. But it's worth a shot."

Dobbie nodded and dropped his arms. "Okay then. Why didn't you guys say that earlier? I don't have meaningful parts to show you. But, you said 'she jumped because the satellite exploded.' I don't blame you for not believing that reasoning, and I can say she didn't take her life because of the launch failure."

"Why is that?" Prosser asked.

"Because," he took a deep breath in, "she had insurance."

"Insurance?"

"Just like you have on your car. Except she didn't buy her's from a gecko, and it cost taxpayers millions of dollars."

"Are you saying that insurance would provide the funds to rebuild?"

"She had what's called 'launch-plus-one.' It covers the launch and one year in service. So, yes. She could have rebuilt. I assumed that's what our company would do when I saw the explosion, but then I heard the news about Katherine. I was in such shock that I got the text about her death before I had the chance to reach out to her."

"So it was something else. That's what I thought." Prosser's gaze remained locked on the revelation. He turned to Dobbie. "Do you have any idea what it might have been?"

"We only discussed work." He placed his hands on the arms of his chair. "I don't know what was going on in her personal life. Perhaps she had other challenges."

Reed shook his head.

"Thank you, Mr. Whitmire. You've been very helpful." Prosser stood and held a hand out to Dobbie.

* * *

Reed lost himself in the outside world that whizzed by as they traveled down the interstate. The trees looked different to him, as did the hills and sky. They seemed smaller, less significant. *Ants may feel the same of their hills when encased in glass*, he thought. *The mounds of dirt are there, along with their passages through earth to nurseries or storage dens, like our roads home. Do they recognize the eyes watching?*

The following Suburban in the side mirror caught Reed's attention. He gripped the handle by the top of the window and squeezed it. "Why don't you pull over so I can say 'hello'?"

"They know we see them. They aren't trying to hide." Prosser said as he drove with one hand on the wheel.

"Exactly."

"I'm not pulling over, so let it go. I'm not risking an assault charge so that you can make a point."

"Like they would file a complaint." After one more squeeze of the handle, Reed placed his hands at his side. He looked at Prosser. "What do you think of what Dobbie said?"

Prosser nodded excitedly. "We're on the right track. Something else made her jump."

Reed turned back to the road. "I know you don't believe me. Not really."

"Sarah does." Prosser gave Reed a quick look. "It's not something you hear about every day."

"Yeah, because people aren't believed. Why talk about it?"

"Maybe. But I'm trying."

"Thanks. I guess."

Prosser lowered the radio volume. "When did this all start for you?"

"Hmm, at first I thought it started when I was eleven and saw a UFO. But there are certain things from my childhood that I wonder about now. Like they aren't what they seem."

"Like what?" Prosser asked with his eyes still on the road.

"Some dreams. I don't know what yours were like, but I had these dreams when I was real young that stuck with me. They still itch at me. They were terrifying. Not because of what they were, but the feeling I had."

"Not sure I'm following."

"There was one where I was outside, in the front yard of our old home. And I had to count all the blades of grass on our property. No one told me to do it, but I knew I had to. It seemed easy on the surface. But the more I stood looking at the yard, the more I realized it was impossible. Because by the time you finish counting, new grass has sprouted, or some has died. And there's the problem of the boundaries with neighbors. Who's to say if a blade is yours or a neighbor's? And so pressure builds on my chest and in my hands. I could feel the shape of it. It was a sphere. Like a cannonball was resting on me, and shot-puts in my palms. Heavy. Round."

"That's weird, Reed."

"Sounds weird. But the thought was absolute terror. I'd wake up and run into my parents' room screaming, and they couldn't calm me down."

"And now you think it was something else?"

"It's possible. If only because that terror doesn't match the dream."

Prosser shifted in his seat. "Okay, I can see that."

"Then, when I was eight, I was sitting on this rough concrete bench, waiting for my mom to pick me up from school. The kind of bench you always scraped yourself on as a kid." Reed watched a bird cut across the glass and vanish into the treeline.

"I remember those."

"This intensity came over me. Screaming at me to slide to my left. I couldn't ignore it. So I did."

"And?"

Reed glanced at Prosser. "A bird shit right where I had been sitting. Barely missed me."

"What?" Prosser looked at him and laughed.

"Yeah, no joke. A bird shit right there."

Prosser opened the hand that rested on the steering wheel. "But what does that have to do with this?"

"At the graduation ceremony for the academy, I was walking with my class to our seats, you know, at that ball field where they hold the graduations. And I was walking down the line of folding metal chairs when a bird shits right on the one I was about to sit on. Right then. Right when I was about to sit."

"What did you do?"

"I was lucky. Someone didn't show, so there was an empty seat. But that's not the point. It's like it was trying to remind me. Like something was trying to get me to think back to that time as a kid."

"Or there's some old bird out there that wants to shit on you."

Reed placed his head against the headrest. "Sounds stupid, I know. But these odd events just have me wondering if all isn't as it seems. Masked memories...altering of reality...psychic impressions. All the BS I never believed before."

"Then you get why I'm skeptical."

"Sort of. But only sort of. Now you need to decide if you think what I'm telling you is true, or if I'm lying or hallucinating. You have to pick a side."

"Why?"

"We've been spending a lot of time together. The bird's going to shit on you."

The two sat in silence, their eyes drifting from the landscape to the traffic to the Suburban tail.

* * *

From their back deck, Prosser threw the football underhand, sending it spinning toward Charlie. The boy made a dramatic dive to catch it.

"You see that, Daddy?" With a giant smile, Charlie popped to his feet.

"That was good effort!"

Charlie ran to the ball that had bounced toward the swing set in the family's backyard.

Sarah sat on the steps to their deck, enjoying a steaming coffee. "They're still following you?"

"Mm-hmm."

She kept her eyes on her husband. "Is there any danger?"

"Naw. What are they going to do?"

"I'm not sure I want the answer to that," she said before sipping her drink.

They watched as Charlie pretended to throw, rush, and catch touchdowns, accompanied by his own exuberant cheering.

"What about what Reed is saying?" Sarah's tone had changed to reflect the inquisitive one that Prosser had found so endearing early in their relationship.

"What do you mean?" he asked.

"About his experiences."

Prosser shifted his weight, moving himself back an inch. "Oh, haven't thought about it."

"Haven't thought about it? How can you not think about it?" Sarah's surprise came through in her increased volume and the lowering of her mug.

"Just haven't. I'm focusing on why the feds are interested in all this."

"So you don't ever think about what he's saying? The experiences?" She turned her body to face him.

"No."

"Do you believe he's being honest?"

Prosser shrugged. "No idea."

"Jesus, John." She returned to her coffee and watched Charlie.

"What?" He placed his hands behind him and leaned back.

"Uh, let's see. You're a detective, and this is maybe the biggest mystery you could possibly have."

"I've got to concentrate on the Fed agenda. Not the paranormal mumbo-jumbo."

Sarah shook her head at her husband.

"What?" he asked with a chuckle.

"It's intellectually lazy. You have something profound, potentially the *most* profound, and you haven't thought about it?"

Prosser pushed himself forward and dusted off his hands. "Damn, Sarah."

Sarah dropped her voice and stole a glance at Charlie, who was balanced on the swing with his arms flung wide, a backyard Superman.

* * *

Reed opened the door to his home and stepped inside. He glanced back at the Suburban two hundred yards down the road and parked at the side. "Assholes."

The door slammed behind him, and Reed walked to the kitchen for water and tossed leftover chicken in the microwave.

The appliance hummed. Reed leaned on the counter and rubbed his eyes. *Launch-plus-one,* he thought. *Those aliens would shoot down another, anyway.*

The microwave beeped. He pulled out the plate, grabbed a fork, and carried it to the living room. The setting sun beamed across the front yard, bringing the day's last light in. Reed sat on the couch and took a large bite of the dinner.

His cell buzzed from his back pocket. Between mouthfuls, he retrieved it to see *Wendy*. Reed answered, holding the phone to his ear as he continued to eat. "Hey."

"Hi."

"What's up?" Reed asked.

"We have to talk." Wendy's tone was direct. Cold. Cold enough for Reed to place his fork down.

"Okay."

Reed heard Wendy take a breath. "This isn't what I want in a relationship, Reed."

"What do you mean?"

"I need someone strong. Someone who will support me and be my rock. I hoped that would be you, but I've thought a lot the last few days, and you're just not."

Using one finger, Reed dragged the fork to the edge of the table. "You're breaking up with me?"

"I'm sorry. I just can't do this."

"You're not doing anything. You're at your apartment."

Wendy continued. "All the...all the...the shit that happened, and you call me to talk about people following you. About beings taking you. It's weak. Weak and kind of pathetic."

Reed looked to the windows, and the thought struck him that his Suburban friends might be listening to the call. "I'm here. If anyone thinks I'm weak, they can knock on my door."

"What?" Wendy's tone reflected her confusion.

Reed picked up the utensil and continued eating. "Yeah, let's break up, Wen. I actually think that's the right call. Strength is exactly what this is about."

"Um, okay."

"K, glad we agree." Reed tapped *Disconnect* and tossed the phone down.

He looked at the fireplace that he wished he had lit.

Reed built himself with hard work, routine, and a focus on health. Now he found himself alone in his mother's abandoned house, with no girlfriend, a dog away at a kennel, and only wishing he had a fire. A fire and someone else to share it with.

Self-control, he told himself. "I'm going to figure this out."

A passing vehicle broke the dying day's light. Its shadow moved across the room.

Chapter 39

Sarah opened their front door to Reed, who had one arm on the threshold and his head low. "Reed, you look like hell."

Reed stepped in, his eyes glazed. Sarah shut the door to the sunny day behind him, keeping her gaze on Reed's dark eyes. The stomping of little feet grew louder as Charlie ran through the kitchen and into the foyer. He wrapped an arm around one of his mother's legs.

"Hi, Reed!" Charlie's wave shook his entire body.

Reed lowered his body to talk to the boy. His voice was gruff, like he hadn't slept. "Hey, little dude! You taking care of my forklift?"

"Mm-hmm. It's with the steamroller."

"Whoa, that sounds pretty cool."

"It's pretty cool." Charlie nodded in agreement.

"Okay, Char-Char, go back to those blocks, and Mommy will be over in a sec." Sarah patted his back.

"Okay!" The stomping resumed as he ran off.

"Sorry. How are you?" Sarah asked as Reed stood.

He tucked his hands in the back pockets of his jeans. "Wendy called it off. Been a rough few nights."

"Oh my God, I'm so sorry!" Sarah placed a hand on his arm.

Reed shrugged. "Yeah, thanks. It's fine, though. I've got a lot that I need to focus on."

Sarah removed her hand and motioned to the kitchen. "You want some coffee?"

Reed smiled. "That would be great. Thank you."

"Anyway, John's in our office. You know where. I'll bring you guys the coffee."

"Thanks." Reed crossed the kitchen, watching Sarah as she made her way to the cupboard. The remnants of a toddler's breakfast made a mess of the counter. He continued to the office where Prosser sat with Katherine's box open in front of him. Three small screws rested in a pile at its side, next to her laptop.

As Reed entered, Prosser looked up at him and then pushed himself back from the desk. "You okay? You don't look so good."

Reed shrugged. "Been better."

"You want to talk about it?"

"Thanks, but not really." Reed motioned to the box on the desk. "You opened it?"

Prosser slid the object to the edge of the desk. "Look."

Reed approached and leaned over the device. Its innards contained a collection of tubes, microchips, and a vial of green liquid soldered in place. "What is it?" Reed asked.

"Your guess is as good as mine."

"Looks like some small vacuum tubes."

Prosser moved his glasses to rub his eyes. "I thought the same. See anything familiar, though?"

"Hmm, what?" Reed looked more closely. "The 'H'."

"Yep." Prosser tapped Reed's shoulder.

Reed stood upright, turning his attention to Prosser. "What the hell does Hephaestus have to do with this?"

"That's what we're going to find out. I called them a few minutes ago. We're meeting with someone there tomorrow."

"You're kidding!" The news seemed to energize him.

Prosser shook his head. "Nope."

Reed pulled a chair over and sat as Prosser snatched the tools and reconstructed the box.

The Hephaestus headquarters commanded acres of land. The singular building, stationed on a low rolling hill, was a common feature in Bridgewater tourism materials. The multi-billion-dollar company elevated the local economy, offering high-paying jobs and supporting small businesses in the city. The company's other buildings in the region all specialized in various scientific endeavors. But HQ was where the big brains worked.

"What do we do now?" Reed asked.

The detective didn't answer.

Reed watched as Prosser's eyes focused on the task, then slumped further into his chair. "We need some answers. I don't want to just wait until tomorrow."

"I thought you wanted to be a detective?" Prosser asked through a bemused grin.

"I do."

Prosser pushed the box to the back of the desk and quarter-turned in the chair. "Get used to it then."

"Okay. So?"

Prosser rested his elbow on the desk and tapped Katherine's laptop twice. "I still feel like there's something with her research we're missing."

Reed huffed. "There's a shit-ton about her research we're

missing."

"Something about it that is tied to what's going on."

"Sure, but it might as well be written in a foreign language."

After a minute of silence, Prosser looked from the computer to Reed. "Who else could we talk to then? Who would be someone who would understand it?"

"Boys." Sarah interrupted and placed a mug on each desk.

"Thanks, hon." Prosser gave Sarah's hand a quick squeeze.

"Thank you, Sarah."

The men each took a small sip of the steaming brew.

"I'm going out with Charlie. Don't get in trouble," Sarah shared.

Reed watched her leave the room, then his eyes drifted to the carpet. "We talked to Dobbie. Maybe someone else knows."

The statement perked Prosser up in his seat. "You mean someone we could ask who might know who Katherine discussed her research with?"

"Yeah."

Reed watched as Prosser swiveled the chair around and reached for the notepad on the desk. He flipped a few pages before stopping and pointing at something. Grabbing his cell, he tapped a few numbers and then put it on speakerphone. Prosser leaned back and waited.

It rang three times before a woman answered. "Hello?"

"Hi, Louise?" Prosser asked.

"Yes, is this Detective Prosser? I remember your voice." Her friendly tone filled the room.

Prosser glanced at Reed. "Yes, excellent memory. How are you and Liam?"

"We're fine, dear. We miss Katherine, but are getting by."

"I'm sorry...again. It must be hard." Prosser placed a hand

on the side of his face.

"But, why did you call?"

As if trying to remain silent, Reed eased his seat closer and leaned forward.

Prosser sat up and crossed his arms on the desk. "I'm hoping you can help me find someone that Katherine would have talked to about her research. Someone who would understand it."

"Which research? She seemed into everything under the sun."

"On dark matter. Who might she have talked to about it?"

"Oh. That would be Wimp. He was the only one who understood what she was saying."

The men's attention darted to one another. Prosser's eyes widened. Reed raised his arm to point at the word as if it hung in the air.

"Who?" Prosser asked.

"Wimp. That's what she called her brother," Reed mouthed quietly.

Prosser held a hand up in a stopping motion to Reed. "And what's her brother's name?"

"Sean. He's down in Boston now. Would you like his number?"

The men grabbed their coffees and smiled triumphantly.

"Yes, that would really be great. Thank you." Prosser said as he snatched a pen with his free hand.

Reed whispered, "Dobbie said Wimp was the key."

Prosser nodded and wrote the number Louise recited, then thanked her before hanging up.

The men locked eyes as they sipped.

* * *

Stars pin-pricked the sky on the cloudless night. They twinkled around the half-moon and above the four tiki torches on the Prosser's deck. Sarah sat with a blanket over her shoulders while John wore his favorite Billings' Notch sweatshirt. Each held an iced tea.

Earlier, the family had ordered pizza and sat around the table laughing and sharing stories with Reed. The cop sat next to Charlie, giving the kid his pepperoni and telling him about the equipment he used at the Collins' farm. After the meal, Reed left, and the Prossers tucked Charlie into bed.

Now enjoying the serene evening, Prosser reached across the small gap between their cushioned wicker chairs to place a hand on his wife's thigh. "We're going down to see Sean O'Reilly Thursday, do you mind?"

"No, that's fine. But you should set aside some time for Charlie." Sarah moved her hand to cover her husband's.

"I will. How's work, hon?"

Sarah chuckled through her smile. "Please, you're going to ask me about project management when you're looking into aliens and dark matter? I don't think so!"

"Well," Prosser paused. "It has taken a lot of my time, but I'd like to know how you're doing."

Sarah waved her arms. "Oh, no. I wasn't saying you need to be more attentive to me, but that's sweet, honey. I'm saying if we're going to talk, then I want to talk about your stuff."

Prosser laughed. "Okay. What about?"

The chair rattled against the deck as Sarah adjusted herself to sit cross-legged. "Like, what the hell was Katherine doing?"

"I'm not sure."

"Guess then." Sarah poked her husband.

"I can't even..."

Sarah blurted, "Yeah, you can't because you don't want to admit that all the alien stuff is real."

"I'm not sure it is!"

"If you were investigating a murder and had an eyewitness as confident of what he saw as Reed is, wouldn't it be a closed case?"

Prosser picked up his drink. "Close to it. We'd still need corroborating evidence."

"K, let's assume what Reed is saying is true. He's seeing aliens, and you know that a UFO took out the satellite."

"Fine." He sipped his tea.

Sarah placed her elbows on her knees. "Then what's your gut say?"

With a grunt, Prosser scratched at his chin. "She was on to something. And the Department of Defense was helping her. The aliens didn't like it. Something with her research into dark matter and that satellite, that's why we're talking to Sean."

"Like the satellite did something to the aliens. Or maybe stopped them somehow."

"It's not a weapon." Prosser reminded Sarah. "It's research. Measurements."

"How do you know?"

"It was to help us understand dark matter."

"Says who?"

"Says all the articles online about it. Says Dobbie Whitmire."

Sarah smiled again and dropped her feet to the floor. "Those same news outlets will tell you aliens don't exist. Or at least aren't here. And Dobbie, who you said" Sarah threw up her arms, "didn't have any idea how the thing worked."

Prosser returned the drink to the side table and scratched at something he pretended was on his palm. "That doesn't mean it's a weapon."

"It means there's truth, and there's what we're told. I'm interested in truth."

The excitement on Sarah's face had Prosser smiling. "I see that. Me too."

"What was the name of the satellite again?"

"Elisha."

"That's a weird name, right?" She punctuated the point with her hands.

"I guess."

"What does it mean?"

"Hmm, I don't know."

Sarah snatched her phone from the table and started typing.

"Here we go. Elisha. It's biblical. Old Testament." She dragged her finger along the screen and summarized the article. "Elisha was a prophet. He was surrounded by an army that wanted to take him. He could see what others couldn't, and when the enemy attacked, he called on God's invisible army to protect them. Elisha is closely associated with the prophet Elijah. Elijah asked God to make Elisha a prophet, and he did. And when Elijah died, Elisha asked God to give him double of Elijah's powers, and God granted it to him."

Sarah raised her gaze from the glowing screen to Prosser.

"So?" Prosser asked, wanting to understand the significance.

"She named it Elisha for a reason. Is there any other 'Elisha'? Like a family name?"

"No." Prosser turned his chair, enough to show Sarah his growing interest in her line of thinking.

The cell clanked against the glass as she placed it down. "Seems to me she named it that because Elisha was so powerful. Elijah made him a prophet, then he got double Elijah's powers, and saved a city because he could see this invisible army."

Sarah smiled at her husband. The blanket had slid down her back, and she lifted it over her shoulders. "I think I solved it for you."

"Okay." Prosser nodded. "So why did she jump? And why was the CIA there? Because that's what I've been trying to figure out. How does this story of Elisha tie in?"

She stared out at the trees and knocked her tongue against the roof of her mouth. After a moment, she turned back to her husband. "You're going to have to talk to her brother."

Prosser smiled before looking up at the stars. "You would make a good detective."

"Oh, I know."

The couple clinked their teas and watched satellites traverse the sky.

* * *

With sunset passed, Reed and Sadie sat on the small stoop looking out at the maple tree that the two had played under decades earlier, and the barren fields of the Collins' farm beyond. An uncovered lightbulb shone from the overhang above, attracting some early evening bugs.

"They told me they would recruit for another search party," Sadie said as she picked at her fingernails.

Reed examined her. Simple diamond studs, torn jeans that bared her tanned knees, a black crop top under a black jacket, hair pulled into a loose ponytail. She wore the whole thing like she hadn't thought about it once.

Sadie turned her head to him, and Reed looked away. "I know you have a lot going on, it's totally okay if you can't join the search," she said.

Reed took his turn fiddling with his fingers. "I'll try."

"He's gone anyway. I know it."

"You never know, right?"

"I'm not blind, I saw the indentation in the field." She made a popping sound with her lips. "Poof."

"You can't lose hope."

"Don't get me wrong, I'll still search." Sadie vigorously scratched her head, as if resetting her thoughts. "So, what's good ol' Reed up to anyways? Besides the case, please."

"Asked me a few weeks ago, and I would have had an answer. These days I'm not so sure." Reed moved his gaze to the stars. "No girlfriend. Dragging ass at work. And, looking into the crazy shit."

"You'll get through it, in a way. Once you accept it."

"What about you?" He looked at Sadie, whose sparkling green eyes met his. "What's life like? Anyone special?"

"Not special. He comes and goes. Mostly goes."

"Fuck him, then." Sadie turned away and dug a toe into the dirt. What smile she had now faded; he had touched a nerve. He nodded toward the tall tree. "That's what I remember." Their arms touched as he raised a hand to point at the maple. "The thing in the sky over the branches. The tree was smaller then."

"Yep."

"I know you said you didn't want to talk about it."

Sadie bumped her knee against Reed's. "It's cool. But first, tell me what this shit is?" She flicked the leather rope around his neck. "Since when do you wear jewelry?"

"Oh, this? It's a talisman."

Sadie hugged herself as she leaned back, laughing. "Won't do shit. Toss it."

Reed accompanied her, chuckling. "Yeah, I guessed as much." He made a mental note to throw it away and tucked it into his shirt.

"So, anyway," Sadie's voice raised, "that day. You want to know what happened. They took me. Took me up in that thing. One moment, I was here. Next, I was somewhere else."

"What did you see?" Reed leaned closer to her.

"That day, nothing." She looked at him. "You sure you want to do this?"

"What?" Reed asked with a furrowed brow.

Sadie dipped her head. "You really want to get into the phenomenon?"

The question echoed in his mind. Reed nodded.

Sadie stood and stretched. Taking a position in front of Reed, she peered down at him. "Tell me what you remember."

"A triangle. In the sky, but low. Above the maple we played around."

"Mm-hmm." She crossed her arms.

"It was terrifying."

"Don't I know it," she said pointedly.

Reed searched her eyes. "I remember you screaming. They brought you up? Put you in their ship?"

"Ship?"

"Yeah, their...spaceship. The UFO." He picked up a blade of grass and tossed it.

Sadie sighed. "You call it a 'ship.' You don't know what it is."

"So, what is it?"

"Like you said. A triangle. One side of the pyramid."

Reed slid back an inch and stretched his right leg out in front of him. "It's not a ship? It's some...alien shit."

"You don't even know that."

"What do you mean?" Frustration peppered Reed's tone.

Sadie dropped her arms. "You're a cop. What would you say to a witness who told you this?"

"That they're crazy."

"To a reliable witness?"

Reed thought another moment. "That I don't know what it was."

"Bingo." Sadie bent her knees and pointed at him. "You saw a pyramid. Could have been a ship, or a portal, or a refrigerator."

"But it was more than that."

"Oh, sure. But what exactly you can only guess."

"It has to be alien."

"Well, it's alien to you." She moved closer to him. "But that doesn't mean what you think it means."

Reed stood and took a step toward the tree. "You're speaking in riddles. Of course, it's E.T."

Sadie followed. "Maybe. Or maybe they've always been here. Or are us from the future. Maybe another dimension that sits right next to ours."

Reed rubbed the back of his neck. "And what about all the other bullshit going on?"

"What's that?"

He pressed a hand against the maple's bark and closed his eyes for a moment against the flicker of dreams and odd occurrences. "These things happening to me. Things that make no sense."

Sadie teased him. "Like?"

"The weird people. They say things wrong and do things people don't do. Like that woman in the library."

"Stay away from them. They'll mess with your mind. Have you doubting everything. Or worse, will..."

"Who are they?"

"Another unanswered question, buddy."

"I want to punch them," Reed said as he made a fist and pounded the tree.

"Then do it." Sadie shrugged.

"What?"

"Not like they're going to call the cops. And maybe it will help you understand."

"Understand what?"

She leaned on the tree and tucked her hands in her jeans. She tilted her head at him, patient and pitying, the way you'd look at a child crying about a skinned knee. "That you'll never understand."

"No, I can't accept that." Reed squared his shoulders to her.

"This isn't like other things. This isn't something you throw

Reed Jacobs Senior at."

"Then who can help me?"

Sadie raised an arm, rotated her wrist, and opened her palm, releasing the question into the ether. "There's no one."

Reed shook his head. "No. No, this is BS. You know more than you're telling me."

"I do, and I don't." Sadie twirled to look out at the field. "I know the pain they inflict. The cruel games. But I can't tell you who they are. Where they're from, if they're from anywhere at all, or anything else."

"But you've seen things. Seen them, right? So you must learn something from that."

"I've seen what they want me to see. You will too."

"No, I'm done."

"You're done when they have no more interest. They've been with me for a long time," Sadie's voice grew faint. "You're dealing with something far beyond what we are capable of understanding. You simply survive, or you don't."

"I can't accept that." Reed stepped over the thick protruding roots to stand next to her. "Your dad brought this on, you know."

Sadie took a deep breath. "He didn't start it. He can't do that. Maybe you're just aware now."

Looking out across the field for what Sadie might have been staring at, he found nothing but the landscape. "So, what do you do about it?"

"Help others and spend Dad's money."

"Shopping?"

"Close. Shopping, shrinks, and drugs."

"So it's always like this? I go on being tormented all the time?"

"Naw, they come and go. They might get you every night for a month, then disappear for a year. It's called a flap—the times they come a lot."

A moment passed in silence.

"They take you, do terrible shit, and drop you off like recycling?" Reed turned back to her.

Sadie glanced at him before returning her eyes to the scenery. "No. Sometimes they act like they give a shit."

"What do you mean?"

She took a deep breath. "A couple of times they've taken me for a walk around the ship, or whatever it is. I get the feeling that when they take you in, they are actually taking you to an entirely different area of the universe. I don't know that, though. Anyway, they'd say things."

"Like what?"

"Like, somehow I was a part of something special. Or they'd share things that humans don't know. Probably to gain trust. They told me the universe is older than we think. Not billions or trillions of years but eternal. They talk about life being special. But it means nothing. The whole thing is fraud. Subterfuge. So you can't trust them. Who knows, maybe it's true. But if they were on the up-and-up, they'd knock on your door at noon, not take you from your bed at night."

"Maybe what they say is true." Reed's eyes drifted above the maple.

"Right, and they share it with a farm girl. When's the last time you told that dog of yours about the rings of Saturn?"

The two old friends stood in silence for a minute. A mouse darted from the field and froze at the foundation of the house, rising onto its hind legs. Above, a hawk turned slow circles. The mouse slipped through the latticework and was gone.

Sadie brushed some strands of hair behind her ear. “Why not stay? Run the farm.”

Sadie shook her head. “No. The Collins’ farm is all bad memories and corn. And I don’t like corn.”

The field stretched into the darkness of the night and called for Reed’s attention again. Playing out across it like an old movie, his memories of the Collins’ farm brought him warmth. Time with Sadie exploring nature, having adventures, and eating the apple pies her mother made. He couldn’t imagine bad memories here. The old film stopped as he thought about Sadie’s horrors eliminating the pleasant memories they should have shared.

Chapter 40

The five-story glass headquarters, shaped like an H viewed from above, reflected the lush landscaping around Hephaestus. At one end of the complex, reproductions of classical sculptures surrounded a pristine pond. Tall, manicured trees dotted the grounds in careful symmetry. And at the center of the H, stacked above the top level, a cylindrical structure commanded a view of the area. Its prominence gave it the appearance of an executive suite or boardroom.

Reed navigated the winding road up to the visitors' parking by the front entrance. Prosser kept his eyes on the shining edifice. As they got closer, the skeletal framework became apparent. Made of wood and stone, it created the effect of the glass construction emerging from a natural environment.

"You ever been here?" Reed asked.

"Never. You?"

"No. But something about the place always gave me the creeps."

"Why's that?"

"I meet a lot of people who work here, but they never say what they actually do."

"They have a lot of pull in local politics. We need to be gracious." Prosser examined Reed.

As he rounded a bend, Reed caught Prosser's glance. "Rumor is they build weapons."

"I'm not sure that's the case. I looked at some of their marketing materials. They weren't easy to find. They were all about solving the 'most challenging scientific problems'."

"Sounds like weapons to me."

The visitors' parking section was empty, so Reed pulled into the closest spot to the entrance.

Prosser grabbed his door handle. "Let me do the talking."

"Yeah, fine. But if you're not up to being Presser, I'm going to jump in."

"I'm serious. The executives here are big deals. They could bury us if they cared to."

The men walked to the front doors, which slid open with a pleasant *whooshing* sound as they approached.

"Holy shit," the words dripped from Reed's mouth.

The atrium stretched out like the grand hall of a modern-day fortress, its expanse bathed in the soft glow of the sun and lighting concealed behind opaque white film running down support beams.

At the back, a solid piece of black marble ran from floor to ceiling, up multiple stories. It stood thirty feet wide. Water poured down it in trickling straight lines, lighted a glowing blue from above. The floor was a chessboard of large, gleaming tiles that reflected the waterfall to the feet of all who entered.

The reception desk appeared to be made of matte black carbon fiber. It made a clear statement—don't mess with those behind it. Attached to its front, a bold and backlit bronze

"H". There were two individuals manning the station, a stern-looking woman in a clean security uniform and another, more pleasant one with a transparent headset.

At each side of the desk, elegant curving stairs to the second level and a glass elevator waited. Comfortable-looking chairs circled small tables at the sides of the foyer. Above, a black ceiling with twinkling LED stars.

The men approached the receptionist, Reed's eyes seemingly taking in everything, while Prosser focused on the woman.

"Hello. I'm Detective Prosser, and this is Officer Jacobs. I called yesterday about a piece of technology created here and was told I might be able to speak to someone about it."

"Of course, Detective." The woman smiled. "I remember your call. You worked the Katherine O'Reilly case."

"That's right."

The young woman in the red blazer shook her head. "Such a tragedy. Let me ring Mr. Hemsey. Give me a moment."

"Mr. Hemsey?" Prosser asked.

"That's right. Allen Hemsey, our CSO."

Prosser placed his hands behind his back. "I hate to use his time if it's not absolutely necessary."

"He was made aware of your call and asked to personally handle it. I assure you, if he didn't deem it valuable, he would not have set aside the time."

"Thank you." Prosser turned, snagging Reed's elbow to follow him as he stepped toward the doors.

"Look, Allen Hemsey is one of the founders."

"I know." Reed stood close to Prosser. He kept his eyes ahead as he whispered. "The guy's a billionaire."

"I've heard stories about him. He's...intense. We need to

be straight and very deliberate with the words we choose. No rambling."

"Yeah, yeah. No problem."

Prosser turned and smiled at the receptionist.

"He's on his way," she said as she pressed a button on the device in her ear.

After a couple of minutes, a soft chime broke the silence. The elevator on their left hummed to life. From the top of the atrium, a man in dark blue slacks and a white button-down shirt stared down at them through the glass. Unhurried, watching, like a god descending from Olympus.

It reached the bottom, and the doors opened. He stepped out as the receptionist stood.

"Mr. Hemsey, Detective Prosser, and Officer Jacobs." She returned to her seat.

Allen approached. He stood just short of Reed, with a frame almost as intimidating. With his salt-and-pepper hair, he looked like he belonged on the cover of an executive magazine. The tapping of his polished black shoes against the tiles echoed in the room.

With a cordial smile, Allen extended his hand in greeting. Prosser and Reed took turns shaking as they introduced themselves.

"Please, let's sit." Allen motioned to the seating area.

The sun beamed in, washing the group as they moved. Allen sat in a chair that allowed a view of the entrance. He crossed his legs and raised a hand as Prosser and Reed sat facing him. "Before you begin, I understand you're here as part of an investigation into Dr. O'Reilly's passing. I'll forewarn you, I am under an NDA relating to our work together, so I'm limited in what I can share. Even though she is no longer with us, we take our NDAs very seriously."

"That's fine. Before I jump in, I'm impressed by the space. What do you do here?"

As if used to the acoustics of the room, Allen projected his voice in such a way that the desk attendants couldn't hear. "When an organization faces what seems an impossible scientific need, they hire us. We have experts from multiple disciplines. They work together to find unique solutions. What we do can lead to breakthroughs that advance our scientific knowledge."

"Wow. That's intriguing. I'd love to hear more, but I'm afraid of wasting your time. So, if you don't mind, can we start with your relationship with Katherine?" Prosser asked.

A single nod from Allen followed Prosser's question before he answered. "There's a small circle of scientists in Bridgewater, largely thanks to the work of U of B and Hephaestus. Because of that, yes, I knew Dr. O'Reilly. We were professional acquaintances. We've met a few times over the years. That's the extent of our relationship."

"And I assume you met her as a part of your work for her?"

"Correct. We met once in consultation."

Prosser leaned forward. "How was she in your meeting?"

"Pleasant. Kind. Professional. I felt nothing out of sorts."

"When was it the two of you met?"

"Oh, let's see now." Allen's gaze drifted to the windows, a pause that felt less like a moment to think and more like disinterest. He turned back to Prosser. "That was February 20th. The product was delivered a month later."

"It sounds like that was the only time you met for this project. You didn't see her after? Does that mean you didn't do the delivery?"

"Courier." The answer came quickly.

"So you don't know if her demeanor may have changed in that month?"

"Correct."

"Apologies if this sounds strange, but were there any odd characters or Federal Agents around this effort? Perhaps you saw them in the parking lot when you met with Katherine. Or maybe they called inquiring about what you might have been doing for her."

"I can't say there was anything untoward."

Prosser leaned back. Now with the sun shining in his eyes, he raised his left hand and placed it at the side of his face. "We believe we found the device that Hephaestus made for Katherine."

Allen shook his head. "We didn't make a device. I say 'we', I was the only one on the project. What I provided wouldn't do anything on its own. Dr. O'Reilly's work was additive to what I developed to make something functional."

"What you developed. What did it provide Katherine?"

"NDA."

"What was it she asked for?"

"I cannot divulge that."

"Understood," Prosser said as he shuffled in his seat for a spot where the sun wasn't shining in his eyes. "What about Dobbie Whitmire? Did you ever do any work with him?"

"Donald. Yes, we've worked together in the past. Talented engineer."

"Mm-hmm. We met with him. Nice guy. Did your work with Katherine overlap with his? His company built the Elisha."

"No. Mr. Whitmire's efforts at A.D.E. were limited to the Elisha. "

"Did you, or Hephaestus, work on the Elisha?"

Allen smiled. "This is an unusual line of questioning for a death investigation."

"We need to look under every rock. I'm sure you understand."

"Indeed."

"Well?"

"NDA," Allen replied with a tilt of his head.

"Got it. We're also talking to Sean, Katherine's brother. You ever work with him?"

The silence slammed into the moment. It hung in the air as if shot from Allen's glare. Then the man spoke, brushing his pants. "I've worked with Sean. Yes. Clever man."

Reed's eyes darted between the men. His fingers began tapping on his knee.

"Worked with him on Elisha in some way?" Prosser asked.

"NDA."

Reed spoke like he had been waiting for a moment to pounce. "What you did for Katherine, was it about aliens?"

With a smile, Allen lowered his leg and stood. He offered his hand as he had earlier. "I'm afraid our time is up. I have another matter to attend to. It has been a pleasure, and I wish you the best in your investigation."

Prosser and Reed followed, standing to shake the man's hand. "We appreciate your time."

Reed held on to Allen. "You didn't say 'no'."

Allen squared his shoulders to Reed, unbothered. With his eyes on him, Allen brought his left hand up and cupped it over their combined grasp. "Perhaps another time, Mr. Jacobs. Until then, stay out of trouble."

After a nod, Allen released his grip and turned for the

elevator. Before entering, he called back to the men. "If you'd like a tour of our headquarters, Ms. Burrow can arrange something. Perhaps you'd like a Hephaestus sweatshirt? Or a mug?"

As if on cue, the receptionist stood. The men declined and exited the building for the Wrangler.

Reed rocked in the driver's seat as he took the vehicle down the long road. The muscles along his jaw flexed and clenched.

"That's not how you keep your cool," Prosser said, his eyes on the passing manicured lawns.

"We weren't learning anything."

Prosser sighed and looked down at his feet. "Yeah, maybe not."

"But he fucking knows something!" Reed bellowed.

Prosser waved it off. "Don't worry about him. He's untouchable. We have Sean tomorrow."

"A fucking mug, you have to be kidding me."

"I would have gone for a sweatshirt."

Reed turned on the radio. Pink Floyd's *Let There Be More Light* filled the cabin.

Chapter 41

Prosser was nostalgic for the day in Boston. He had taken Sarah and Charlie to the aquarium and enjoyed lunch at Quincy Market. The old American architecture added to the city's charm. During the drive, he and Reed discussed their time in Boston and planned how they would address Sean, agreeing to be honest, straight.

When they arrived, they stretched their legs and ascended the brownstone's front steps. Sean answered the door in pressed khakis and a baggy hoodie; the tail of his wrinkled white button shirt poked out. He had gray stubble, thinning hair, and thick glasses.

"Come, let's walk at least," Sean said. The gravel in the man's voice suggested he may have just woken up.

He led them down to the uneven sidewalk and shuffled across the street with his hands buried in his pockets, toward a park with a playground and benches. Sean followed the freshly paved path around it.

"Want to head to the pub? Get some beers?"

Reed answered before Prosser had the chance. "Don't drink. Detective Prosser talked to your mother. She said Katherine would tell you about her research."

"Actually, she said you were the only one who would understand it," Prosser added.

"Jesus, guys, how about a kiss first?" Sean looked at the men to his left. "I'm kidding. Let's back up. What exactly do you want?"

"I'm...*we're* looking into Katherine's death, and we believe there's a connection to her research."

"Why is that?"

"She jumped," Prosser caught himself. "I'm sorry, Sean. I don't mean to sound crude. But—"

Sean interrupted as he placed his hands in the kangaroo pocket of his sweatshirt. "It's okay, I get it."

"She took her life after seeing the rocket with the Elisha cargo explode."

"Gotta say I liked 'she jumped' better," Sean joked.

Reed leaned forward as they walked, looking at Sean. "But that's not why she did. And it looks like a UFO shot it down."

"Reed, really?" Prosser put out a hand to push him back.

To their surprise, Sean nodded in validation. "Yup."

Reed and Prosser looked at one another before turning back to the man. "What do you make of it?" Prosser asked.

"They wanted it down."

"Hold on." The group stopped as Prosser took Sean's elbow. "Are you saying that...that aliens didn't want the Elisha launched?"

"Certainly didn't want it operational, did they?"

"Fuck, I told you!" Reed smacked Prosser's side.

Sean laughed through his nose. "Let's sit. You two sound like you want to get into heavy shit." Turning, Sean brought them across the park. Prosser recognized the wharf ahead.

Boston's Harbor Walk offered a pleasant view. Its brick path had large stones laid by the water's edge, where a heavy chain acted as a barrier. They followed it to the end of Long Wharf, where they sat on a bench with a view across the bay to the airport in the distance.

"Before I tell you guys anything, I need to know where this is coming from. Why you're so interested, and why you think the beings are involved."

"I was assigned your sister's case, and it never sat right. I told you on the phone, but I'm a detective for Bridgewater PD, and Reed is an officer. I haven't determined why she jumped."

"Mm-hmm."

"And the aliens, I found that video online," Reed added.

"So?" Sean asked.

As if suddenly uncomfortable, Reed adjusted his position on the wooden bench. "And I see them."

Sean nodded. "Yeah. I see them too."

The response made Reed sit up. "You do?"

Without answering, Sean pulled an aluminum flask from his pocket, took a swig, and returned it.

"As a part of the investigation, we've met with some folks. Allen Hemsey is one."

Sean looked at Prosser, seemingly eager for his next words.

"He didn't share anything useful. And abruptly ended the conversation when Reed asked about aliens."

"He might be the only one smarter than Katherine, but he's cold," Sean said, turning back to the water.

"Is he dangerous?"

"No. At least not in the sense you're thinking," Sean said. "He's actually an interesting guy. Fun to talk to if you can get past his quirks. But, hydrogen bombs spend their lives in silos doing no damage at all."

A moment passed with the men looking out at the bay. Prosser broke the silence. "We also met with Dobbie Whitmire. You know him?"

"Yeah," Sean said through the wince from the drink.

"He said Wimp was the key."

Sean laughed. "She started calling me that after my eleventh birthday party. She had some magic trick where she could lift this box, but when I tried, it was way too heavy."

"Why are you the key?"

Reed watched the back-and-forth between the two.

"Katherine wasn't the only gifted one in the family. She just held her shit together better." The flask appeared again. "She did her research. I did mine."

"What's yours?"

"Plasma physics, primarily. She needed energy, at a significant scale. I helped her."

"Dobbie said something about energy."

"Mm-hmm."

"Okay, so you could supply energy somehow to the Elisha?"

"That's right."

"Why was that important?" Prosser couldn't look away from Sean, who kept his gaze on the skyline.

"For the Elisha to work. To *really* work."

"What do you mean?"

"I have to spell it out for you guys?" Spittle shot from Sean's mouth and he looked at them, his eyes sharp.

"Please."

"Those fuckers come from dark matter. You could think of it as their dimension. Dark matter permeates the entire universe. They can be almost anywhere and at any time. They have ways to manifest in our ordinary matter. Katherine figured out how to do that, but in reverse. She intended to inject immense amounts of energy into it." He sipped again. "To fry them. Or, at least some around the planet."

"To fry them," Reed repeated.

Sarah was right, Prosser thought.

Reed asked, "Sean, could you take over? Complete your sister's work?"

"'Fraid not. Dark matter was her expertise."

Reed gripped and wrung the metal armrest. "Yeah, okay. At least I know they are aliens."

"It's more complicated than that. They've been here a long time. They're as much a part of Earth as we are. But, the Elisha was to be the first in an array. We're talking about an entire planet here, so there would need to be more satellites in place for adequate defense. And we couldn't test on-surface, had to be in space."

"Why?"

"So not to destroy Earth. When I say significant energy, I mean it."

"You said you see them. The aliens. Katherine was protecting you." Reed's tone elevated.

"That's right," Sean said.

Reed turned to the water and spoke to himself. "She was going to protect us."

"Do you think that's why she jumped? Because they would just keep stopping her plan?" Prosser asked.

Sean turned to him. "Did you interview David Jarrow?"

"Yes."

He turned back to the water. "God, what a fuckwad."

"Won't argue with you there."

"At her memorial, he went on and on about Schopenhauer.

Fucking clueless to the fact that everyone was grieving." He drank again. "You know what is most annoying about Jarrow?"

Prosser shook his head.

"That he's fucking right. Asshole. The only reason that one commits suicide is because the prospect of going on is much worse than the unknown of death. Worse than death being non-existence. And the Elisha's destruction was an obstacle. My sister would keep at her research until she found another way to deliver the payload. She was nothing if not irritatingly relentless."

"Something else happened then. Something we don't know." A plane emerged from the distant airport and rose into a cloud. "Do you know what might have made her do it?"

Sean placed his shining flask in front of the men. "I don't know. But it was worse than death."

Chapter 42

Prosser and Reed sat across from each other at a bench table at the center of the diner. To one side, a row of windows out to the parking lot, along with more benches, and to the other, the kitchen and a long aluminum bar.

The pair stopped at the restaurant between Boston and Bridgewater after their talk with Sean O'Reilly. They had walked with him back to his townhome, and he offered whatever future support they needed, only asking that his name remain out of anything official.

A waitress stood by their table, her hair up in a tight bun, with a notepad and pencil ready.

"Water, please."

"Same," Reed said, feeling like he couldn't get the word out fast enough to get rid of the waitress.

"Sure, guys. Will be right back with those," she said as she tucked her notepad into her black apron pocket and walked away.

"She fucking did it. Figured it out. I told you," Reed whispered excitedly across the table and over the laminated menus.

"Told me what?"

"That somehow there's a way. You can stop them." Reed's eyes were locked forward.

"You never told me that."

Reed leaned back. "Oh, I must have said that to one of the other assholes that didn't believe me."

"I think I believe you."

"Think?"

Prosser shrugged. "Look, that's as good as you're getting right now, okay?"

"Waters." The young waitress placed them on the table and opened her notepad to a fresh page. "You guys ready to order?"

"I'll just have a burger and fries," Reed said as he handed her his menu.

"Yeah, same."

"Easy enough. Anything else to drink?"

"No, thanks."

The two watched as she took the menus and returned to the counter.

Reed leaned closer again. "Katherine knew how to stop them, John. Don't you understand how big that is?"

Prosser opened his hands. "But she killed herself. I'm not sure how much good this will do you."

"It's possible. That's all I care about. There's a way to kill them."

"Which requires massive amounts of energy."

Reed's arms fell to the table. "Fuck, man. I'm riding this wave right now. Just let me."

The little bell over the diner's glass door rang.

"The fuck?" Reed saw them first. The blond CIA agent,

Ethan Boyd, approached with another man. Boyd was dressed in expensive jeans and a polo. His friend in a gray suit, a matching brimmed hat, and a slim black tie. The man's pale skin made his blue eyes shine, and the black hair that poked out from under the hat appeared fake. He walked stiffly.

"Gentleman. Mind if we join you?" Boyd asked.

But before Prosser or Reed could answer, the men sat—Boyd next to Reed and the mysterious individual next to Prosser.

"You're blowing your cover," Prosser spoke to the agent after a quick inspection of the odd man.

"Am I? Nice trick back at the garage, by the way." Boyd said with a smile. "I have tricks, too."

"Fuck off," Reed said.

They stared as the unknown man placed his white hands palms down on the table. Boyd leaned back and cupped his on his stomach. "So, what's good here?"

"Boyd. Is that a pseudonym?" Prosser asked.

"Does it matter?"

"The fuck you want?" Reed asked.

Prosser raised a hand. "Easy, Reed."

Boyd ignored the question. "How was your visit with Sean?"

"Enlightening."

Boyd nodded, then moved closer. "You know, not everything is worth looking into. Know what I mean? Like when you're in junior high, and you want to know if your crush likes you. Sure, you could ask. But that would mean getting an answer. And you might not like the answer, so you don't ask."

"Jesus, stop the mysterious bullshit. I'm doing my job." Prosser said with a chuckle.

"Your job was to identify the manner of death. You filed that already. I read it. You did good. Clean."

"I'm curious about the cause. Why did she do it?" Prosser asked.

Boyd responded, "Curiosity killed the cat."

The strange man sat without shifting, without blinking. His clothes looked fresh off the rack, his skin smooth and poreless as poured resin, shining faintly like wax left under a heat lamp. When he smiled, the expression arrived in the wrong order, lips moving before the eyes caught up.

Prosser insisted, "Say what you want to say. That way, you can go, and we can eat."

"Charlie and Sarah are at swimming class. You're at least a couple of hours away," Boyd whispered.

Prosser leaned close to the agent. "Let me be clear with you. If you touch my family, I will kill you."

Boyd smiled without backing away. "You do not know who you're dealing with."

Something ate at Reed, a familiar itching at his mind. And he felt the only way to scratch it was to look at the strange man's feet. He couldn't explain why, but he couldn't escape it.

Reed leaned back, and his eyes drifted under the table. He tilted his head and squinted, then ducked his head under to get a closer look. Three inches of space between the man's socks and the bottom of his pants revealed dark gray flesh with thin black veins under its surface.

With one rapid move, Reed grabbed the fork from the table and slammed it into the middle finger of the man's left hand. The three prongs stuck into his flesh. The handle stood upright and unmoving. Diners stopped their chattering. Prosser and Boyd looked at Reed, then at the hand.

The cuts of the pasty flesh held tight against the fork,

wrapped around the prongs like rubber. No blood emerged, and the finger lay like a deflated balloon.

Reed launched himself up from the table. With the other patrons all gawking at him, he pointed to the smiling man. "That motherfucker's not real!"

"Now, why did you have to go and do that?" Boyd gripped the fork and pulled it from the man's hand. The flesh rebounded, soundlessly covering the three small wounds.

Prosser stood and pulled cash from his pocket, then placed it on the table. "We'll finish this another time."

Boyd watched the men leave.

* * *

"What was that?" Prosser opened the car door and got behind the wheel.

"Did you see that guy?" Reed blurted as he took the passenger seat.

"Yeah."

"He was...he was...not human. I've seen one like him before, at the library. Like something wearing a skinsuit, but there's nothing in the middle finger. Like they have fewer fingers or something."

The Explorer bounced as Prosser pulled onto the main road toward the interstate. "A skinsuit?"

"Yep. There's something inside. Something...other."

"What you were calling 'wolves'."

"That's right."

Prosser nodded. "You know what that means?"

"What?"

"Boyd wasn't fazed by what happened. He knew. So, if that thing was alien, then they're working with the CIA."

"Holy shit." Reed's eyes locked on the horizon ahead. The heaviness of the realization barreling toward him for a head-on collision.

"I wonder if Katherine figured that out."

"Do you think that's why she did it?"

Prosser shook his head. "No, I believe Sean. Just another obstacle, right?"

"Maybe she discovered the wolves were working with someone in our government when the rocket went down."

"How you figure?"

"Like she worked out that someone must have given the aliens information on the Elisha. Told them when it would launch and from where. They knew to shoot it down."

Prosser drummed his fingers on his knee. "Yeah, that's possible."

"I need my dog." Reed looked out his window. He wanted Badge at his side, his non-judgmental and supportive partner through hard times.

They drove in silence for a minute, Reed letting his nerves settle. Then the alert appeared on the dashboard's screen: a call from Oberman. Prosser punched the green answer button. "Hey, Chief."

"John, where are you?" Oberman's anxious voice filled the vehicle.

Prosser glanced at Reed. "I...I went to Boston for the day. On my way back and am a couple of hours south."

"We got a call, John. You need to get to the hospital now."

"What? What's going on?"

"I'm sorry, John. I'm so sorry."

"Lesley, tell me what happened," Prosser yelled to the screen.

"It's Charlie. We got the call. I'm so sorry." The men could hear her sobs through her words. "You need to get to Bridgewater ER."

* * *

Charlie rubbed his eyes. The swimming pool water made everything hazy, and the heat and humidity from the indoor facility made breathing hard. Condensation fogged the windows along the two outside walls. The bright lights on the ceiling bounced off surfaces, giving everything a halo-like glow. Rows of cheap, white, plastic chairs sat empty as kids and their accompanying parents splashed about. A lifeguard sat on the stairs into the pool.

Charlie kicked his feet, sending water up over his head.

"You're doing good, Charlie-P!" Sarah said. She braced her son under his arms as he rested his on her shoulders. He did his best to kick underwater, but he liked the splashing when he didn't.

Charlie kept his eyes fixed past his mother, on the one woman not in the pool. She stood at the far end, on the corner edge, feet spread in a wide V like he had seen a ballerina do. Her arms hung still and straight at her side. Her black hair was so perfect that it reminded him of his Lego figures. The white dress she wore didn't reflect light like other surfaces, making it harder for him to look away.

The woman's eyes seemed wrong, and they fixed on Charlie.

The instructor changed the routine. Now, kids swam the width of the pool, a guardian in the water and walking along at their side with arms ready.

"Ready, Charles?" his mother asked as she released her grip and let her son swim on his own.

Conversations, laughter, and splashing all echoed and mixed into a cacophony of meaningless sounds. Water rushed into Charlie's face. He moved his arms and feet to propel himself forward. He pushed them harder as he felt his body sink a little. With his eyes still on that woman, his muscles tired. He drew deeper breaths.

Why is it here? Charlie wondered. Though he had never seen the woman before, he knew it well. The burning between his collarbones brought that unmistakable sickness to his stomach. Only one thing did that. The tall monkey. The one who directed the others. But not the one really in charge.

Why is it...wearing that?

* * *

Prosser hit the disconnect button and pushed the accelerator.

"You want me to drive, John?" Reed asked.

"No. Fuck no!" Prosser slammed his palm against the wheel. "Fucking Boyd said it! He said Charlie was in his swimming class."

He turned onto the highway ramp and pushed the Explorer. The engine roared. The cabin shook as he checked his side mirror and slid into the furthest left lane. Prosser pressed a button to call Sarah.

Busy signal.

"Shit."

Then the screen came to life again, notifying him of a call from Sarah. He hit *Connect.*

"Sarah?"

"John! Oh, God, I don't know what to do." Sarah's throat sounded sore and her words wet.

"Sarah, what's going on? Where are you?" Prosser asked.

"It's Charles. Charles drowned."

Prosser held the wheel with both hands. "What? What, Sarah? How? WHAT HAPPENED?"

Sarah's tone transformed to what seemed a shocked awareness. "Oh, oh my god! Not Charlie, John! Charles Lancaster. From swim class. Char-Char witnessed it, and I don't know what to do."

"Wait, Charlie's fine?"

"Yes, but no. He's torn up. He saw a friend have CPR done. He's traumatized!" Sarah cried.

Prosser whimpered, "Jesus Christ, Sarah! Jesus fucking Christ, Sarah! What the fuck? You call me and say Charlie dr-drowned?" The tears of relief poured from him, making him stutter.

"John, I'm sorry. I'm so sorry! Charlie's okay. There was confusion on the 911 call, too. The lifeguard said the wrong name."

"Fuck, Sarah!" He wrung the leather wheel, tried to break it.

"Sorry, John. I didn't mean to freak you out."

Prosser punched the screen, disconnecting the call. He yanked the SUV to the far right, tires biting gravel as he stood on the brakes.

"Fuck!" he screamed at the windshield before opening the door to blaring car horns and rounding the Ford to the grass and the small ledge of rock. The road spun around him as he pressed his hands to his skull and paced in tight circles. He tried to catch his breath.

"Oh, fuck." The ground felt soft as he collapsed to his knees. He tore his glasses off and vomited. The sobs came up the same way, all at once.

"Hey, man." Reed emerged from the car and knelt next to him. He placed a hand on Prosser's shoulder. "It's okay. Let it out. Let it all out. Your son is fine."

Reed watched and said nothing more as Prosser expelled the horrors that had ravaged his thoughts.

Chapter 43

Prosser peeled out of Reed's driveway and raced toward home as Reed grabbed the keys to his Wrangler. He needed Badge back, his sidekick, his shadow, his best friend. On the way, he would stop at Sally's to find out when Patch worked next—to discover if the clerk had been experiencing any more strange events.

He entered the gas station to find Elly, the manager who provided the video footage, organizing behind the register. "Hi, Elly."

She turned to see Reed and smiled. "Should I ring up another USB drive?"

"Not this time. Can you tell me when Patch works next?" Reed put his hands in his pockets.

"He quit."

"Quit?"

"Yup. Moved to South Carolina. Said he was going to work with snakes or something."

"Python?"

"Mm-hmm."

Reed nodded. "Good for him. Thanks." With a smile and a wave, he returned to his car, happy that the young man left to make something of himself. Reed decided he wouldn't track down Patch. The kid deserved peace.

After a short and uneventful drive, Reed approached the kennel. The building was turtle-shaped—a small room at the front designed for drop-off and pick-up, with a much larger warehouse at the back for the dogs to play in inclement weather. From the indoor space branched outdoor pens with natural grass and dirt.

Reed had used Bridgewater Boarding several times for Badge. As the dog would see the facility, he'd get so eager to play that his butt would wag faster than his tail.

Reed didn't receive the usual welcoming smile from Claire, the co-owner and woman who manned the front-of-house, when he entered. Instead, she looked confused.

"Hey, Claire. Here for Badge," Reed said as he approached the counter.

She shook her head. "What? You already picked him up."

"What do you mean? He's been here a few days now. Haven't been in since."

Claire shifted her weight from one foot to the other. "You picked him up this morning. I went back and got him."

Reed placed his hands on the counter and took a deep breath. "I didn't get Badge this morning. I was out of town."

She only shook her head.

"Can you go back and look?"

Her eyes examined his for any sign of a punchline. "Yeah, you said you were out of town. You went on and on about talking to some guy about plasma physics. I thought it was weird. So unlike you. You paid and everything."

"Claire, seriously." Reed's fingers curled into fists. "I hear you, but please go check for me. It's an emergency."

"Yeah, sure. Okay." She retreated through a door to the boarding space. The barks got louder as it opened.

Reed paced the room and ran his fingers through his hair. Badge had to be here. He *had* to be.

The sound of barking caused Reed to turn his head, his eyes widening in anticipation of seeing Badge. Until Claire closed the door behind her, the barking muffled, and with no dog at her side.

Cautiously, she moved to the register. "I'm sorry, Reed. He's not here. Like I said."

Reed approached the counter again. Heat flooded his face, his pulse hammering at his temples.

"Are you okay?" Claire whispered.

Reed erupted. "No, I'm not okay! I need Badge NOW!"

"I handed him to you."

"No, you didn't!" Reed slammed both fists down onto the table. The small rotating display of dog tags, rolls of poop bags, and treats tumbled to the floor. A thick crack appeared along the long wooden top. The register's bell rang a solemn ding.

Claire stepped back and looked at the damage. As she shook, her eyes moved up to Reed. "You need to leave."

Reed's arms and hands locked rigid. He rounded the counter and drove his shoulder through the warehouse door. Inside, some dogs ran amok, while others napped tucked into various nooks. Workers managed the virtual chaos.

"BADGE!" Reed called out as he walked to the center of the space. "Badge?"

He stopped and turned in place. His heart pounded in his throat. The room spun, dogs, workers, the aluminum walls swirling like a merry-go-round. "Badge!" Reed dropped to his knees. Various dogs came to sniff him, but none were familiar. None was his.

Claire's voice came from behind him. "I'm calling the cops if you don't go. I'm guessing that wouldn't be a good look for you."

Reed's muscles strained against his body as he stood. He glanced at Claire before walking into the lobby and kicking the door open to the parking lot. With methodical steps and eyes radiating fury, he continued to his Wrangler.

"I...will...fucking...kill...that...man." The door handle creaked as he pulled at it. He slid behind the wheel and called Prosser. "I need that address," he demanded.

"What address?"

"For the CIA guy." Reed backed out of his parking spot.

"Why?"

He shifted into Drive. "Don't fuck with me, John. Not now." Reed's blood boiled, and his teeth clenched.

"What's going on?" Prosser asked.

"He fucking took Badge. He took my fucking dog!"

"Jesus."

Reed spoke with an unnatural calm. "Give me the address."

"Yeah, one sec. Hold on, I'll text it to you."

Reed hung up and pulled onto the road.

* * *

Prosser sat on his living room floor next to a fabric mat with printed roads and trees between him and Charlie. Toys were piled up next to them with their empty bucket close by. Prosser moved a small die-cast car along a street as Charlie stomped around it with a dinosaur.

"You doing good, buddy?" Prosser asked his son.

"Mm-hmm."

Prosser rubbed Charlie's back. "I know today was scary."

"Yeah." The boy didn't move his attention from the creature.

Sarah rested on the couch next to them, watching the two play. "I talked to Charles Lancaster's mom, he's going to be okay. It was just really scary, right Char-Char?"

Prosser gripped Charlie's arm. "We love you, Charlie-P. We won't let anything happen to you."

"Your Dad's right. And you can ask us questions if you need to."

Charlie made the triceratops jump, run, and growl. The low evening light added to the somber mood. Sarah studied her husband. Prosser had rushed home and hadn't even taken off his shoes. "No more of that case," she asserted.

He shook his head. "No more."

"You mean it?"

"It's done."

Prosser grabbed two dinosaurs from the stack of toys and slogged around Charlie.

* * *

Reed drove for hours on the highway to Boyd's while his body trembled with energy needing a release. Anger coursed through the veins in his arms and down to his toes resting on the accelerator. It clouded his mind. Turned him into a heat-seeking missile. He only hoped he'd get his hands on Boyd before he exploded.

Reed stopped the car outside the two-story brick home in Manchester and didn't bother turning it off or even shutting the door as he exited. He walked the path to the door, passing under a glowing old-fashioned street lamp as dusk had settled in.

The ground-floor lights were on. He knocked three times, then dropped his arm, standing with his chest out and fists at his sides.

The door opened to reveal an elderly man. A woman of about the same age accompanied him from behind. "Hello, can we help you?"

Reed studied them. A gray-haired man in a button-down and khakis, the woman in a green blouse and skirt. They looked like they'd just come from church.

Another trick.

But the rage wouldn't let go.

"I'm here for Badge."

"Who?"

"My dog. Badge."

The woman spoke from behind her husband's shoulder. "We don't know your dog. Did you lose him?"

"No, I didn't lose..."

"Jacobs?"

The familiar voice echoed from further in the house. Reed couldn't make her out through the darkness of the long hallway. As she stepped forward, he saw her clearly. "Chief?"

"What are you doing here?" Oberman positioned herself next to the old man. She was wearing jeans and a sweatshirt. Reed couldn't remember the last time he saw her out of uniform.

The words escaped Reed. He stood there, jaw slack, speechless.

"He said he was looking for his dog," the old woman shared.

"Badge?" Oberman asked the group as she wiped her hands on a small towel.

"Yeah, have you seen Badge?" Reed asked sheepishly.

Oberman placed her hands on her hips. "Why would he be anywhere near here?"

Reed relaxed his fists. "I don't know where he is. Why are you here?"

"Me?" Oberman sounded surprised. "I picked my aunt and uncle up from the airport to bring them home. We just had dinner together. What are you doing here, Jacobs?"

Reed shook his head. "Airport?"

The old woman spoke again. "We had a lovely cruise around northern Europe." She turned to Oberman, "Is this the young man with the child?"

"Oh, no. That's John Prosser." Oberman smiled and spoke to Reed. "There was a scare with his son and a mix-up at dispatch, but he's okay."

Reed nodded. "I'm sorry, my mistake. I guess I have the wrong house." In a moment of clarity, Reed pointed to the man. "What's your name?"

"Ethan," he said.

"Ethan what?"

"Boyd."

"Thank you." Reed nodded and hurried to the Wrangler, ignoring the murmuring from the doorway. With the engine still running, he wasted no time driving the vehicle around the corner and out of sight. Questions flooded his mind too quickly to recognize them. Reed had no sense of where to begin in unraveling the riddle.

As he approached a small park, he pulled over and called Prosser. "He's still fucking with me."

"What are you talking about?"

"Agent Sanders, Boyd, or whatever his name is. The house, the address you gave me?"

"Yeah?"

"It's Ethan Boyd all right. An old guy who just happens to be Chief's uncle."

"Aw, shit. He knew."

"Exactly." Reed sighed in defeat.

"Sorry, Reed."

"You saw him here, right?"

"Yup. But it doesn't matter. It's all a trick to distract us. He's CIA, regardless of where he lives or what his name is."

Reed put his hands on his head. He slid down the seat of the Wrangler an inch and looked at the roof. "Everything's gone, man," Reed conceded. "Everything's gone, and I don't even know why."

"It's a hard time for you. I hear that. Things can turn around."

Reed turned his head to the small park. It remained empty in the night. He imagined children on the swings, families at the picnic tables. Not now.

* * *

Reed breathed through clasped teeth as he jolted awake. His eyes darted side to side. Beads of sweat pooled on his forehead. And words would not come. He could not move. The fear was instant, a flash from his gut to his throat. As before, he tried to kick and scream, but failed.

Light danced from the open window at his side. The air rushing in did nothing for the smell. Ammonia, sulfur, and a lazy screen of citrus. It burned.

Organic clicking sounds arrived, followed by an electric whirring. His body rose from the bed. The white sheet caught on his feet, then slipped free and flittered away.

Oh, my God. The tendons behind Reed's eyes ached from the pressure he applied to keep them open.

His body moved to the window frictionless, effortless.

No.

Reed's body continued. The bottom of the wooden frame brushed his nose as he passed through it.

Outside, he bore witness to the dark pyramid with the concave center. The craft was blacker than the night sky above his home. It hovered as still as a mountain. He rose to the looming craft as if strapped to a board.

No. No, please.

It swallowed him into a darkness beyond space, void of light.

Inside, the invisible force lowered him onto a stiff, cold surface.

What are they doing? Where ARE they...

He heard a shuffling at his side, and the smell of spoiled earth struck him. Something rough ran along his chest and down to his navel. Commanded by something other than his own will, his arms moved from his side. They stretched out to form a T, and his palms opened to the unseen sky. Then he felt the pressure of what seemed like heavy metallic balls, one in each hand. Another, heavier one, took its place on his chest and promised to crush him. A familiar sensation from his childhood dreams. Yet he could still only see black.

A coarse and irregular ticking sound came. Reed could sense the source was a being hidden by the cloak of darkness. Something communicated. It was meant for him.

The sound intensified, intervals tightening, volume climbing, until Reed could no longer tell whether the source was in the room or somewhere behind his own eyes.

In the darkness, a form began taking shape—the metallic sphere on his chest. Polished to an unnatural perfection, Reed glared at it. A reflection emerged. A reflection of...something.

Reed struggled to make sense of the shapes. He tried to raise his head for a better view, but failed. He tried squinting and was just able to move the muscles around his eyes enough to make it work. Reed focused on the space a foot in front of his face. The spherical warping of the reflection of something that moved behind his head.

Contours began making sense to him.

Reed tried to shake his head. His eyes opened further still. The breath in his lungs roared to him to scream, but none came.

Though shrouded in darkness, the form grew clear to him. Two elongated black eyes the width of basketballs. The eyes of a giant mantis-like creature. Reed saw its mandibles open vertically. They revealed slender tendrils that writhed and reached forward as if to grab Reed and pull him into the razor-like teeth that encircled its pulsing throat.

Reed didn't know how the information came to him, but he recognized the mantis as the dominating creature. The thing in command.

Then something dropped onto Reed's face, covering it and contouring around his features. It cooled his skin like metal or stone. It was heavy with holes for his eyes to look through—to continue gazing at the beast who moved as if wanting to feast on Reed's essence.

The mantis spoke to him in his mind.

Endure.

Reed pressed his eyes closed. Squeezed them so tightly he thought he might rupture blood vessels. Then he opened them to the tendrils licking at the mask. The part of Reed that knew how to fight broke.

Chapter 44

Reed crossed the parking lot to Prosser, who waited at his Explorer. The thick clouds leached the color from the parking lot, leaving everything the same dull pewter. Reed stretched his arms as he walked, then rubbed his eyes. "Hey, what's up? Why didn't you come inside?"

"I have something for you in my car." Prosser's hands rested in his jacket pockets.

"Something for me?"

Prosser opened the back door to reveal a covered cardboard box on the seat. "Put it in your Wrangler. Lock the doors. I don't want you talking about it to anybody. I'd be in serious shit."

"You going to tell me what's in that?"

"The only evidence we had. The laptop and the box."

"O'Reilly's?"

"Not so loud!" Prosser looked around the Bridgewater Police Department's lot.

Reed reached into the SUV and lifted the lid of the box to peek inside. The laptop lay flat at the bottom, the mysterious black device on top. And next to it, a little yellow excavator. He picked up the toy and showed it to Prosser. "What's this?"

"Charlie wanted you to have it."

Reed closed his fist around it, held it a beat, then tucked it into his pocket. "Okay, and this other stuff. Why are you giving them to me?"

"Because I'm out. I'm done." Prosser rested a hand on the top of the door.

"What do you mean, you're 'done'?"

"I'm not doing it anymore. Yesterday they made it clear—they are not above hurting my family. It got real."

Reed stretched his arms out. "It has been real for me! It still is!" He pointed to the detective. "You're the only one I've got helping me on this. They took me again last night, John!" Reed's jaw trembled. He shook his head. "I will spare you what they did to me."

"I'm sorry. This is it. Take the stuff and tell nobody. Or I will mea culpa them into the evidence room right now."

Reed grabbed the package and pulled it from the car, hugging it tight to his side with one arm. He stepped into Prosser's space. "So much for 'Presser'. You didn't even figure out why she jumped. That's all you cared about before."

Prosser shut the back door of his vehicle and opened the driver's. "I hope you figure something out. Something that helps you, whatever it is. But Charlie's everything, Reed. He's only five. I hope you understand."

Prosser entered his vehicle and started the engine. Reed stepped aside and watched the detective roll to the main road and drive away.

Reed walked to his Jeep. A laptop full of high science he couldn't read. A black box that did nothing. He had no idea where to start. Inside the Jeep, he pulled the little excavator from his pocket and set it on the dash.

* * *

Reed stood in his living room with his arms crossed. The distressed coffee table held the few objects that he had to work with. Next to Katherine's laptop, a yellow sticky note with the computer's PIN and password. Next to that, the black box and the iron mask. Without Prosser, he'd need to work out for himself any potential solution to what tormented him.

The room's lamp did little for the space. The dark wood of the ceiling and the brick of the fireplace absorbed the light. And through the windows, with all the snow melted and a cloudy sky, the darkness of space loomed.

"What now?" he asked himself. "What would a detective do? Where can I start?"

Reed opened the coffee table's drawer and pulled out a pad of paper and a pen. He sat to write notes.

"Take inventory, Prosser said." Reed looked at the items. "Check."

He scratched his head. "Okay, from the beginning."

Chapter 45

From the side of Route 4, Reed sat in his cruiser with the glow of Katherine's laptop illuminating the cabin in the dark night. With it on the passenger seat, Reed snuck time into research while on duty. He had the file management program open and performed various searches of the computer's contents. *UFO, alien, triangle, pyramid, unidentified flying object, UAP, unidentified aerial phenomenon, extra-terrestrial, mantis...*

Nothing.

Behind the computer's raised lid, the odd black box with its crooked antenna sat silent. His cooler of food and drinks waited on the floor. As did the mask. Reed drummed on his knee with his right hand. *What else?* he thought.

He looked out the window at the vacant road ahead. The radar on his dashboard registered double zeros as nothing passed. Thick and rolling clouds dominated the sky.

There has to be something on this laptop. Has to be.

A Tesla turned a corner onto Route 4 and headed toward Reed. He kept his eyes on it. His stomach churned. His skin prickled with electricity. Reed readied the accelerator and gripped the shift knob. Beads of sweat appeared on his forehead as the car approached.

The box on the seat next to him ticked. Slowly at first. Then, as the car neared, the static fracturing of the peaceful cabin became frantic.

Reed could now see the driver. His heartbeat and breathing quickened. That black hair. The pale skin. *That woman.*

The Tesla passed, and the ticking of the box slowed. Reed scratched his scalp and pressed his eyes closed. "Goddammit!" He grabbed the wheel and put the car in drive, moving onto the road and backing up to turn around.

He pushed the vehicle to catch up to the woman, getting close enough to recognize her in the Tesla's rearview mirror. She didn't move her attention from the street. The sagging of flesh under her eye revealed the darkness beneath.

Breaking protocols, Reed turned off his radio. He also tossed the radar to the floor next to his food.

Reed rocked back and forth in his seat. "What are you doing out here?"

He made note of the license plate for a registration check later.

The red brake lights and the right turn blinker engaged. Reed did the same and followed. The cars wound through a long stretch of road lined with tall trees as they ventured farther from civilization. The moonless night made it darker than usual.

"Where are you going?" he asked. Reed placed his hand on his hip and felt the cold steel of the pistol. He touched each finger to it.

Following the car for miles, his mind wandered. *How far am I going to follow her for? She doesn't seem to care. She must know I'm behind her. Will she disappear like those guys? What if she stops and comes up to my car? Do I hit her? Shoot her? Run?*

Reed slowed to allow more space between him and the Tesla. He knew the route they were on; it went up to Billings' Notch and down the other side of the mountain. A scenic drive for visitors to the area. *But not this kind of visitor.*

The cars weaved through turns, and the Tesla slowed. She pulled into a dirt parking area, and Reed followed, keeping his car back and his foot ready on the accelerator.

The vehicle parked in front of the weathered split-rail fence near the beaten path that led to the collection of shallow caves where tourists took their selfies.

Reed stopped the cruiser thirty feet behind her and watched.

The Tesla's lights turned off, and the driver's door opened. The box's ticking returned. Reed's eyes widened. He put a hand on the shifter, ready to pop it into reverse.

"What are you doing?" he asked himself.

Her leg emerged. She planted her foot, in its black leather flat, on the ground. Her arm appeared, and she placed her hand on the side of the car. Reed watched as she lowered her head an exaggerated amount and pushed herself out of the vehicle.

She turned to the path, stepped back, and shut the door.

Reed shook his head. *She didn't look, but she must know I'm here.*

The woman began walking into the woods, following the path marked by a small signpost. *Billings' Notch Caves.*

The images from Little Red Riding Hood flashed before him. The girl on her way to grandma's and encountering the wolf. The wolf buys time by tasking her to collect flowers, then consumes the old lady and eventually the little girl.

Reed placed a hand on the door handle. "Jesus, Reed."

The woman walked around a dark corner and disappeared into the forest.

"Damnit!"

Reed jerked the door open and rounded the car. He jogged to catch up as his shaking hands unsnapped his holster. He crossed the lot and passed the entrance sign.

As he approached the corner where she disappeared from view, Reed slowed. He pulled his flashlight from his belt and pointed it ahead. The beam lit the path and some facing trees while sending everything else further into an abyss. Crisscrossing the beam, he searched along the sides of the narrow passage for any hiding places or crouching were-people. Downed trees, piles of dead leaves, and the occasional plastic bag littered the area.

Reed noticed the quiet. No hooting owl, no scattering squirrel, not even crickets. Everything with sense had already left. *Smart*, he thought. *Then what am I doing?*

He moved the flashlight to his left hand and pulled his pistol with his right. He aimed it at the ground ten feet ahead. He quickened his pace.

Though the night had been warm, his breath started to fog. Each breath ghosted by him. He tucked his bare arms closer to his sides.

The beam flickered off something white, jolting his muscles. His legs stopped, and he forced them forward again. Faster. His heart raced.

The light struck again, and he saw the back of the woman as she walked. Centered perfectly on the pathway, her arms didn't sway with her stuttering steps. Her hair didn't wave either.

Reed adjusted his grip on the pistol, pressing his trigger

finger against its side. He followed for another minute as they walked down the trail. Ahead, the sky came into view over the rocky outcropping that was the Billings' Notch cave system. The half-dozen caves offered little for exploration, with the deepest only going back sixty-five feet.

Fuck, he thought as the woman continued in the direction of the nearest cavern. He watched as she stepped to the right and up on a rock just 10 yards from a cave's ominous mouth.

Reed raised his weapon, aiming at her back. Then she stopped. Reed did, too. He held his breath and kept his gun trained on her.

His hands shook. The light bounced and jostled around the trees and the wolf's back. He opened his mouth, and a soft cry escaped. Reed took a step back, and as he did, the woman turned her head enough for him to see the side of her face and her wilting eyelid and lips.

The stone ground against the soles of her shoes as she half-turned to Reed.

Reed bent his knees and straightened his arms.

"What are you?" he called out as he moved his finger to the trigger.

She completed her turn to face him. The slender and pale woman in the sleek dress stood still. Reed could see how her skin hung on whatever was beneath it. She had no collarbones. Her knees reminded him of those of a doll.

"Come," she said as she raised an arm. But her mouth didn't move. The message came to Reed's mind.

Reed shook his head.

"Come to the caves. There are many wonderful things to show you there," the thought message came. She stretched out a hand. Her middle finger drooped down like an empty banana peel.

"No," Reed said as he stepped back. "No, I'm not going with you."

A wide grin stretched over the woman's face while her eyes sank as if dead. She extended both arms to beckon him.

"Don't. Don't move!" Reed raised the gun. His eyes trained on the thing under the skin. He tried to make out details, anything to give a hint on what hid behind the human shell.

A light engulfed the area from above. The space between trees lit up like daytime. No creatures scurried about.

Reed looked up. The black object towered above the trees. A hole at its center sent the white beam of light on him.

"No!"

The machine began rotating. Reed's eyes went from it to the wolf and back again.

Come.

"Stop! Stop!" he cried out. The flashlight got in his way as he tried to clutch his hair. His breath crystallized and fell in a glitter of ice.

Reed closed his eyes and raised his pistol. His finger pressed against the trigger and he squeezed.

clunk

Reed opened his eyes to the woman standing on the rock. He pulled the trigger again.

clunk

"What the?"

clunk clunk clunk

"Shit."

He turned his attention back to the woman, the wolf that coaxed him. Her arms now hung at her side like dead weights. Her skin was like a wet towel.

Movement in the cave startled Reed. He looked up to it, where the light from the craft penetrated the threshold by a few feet. Just at the shadow's edge, and bathed in darkness, the seven-foot-tall mantis stood.

Reed could feel its black eyes, which seemed to consume all the light that approached them. They pulled at him. Reed stumbled. The urge to go to the cave came. It teased him. It promised rewards of glorious sights. But his fear fought it.

"No..." Reed shook his head and took longer steps back. "No."

The scent came to him. Even in the pristine natural area, the smell scorched his nose.

The mantis extended its neck. It opened its jaw to expose the writhing tendrils inside. They moved like snakes, seeming to want to drag Reed toward the creature.

Something snapped in Reed's mind. Like his primal brain woke and took control. He turned and ran. With adrenaline pumping, his breathing remained steady as his legs pushed him faster than he had ever run.

He turned a corner, and the light that drowned the wood flicked off. Reed didn't glance up or back, he kept moving forward. He focused on getting out, getting to his car, and back on the road. As he ran, his flashlight darted up and back, across trees and track. The fear of the light finding the woman, or that thing, was beaten back by his desire to be in the cruiser.

Turning another corner, he saw the back of the sign and the parking lot. A few more steps, and the Tesla and cruiser beyond came into view. He changed his course to go straight to it and jumped over the low fence. In five leaps, he crossed the parking lot and stumbled across the hood of his car. The sound of his body against the metal grumbled into the air. He grabbed the frame around the driver's window and jumped inside, slamming the door behind him.

Reed tossed his pistol and flashlight on Katherine's laptop and locked the car. He started it. Reed looked up through the windshield. The sharp edge of the ship teased him.

"Fuck this."

Reed pumped the vehicle into Drive and slammed on the gas. The rear end swung wide before the tires caught and the car launched forward.

He turned the wheel. The car rumbled over dirt. It jumped the lip to the road. Looking at the dust behind him, he saw the pyramid drifting away. He moved his body forward, close to the wheel, and willed the vehicle to go faster. Reed knew the wolves let him go. He understood that could be the only explanation for his escape. But he raced nonetheless.

Chapter 46

"Wow, Dad! Check out all the stars!"

Charlie turned in place, his eyes scanning the planetarium. Countless bright pinpricks of light dotted the false and dark blue sky. A radiant digital comet raced across the dome and vanished.

The two weeks since he'd given Katherine's evidence to Reed went by with no hint of a spook or danger to his family. It took a couple of days for Sarah to settle, and for Charlie's nightmares of his friend drowning to fade. But Prosser felt so at peace that he ran the numbers on his pension. He had taken his son to the aquarium, the toy store (again), the park, and to see a dinosaur exhibit at the museum. After being hounded by Charlie, which earned the boy the new nickname "Little Presser", Prosser agreed on a trip to the Bridgewater Planetarium.

"Look!" Charlie pointed toward the floor, where a projection of Antarctica rotated. "I want to be an astronaut, Dad."

"Study hard, and you can be."

"Have you ever been to space?" Charlie asked with a raised and delighted voice.

"No, that's not something that's been available in my time.

I bet you'll go to space one day, though."

"It's dark up there." Charlie's tone turned serious.

Prosser scratched at the back of his neck, keeping his eyes on Charlie rather than the galaxies overhead and whatever might be looking back. Charlie took his hand and led him to the other side of the room. He pointed up to an area of stars.

Prosser's phone buzzed with an alert of a call. He pulled the cell to see Reed's name on the caller ID.

He answered it.

"Hey, what's up?" Prosser asked.

"Can you come to my place? It's important." Reed's tone was calm and friendly, a sharp contrast from the last time that they had spoken. Reed had seemed to avoid Prosser at work and called out of several shifts.

"I can't. I'm with Charlie."

Charlie spun his body.

"Tomorrow?" Reed asked.

"Yeah."

"Swing over then. I'll be here."

"Why? I'm done, remember?" Prosser looked around the spherical room for any unwanted guests.

"Yeah, yeah, you're done. It's something you're going to want to see. It'll be quick. I'm not pulling you back in, I promise."

"Tomorrow then." Prosser hung up and watched Charlie sketch a constellation in the air with a finger.

Chapter 47

"Come in," Reed said as he moved the door aside.

Prosser entered Reed's home, the old house's rustic charm diminished by the cracked floorboards and paint. The place seemed to be falling apart, as did Reed. He had bags under his eyes filled with sleepless nights, and the walls of the house bowed. He suited the dilapidated building well.

"What's going on?" Prosser asked.

"Follow me." Reed turned and walked through a wide threshold.

Prosser followed him to the living room. The room held the stale, closed-in smell of a place that hadn't seen open windows in weeks. Prosser sneezed.

Reed went to the couch and sat at the laptop on the coffee table. Behind it lay the box and the iron mask.

"Sit." Reed patted the cushion next to him, and Prosser sat. "I'm not going to get into it, but things have been happening. They're not going to leave me alone. It's getting worse."

"I'm sorry to hear that. But, what the hell is this?" Prosser pointed to the mask.

"Never mind that." Reed made a brushing motion with his

hand. "I need to show you something. See, I thought I should try to figure out why Katherine killed herself. Because, like, I'm not going to learn dark matter or plasma whatever. It's not like I will be able to build the Elisha. I can't kill them. So, back to the task you originally had."

"Mm-hmm."

"Right, so I thought if I could figure that out, it was as good a next step as any."

"Sure, sounds logical." Prosser reached behind the computer for the box. He rotated it in his hands.

"I know what that does." Reed looked at the detective.

"What?" Prosser asked.

"It makes a noise when they are coming. Or are here. I haven't figured out how it works, though."

Prosser examined the box again. "Like whatever they do to enter our space, or...be in our matter, it can register."

Reed smirked. "You sound like a believer."

Prosser placed it back down.

Reed continued. "K, anyway. She didn't jump because the Elisha was destroyed since she had insurance. But, she did jump after it blew up."

"Yeah."

Reed's gaze went from Prosser to the laptop and back. "So I put myself in her shoes." He motioned to Katherine's laptop with both hands. "She's watching the feed. The launch happens, rocket's going up, up." Reed raised his fist and opened it dramatically. "Then boom."

He looked at Prosser. "Then what does she do?"

"She took the photo off the wall and jumped."

"Nope. There's still *five* minutes between when the rocket explodes and she drops from the window. It doesn't take five minutes to move that photo and jump."

"You're splitting hairs. She may have been contemplating her life. Wrestling with whether to do it or not."

"Sure, maybe, Detective. But *you* don't know that. And because you don't know that, you keep checking."

"Okay, smart guy." Prosser nodded.

"She did something else, and probably on the laptop. You checked her cell records, right?"

"Yeah, nothing useful."

"Right. I imagine it blew up with calls after the explosion. People wanting to talk to her."

Prosser agreed. "Mm-hmm. No connected calls, though."

"Yeah, we're off track. The point is, whatever she was doing was on the laptop. Following?"

"Yeah."

"So I asked Jeannie..."

Prosser turned to face Reed. "Whoa, Jeannie? I told you not to tell anyone!"

"It's fine. She already knew you had it. And she's cool. I took care of it."

"What do you mean? She hates you!"

Reed rubbed his leg. "No, she doesn't. She really likes me. Anyway..."

"Yeah, you 'anyway' right past that and get to the point."

Reed turned his eyes from Prosser back to the computer. "I asked if there was any way to see what Katherine might have been doing on the laptop at that time."

"And?"

"And usually there's no way to tell. But," Reed pointed up in exclamation, "this is property of the University of Bridgewater. They may not handle inventory well, but they do install monitoring software on all computers as policy."

"Monitoring software."

"Yup." Reed gripped the front edge of the device. "It tracks what a computer was doing at all times. What software it's using. What websites it's visiting. All that."

"Hmm."

Reed scanned Prosser. "Yeah, you had this thing the whole time, Detective."

"You can stop doing that now," Prosser said with raised eyebrows.

"K, Jeannie got access to the software and showed me that Katherine was on the URL for the feed of the launch, and then closed that browser." Reed glanced at Prosser. "She closed it in the same minute of the explosion. We know she was done with the video at that point."

"Okay."

"Then she opens another program." He pointed to the laptop.

"Well? Keep going." Prosser made a circular motion with a finger.

"Wanna guess?"

"No, just tell me."

Reed smiled. "Elijah."

"What?"

"Elijah." Reed placed his hands on his knees. "A program called *Elijah*."

"I know that name."

"I looked it up. Elijah was a prophet, like Elisha."

"That's right. Sarah told me about him. Elisha got his powers or something."

Reed nudged Prosser with an elbow. "Yeah. You should

listen to your wife, man."

Prosser rolled his eyes. "Just keep going."

"Here." He dragged the pointer to the file management program, navigated to a folder, and double-clicked an icon labeled *Elijah.exe.* It opened with two white, vertical boxes filling the screen. At the bottom of the left box, the cursor blinked.

Reed paused again.

Prosser leaned closer. "So, what is it?"

"I didn't know what at first, either. The damn thing sits here like this, right? But there's a cursor, so it wants some input. I thought with Katherine it could be anything—programming, research, whatever. I finally said 'fuck it' and typed."

Reed reached for the keyboard, typed "Hello," and hit *Enter.*

The program responded with a single word in red in the left column. *Hello.*

"It's fucking A.I."

"What?" Prosser perked up.

"It's artificial intelligence. I looked online, *Elijah and University of Bridgewater.* There's an agreement between the university and the Department of Defense for access to the DoD's quantum computer. Jeannie figured out that the communication that goes through this program hits an IP address at the DoD."

"Holy shit." Prosser leaned back.

Reed pointed at the screen. "And Katherine is using the quantum computer for an A.I."

"You mean *was.*" Prosser corrected him.

"Nope. *Is.* You think U of B is bad with inventory. The DoD hasn't even taken down Katherine's access. It still works." Reed moved his hands to the keyboard.

Prosser put his on his head. "If Elijah has access to DoD databases, it might have known something Katherine didn't."

"That's right. Now, watch this." Reed typed again.

I am Katherine O'Reilly.

The response came with text first.

No, you are not.

Followed by an image of her obituary from the local paper in the box on the right side of the screen, and further commentary from Elijah on the left.

Dr. Katherine O'Reilly died on April 13th. You are Reed Jacobs Junior. Officer at Bridgewater Police Department. Sitting next to you is John Prosser, Lead Detective, Bridgewater Police Department.

"What the fuck, Reed?" Prosser placed his hands at his side and pushed into the couch, ready to stand.

Reed smiled and pointed at the small circle embedded in the top of the computer's screen. "It's accessing the webcam. And, like you said, databases. It knows who we are. Who knows what it has access to."

"But it allows us access still."

"Yeah, I can't explain that. Maybe it's just programmed to interact with whoever's in the software. Check this out."

Reed typed: *Were you communicating with Katherine O'Reilly on April 13th after the explosion that destroyed the Elisha satellite?*

Yes quickly appeared in red under Reed's question.

"Holy shit."

Reed smiled and leaned back. "Not bad, right?"

"Yeah. I'd say you should take the NDIT."

"I stopped there. I didn't go any further. I called you. Like I said, I don't expect you to jump back into this. I don't want your family hurt, either. You've got a great kid and an awesome wife. But I thought you might want to know what happened to Katherine. And this thing could probably tell us. We could find the answer together."

"Yeah. Thank you." Prosser nodded.

"Now we can ask for that conversation." Reed leaned forward and positioned his hands over the keyboard.

"Hold on." Prosser reached out and grabbed his forearm.

"What?"

"Let's be methodical. Whatever Elijah and Katherine were... discussing, she killed herself right after."

"Something she learned made her do it."

Prosser released him. "We need to take baby steps."

"What do you want me to ask?"

Prosser looked around the drab room as he thought. "Here, ask this." He eased each word out carefully, "Ask, 'when Katherine O'Reilly engaged you on April 13th after the destruction of the Elisha, without revealing the content of your messages, tell us the nature of your conversation.'"

Reed typed along as Prosser spoke, and the reply came.

Katherine O'Reilly asked a question concerning the phenomenon.

"We need to clarify that," Reed said as he prompted Elijah.

What do you mean by 'the phenomenon'?

Alien visitation and intervention, Elijah responded.

"Okay." Prosser reached toward the computer. "So, do we want to know what she asked?"

Both men sat in silence for a moment, staring at the red text.

Reed spoke first. "I say we ask what the question was."

Prosser nodded. "Yeah, but only that."

Reed gave the command.

Without revealing the answer, what did Katherine O'Reilly ask?

The letters appeared one by one, as quickly as they had before. But time felt like it had slowed. They held their breath as they read the text, watching it come to life.

What do they whisper to those who listen?

The men looked at each other and then away. The question sank into them like a needle. Consumed them like a virus.

"They."

"The wolves," Reed whispered. "It means, what do the wolves say to the humans who are listening to them? The humans who are working with them...The CIA."

Prosser squeezed his hands together. "She saw the rocket destroyed and knew the aliens had something to do with it. She surmised that someone must have told the aliens the true mission of the Elisha."

Reed finished his thought. "So she went to Elijah since it had DoD access, and asked her question. Elijah may have concluded something about the aliens from DoD data that maybe the DoD itself doesn't even know." Reed began typing again. "Hold on."

"Be careful," Prosser said.

"Yeah, I got this."

After you answered Katherine's question, did she input anything else? Reed asked the artificial intelligence.

No. After my answer, Katherine disconnected, Elijah replied.

"Disconnected?" Reed asked Prosser.

"Like Jarrow said. The answer made life worse than death," Prosser said with finality as he leaned on the arm of the sofa.

"Yep. Elijah's answer is the next question to ask."

The men sat side by side in silence, each locked on its response. A response from a program that likely didn't understand the weight of the words "Katherine disconnected." It certainly didn't understand the implications of the message that it communicated to Katherine on April 13th.

For two minutes, they sat motionless and deep in their own thoughts.

Prosser broke the silence. "I have Charlie and Sarah to think about." As if sprung from the seat, Prosser stood and pointed to the door. "I'm sorry, Reed."

A somber smile appeared on Reed's face. "I don't. I don't have Sarah or Charlie. Or Wendy, or Badge."

Prosser dropped his arm. "Reed, think about this, man. This isn't a game. Think about what happened to the professor."

"I understand, John." Reed sat at the laptop as if rooted in place.

Prosser stuck his gaze on his friend. "Whatever that thing knows, it's not good."

"Yeah, I'm okay with that."

"Reed?"

"Seriously, John. I'm good. You go."

Prosser stared at the man he had become close to in their investigation. He didn't blink. He swallowed against the tightness in his throat. "First, give me your gun to take with me."

Reed shook his head. "That's not happening. Go, John. I appreciate what you've done. I wouldn't have gotten this far without you."

Prosser motioned for Reed to stand. "Come on, man."

Reed stood, and Prosser hugged him and patted his back.

"Please take a moment to think about it after I leave, when you're alone. Make sure it's what you want," Prosser said.

"Yeah, I got this. I'm clear."

"K."

* * *

Prosser crossed into the foyer and exited. Reed cleared his throat, and it echoed around the room as a reminder he was now alone. He stood at the window and rested against its frame.

Prosser walked to his car and opened the door. He paused and stood for a moment, looking back at Reed's home. Before getting in the Explorer, Prosser tapped the door twice with his palm. Then he drove down the driveway and turned onto the street.

Reed had a call to make. The bright day and budding trees asked him not to go forward. He tapped his cell. The line rang until he saw her on video.

"Hey, Sadie." Reed smiled.

"How are you?" Sadie appeared to be outside. Bricks formed a wall behind her, and the edges of a white chair emerged from behind her shoulders. Reed's heart skipped a beat. She looked happy.

Reed took a breath and dug his fingernails into his palms. "I'm doing okay."

"You kind of look like shit."

"Haven't been sleeping much."

She nodded. "You taking care of yourself?" Her face grew as she moved closer to the camera.

"I am. I'm sorry about your dad."

Sadie looked off-screen and back again. "Me too. So, what's up?"

"I want to apologize. Actually apologize. I should have been there for you."

"You already did, remember?"

"I said the words, but I was awfully focused on myself. I want you to know that I see what I did to you. And I'm sorry. I wish I could go back."

Sadie shook her head and wiped an eye. "That was a long time ago."

"That's not an excuse. You faced it, and I didn't. That was wrong."

She smiled again. "Well, thank you. I appreciate it. What are you doing today?"

"Fighting." Reed turned from the window and placed a hand at the back of his neck.

"What? Like boxing? That sounds like a Reed thing."

Reed laughed and sat on the couch.

Sadie shrugged. "Well, whatever the fight is, I hope you win."

"Thank you. What's going on at the farm?" Reed cupped his cell phone with both hands.

"Red tape since Dad's still missing. I will go back up in a couple of weeks to search some more."

"Then what?" Reed moved one arm to hug his body.

"Sell it. Live life. Never go back to Bridgewater."

Reed lowered his eyes and nodded.

Sadie whispered, "You sure you're okay?"

"Yeah. I wish things turned out differently." Reed looked up at her.

"Me too."

They looked at each other in silence.

Reed brushed the back of the phone with a finger. "I'm going to go, Sade. I hope you remember our good times."

"You sound so final. You're frightening me." Sadie brought a hand up to her chin.

"You have enough to be scared of."

"Reed?"

He straightened his body. "Like I said, I'm fighting. Just not with my fists anymore. Little Red Riding Hood had to risk being eaten to bring her grandmother food. Love you, Sade."

"Love you too."

Reed disconnected and placed his phone face down. He looked at the laptop and the cursor—the blinking vertical line's patient repose for a command. Elijah rested, like an old friend waiting to be the ear he needed. Like Badge used to do.

Reed noticed the ticking clock on the fireplace mantle, the half-circle timepiece in brass fittings left by his mother. Next to it sat Charlie's digger.

tick tick tick

He counted each measure with the cursor's blink and found them in perfect unison. And the same with the beating of his heart.

The old painting above the mantle caught his attention. Bosch's *The Last Judgment.* Its presence there had become so familiar that he couldn't remember the last time he looked at it. He wasn't sure he could even describe it to someone. His father brought it home one day and hung it without a word.

Reed knew little about it, only what his mother told him.

"God cast out the evil angels and turned them into insects. Jesus judges us all, and Satan torments the sinners," she had said. After those words, she bowed her head and turned on her heels for the kitchen. Young Reed looked at it with a hate he didn't understand.

He didn't delay Elijah any longer.

What answer did you give Katherine?

Elijah replied. The air left Reed's lungs.

Its response lingered. He sat with it a moment, then snapped the laptop shut. He approached the fireplace, his steps easy against the creaking floor. "Miss you, Badge," he whispered to the empty bed.

Reed lifted the art from its place. Dust danced in the light as he tore the painting from its brittle frame. Releasing the wood, it clattered into the hearth. *The Last Judgment* didn't resist his crumpling of the yellowed canvas, and he tossed it in as well. From the mantel, Reed plucked the matchbox. He struck one and watched the flame erupt and settle. Holding it like a delicate flower, he bent to the hearth and emptied the remaining matches onto the canvas. Then Reed set it all afire.

Chapter 48

Charlie opened his mouth in uncontrolled laughter as he tried to squirm away from his father, tickling him with stubby T. rex arms and a semi-ferocious growl. He wiggled free and rolled in the grass as his father watched.

As he stood, Charlie saw his mother sitting on the back patio with a tray of lemonades and crackers on the table beside her. He smiled. Happy bubbles filled him.

He ran to the swings and bounced up, spinning in the air to land on one. The dirt crunched from Charlie's pushing to gain momentum. As he gripped the chain tight, his father sat on the swing next to him.

Charlie let out a bright, rolling laugh. He dropped his head back and raised his legs to gain speed. The sky arched over his vision, and he saw the trees behind. Then the sky returned, followed by his house and the living room windows.

Pulling up, his body swung the other way. Then he rocked back again, higher this time. The chain snapped taut as it raised his body further.

"Careful, buddy!" his dad cautioned.

Charlie wanted more days like this. Sunny days with Mom and Dad outside. No school or work. No picking up toys from the living room floor or putting his barely dirty clothes in that bin. No baths or even washing hands. Just fun. Fun and laughing.

As his body reached its apex, he threw his legs out and extended his arms to lower his head. The wind swept through his hair.

The sky filled his vision again. A wide blue sky with only a few puffy clouds.

Charlie understood they were there. They said they watched. And then, as the motion carried him high again, he saw the pyramid.

CONTINUED IN:
THE MECHANISM OF COLLAPSE

One more thing...

Can I have one more minute of your time? As an author, reviews mean a lot to me. They help other readers and assist in spreading the word. If you like this novel, please consider leaving a review on GoodReads or Amazon.

https://www.goodreads.com/book/show/221287741-the-dark-matter

https://www.amazon.com/stores/Daniel-M-Durick/author/B0CGFVJ3Z1

The Tetrad Cycle

Beneath the world we can see lies another, older and stranger. A structure of reality that physics has only begun to dare glimpse. Most of the universe is made of something we cannot touch or even light. We call it "dark matter" and look away.

But, something within it wants something from us.

The Tetrad Cycle follows that thread down through the layers of existence: past the matter we mistake for solid ground, past the orders of being that move unseen between worlds, toward the field of consciousness from which everything unfolds. It is a series about what the universe is made of beneath the physical, and what it is beyond. It explores what the soul actually is, whether anything of us survives the body, and how far a single human will can reach when it finally understands what it is reaching into.

The cosmos is layered. Patterned. The four books trace its tiers from the material world we know toward the source that shaped it. What waits at the top of that ascent is the question the Cycle seeks to answer.

Some thresholds you don't cross unchanged. The reader is invited through.

About the Author

Dan Durick is a Vermont writer with a young son and a demanding day job as a Director of Digital Marketing and Copywriting for a large tech company. To not go totally insane, or become a "dull boy", he brings universal mysteries to science-fiction/horror novels grounded in a reality we recognize. By combining accounts of unexplainable experiences with philosophical explorations of what is behind it all, he crafts the kinds of mysteries that leave you both contemplative and paranoid. If you're not curious, you will be. If you're not disturbed, you should be. If you're not mesmerized by the macrocosm...*wake up*!

Dan's stories come from his study of Philosophy in college and his forty-year-old subscription to Time-Life's *Mysteries of the Unknown*. He ponders them on family road trips and dog walks. They haunt him in corporate meetings and nightmares. They beg to be let loose upon the populace.

Besides that, he plays with his son, takes the family to get ice cream, and drives with the top down. All good distractions from the multitude of phenomena that could upend our reality.

You can connect with me on:

- https://www.dandurick.com
- https://x.com/dandurick
- https://www.facebook.com/dandurickauthor

Subscribe to my newsletter:

- https://dandurick.eo.page

Also by Daniel M Durick

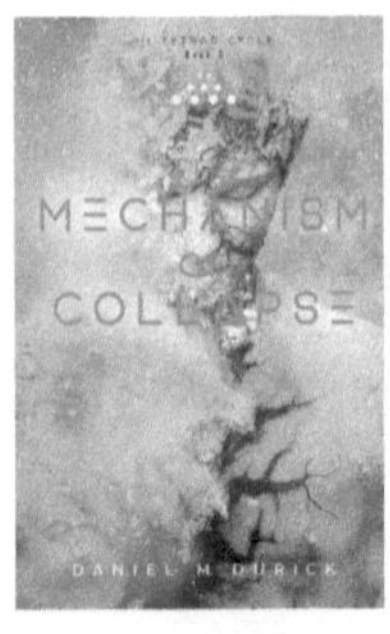

The Mechanism of Collapse
Book 2 of The Tetrad Cycle

Allen Hemsey has made the discovery of a lifetime: a particle embedded in the pineal gland responsible for the collapse of the quantum wave function, and it may be nothing less than the human soul. It's a finding that could reshape civilization, and Allen believes it holds the key to defending humanity against an extraterrestrial threat no one else knows exists. But some truths, once uncovered, cannot be controlled.

Clausen Carey, a psychic television personality haunted by visions of Bridgewater's destruction, drowns his gift in vodka and regret. Estranged from the daughter he can no longer read, Clausen is pulled into a web of missing children, faceless predators, and something evil lurking at the edge of perception.

When Allen's revelation reaches those closest to him, it ignites a crisis of identity that fractures friendships, marriages, and the very meaning of existence.

As a black pyramid descends over the city and the Elm River rises, the fates of a scientist, a psychic, and everyone they love converge in a storm that threatens to collapse everything.

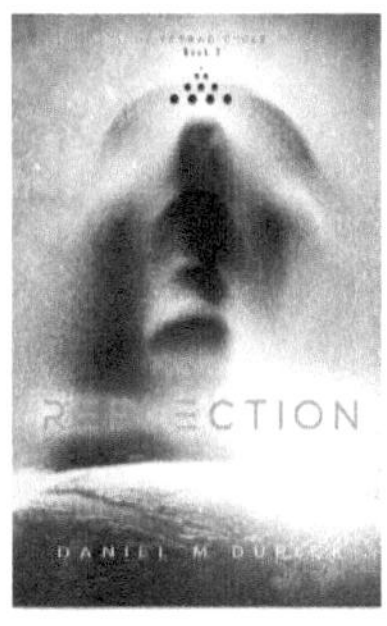

Reflection

Book 3 of The Tetrad Cycle

A missing scientist. A grieving father's deadly secret. A discovery at the edge of the universe. The third novel in The Tetrad Cycle pushes the boundaries of science fiction, supernatural horror, and conspiracy thriller.

Detective John Prosser thought he'd left the shadows behind. But when tech visionary Allen Hemsey vanishes without a trace, the investigation drags Prosser back into a web of government cover-ups, alien encounters, and a rogue CIA operative who plays by no one's rules.

Michael Angelides is hiding something behind his pool house. Shattered by the death of his daughter and the collapse of his marriage, the CEO is summoned to a classified facility in the Nevada desert, where a terrifying revelation awaits. Now Michael must confront an alien intelligence, a soul-shattering scientific discovery, and the consequences of his own unforgivable act.

Meanwhile, psychic Clausen Carey strikes a bargain with a demon to restore his daughter's stolen soul, only to realize he's unleashed something far worse than he imprisoned.

From the corridors of the Pentagon to a secret facility buried inside a mountain, from small-town tragedy to the edge of the universe, *Reflection* weaves UFO phenomena, demonic possession, quantum consciousness, and government conspiracy into a thriller that asks the most terrifying question of all: What lies beyond everything we know, and what happens when it looks back?

Book 4 of The Tetrad Cycle

Coming soon!

Tether

"The Universe seeks balance. With an offering in one direction, you can push it in another. You can never set it off course for long, though. It always finds its way back."

In the intricate web of human connections, where bonds provide comfort, lies a sinister twist. In this occult horror novel, Kristin Fuller, a promising young woman, discovers the malevolent potential of the cosmic threads that bind us. As powerful forces manipulate these connections for nefarious ends, Kristin finds herself in a perilous struggle for survival. With few clues, she and her closest allies confront the looming darkness. In a race against time, Kristin must unravel the mysteries surrounding her and face the ultimate question: Can she break free from the sinister ties that bind, or will she succumb to the forces seeking her demise?

For purchase options, visit: https://www.druidlakeinc.com/tether-book

www.ingramcontent.com/pod-product-compliance
Lightning Source LLC
Chambersburg PA
CBHW030403020826
49168CB00022B/119
9781966053019